"You
After t
Have you l
you may ever have had!"

The marshal's glare sizzled as he growled in her face.

Meri blinked. When had he gotten so close? And how was it possible for him to be so close when they were both still on horseback? She fought the impulse to move her horse away from the growling marshal and instead leaned toward him. "Yes, I *chased* them!"

He copied her movement, leaning in until she felt his breath on her face. He held her eyes for several breaths without blinking. In a low dangerous tone, he asked gently, "Why?"

Meri barely heard him over the pulse thudding in her ears. "Because…"

Why had she chased them? At the moment she couldn't remember. His nearness was making it nearly impossible to think. "Because they made me mad?" she finished lamely, feeling as foolish as she no doubt sounded.

He blinked, and warmer hazel softened the steely gray. Settling back in his saddle, he shook his head. "Remind me never to make you mad."

CLARI DEES

An avid reader by age seven, Clari Dees loved to hang out at the public library, and the local bookstore staff knew her by name. Her favorite books included Marguerite Henry's horse stories, Louis L'Amour's Westerns and Grace Livingston Hill's romances. Her fascination with books and libraries continues, and Clari now works as a public librarian by day and a writer by night. When she's not locating books for an overdue term paper or tracing down a missing genealogy link for patrons at the library, she can be found at her computer plotting the lives and fortunes of hapless fictional characters.

A preacher's kid from a large family, Clari has been in forty-one states and two countries on mission and singing trips. She still travels with one sister to singing engagements, but firmly believes there is no place like home, which happens to be the beautiful state of Missouri. She loves to spend time with her family and the horses, dogs, goldfish, cat, rabbit and bearded dragon that inhabit their country place. You can visit Clari on her blog, cdeesbookshelf.blogspot.com, or drop her an email at cdeesbooks@gmail.com.

The Marshal Meets His Match

CLARI DEES

Love Inspired

Recycling programs
for this product may
not exist in your area.

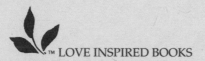

™ LOVE INSPIRED BOOKS

ISBN-13: 978-0-373-82950-7

THE MARSHAL MEETS HIS MATCH

www.LoveInspiredBooks.com

Printed in U.S.A.

He healeth the broken in heart,
and bindeth up their wounds.
—*Psalms* 147:3

Weeping may endure for a night,
but joy cometh in the morning.
—*Psalms* 30:5

To my Lord and Savior, Jesus Christ,
who gave me the desire of my heart.

To my mother, who taught me to read.
To my father, who taught me to love God's Word.
To my brothers and sisters, who believed
I could write and encouraged me along the way.

I Love You So Much!

Chapter One

Little Creek, Colorado
Spring 1883

Meri McIsaac stepped through the doors of Van Deusen's Dry Goods and Mercantile into the enveloping aromas of dried spices, leather goods and pickle barrels and straight into the even more enveloping arms of Mrs. Van Deusen.

"Oh, it's so good to see you. It's been an age since you've been in town." The diminutive, white-haired proprietress ambushed Meri with an exuberant hug. "Are you going to be at the church picnic a week from Saturday?"

Meri shrugged. She'd forgotten about the annual church picnic that heralded the end of a long winter and the welcome arrival of spring. "I don't know, yet. The weather's been so wild lately…"

"Oh, the roads are drying up nicely now, and you just have to be there. The new marshal has arrived, and you *have* to meet him. I've told him all about you. And if you don't like him, there are a several other new single men who'll be at the picnic, as well. You can look them all over and see which one strikes your fancy. You're not getting any younger, my dear, and it is high time you found someone to marry. Your dear mother wouldn't want you grieving for her any longer. She'd say it's time you got on with your life. You don't want to spend your entire life as an old maid, so be sure to come to the picnic where you can meet all the new bachelors at once." The woman's head nodded sharply to emphasize her point as she finally took a breath.

Meri struggled to hide her annoyance at the well-meaning assault, but the old maid comment flicked a raw spot, sparking her temper. Ducking her head and taking a deep breath, she pretended to study the list of needed ranch supplies and hastily changed the subject before losing control of her tongue. She was already feeling guilty for snapping at her father on the ride into town. He'd innocently mentioned a lighthearted memory of her mother, but it had stung the still fresh wound of her loss, and she'd saddened him with a harsh reply. She didn't need another biting retort on her conscience.

"I have a list of things we need at the ranch. Faither asked me to leave it with you. He'll stop by after he finishes at the bank to load the order into the buggy. I've got another errand I need to run, so if I can leave it with you, I'll be on my way." Meri thrust the list into Mrs. Van Deusen's outstretched hand.

"Of course, dear. Are there any special instructions?" The woman was already perusing the list.

"No. I think the list is pretty self-explanatory." She hid a relieved sigh. As pushy and nosy as Mrs. Van Deusen could be, she was also easily distracted by a long list. She prided herself on filling orders to the exact detail and fretted if something was not in stock. If Meri could get away before the proprietress finished reading the paper, she would escape another round of unwanted advice about her unattached status.

Mr. Van Deusen walked out of the supply room and around the end of the long counter. "We'll see to the order, Miss McIsaac. You feel free to go about your other errands. Naoma can catch up with you when you return." His wink went unseen by his wife.

Meri managed a weak smile and a thank-you and escaped out the door. This was supposed to be a fun trip to town to get away from the ranch for a little while after a long, hard winter, but she was out of sorts and already regretting the trip. She'd forgotten Mrs. Van Deusen's escalating matchmaking efforts and the terms *old maid* and *spinster* beginning to be linked to her name. Being twenty-nine years old and unmarried—by choice, mind you—did not make one an old maid!

Feeling her temperature rise as she dwelt on the subject, Meri ducked down the alleyway between the mercantile and the clock maker, taking the back way to the livery stables. She wasn't in the mood to deal with any more nosy, opinionated females at the moment, or she'd have a new title to add to the irksome ones of old maid and spinster. Something along the lines of the *cranky* and *snippy* old maid.

Meri walked past the line of businesses and outbuildings that made up the north side of First Street and reached the pastures belonging to Franks's Livery Stable and Smithy.

Franks, a former slave freed during the War Between the States, had worked his way west during the turbulent years following the war, eventually settling in Little Creek. No one knew for sure how old he was, but he seemed ageless to Meri with his unlined chocolate skin, sharp black eyes, closely cropped black hair with a few touches of gray and an upright frame rendered massive by years of working with horses and blacksmith's tools. He could be intimidating to those who didn't know him, but a gentler, kinder man didn't exist outside of Meri's father, in her opinion, and Franks had become a close friend. He never failed to calm her down when she was riled, cheer her up when she was sad or just be available with a listening ear, a shoulder to cry on and words of wisdom when she was ready to listen.

It had been weeks since she'd had an opportunity to chat with him due to the stormy weather of late winter. Her father had remarked that any other female would want to visit their "women friends" after being cooped up at the ranch for weeks, but Meri preferred Franks's company to anyone else in town.

Franks ran the livery stable and had also acquired enough land to allow him to breed horses on a small scale. No one knew horses like Franks, and Meri loved to discuss every aspect of them and their breeding with him, which would have scandalized the finer sensibilities of the prim-and-proper matrons of town if they could overhear.

She reached the corner of the closest pasture and slipped through the fence boards. Franks's pastures ran almost the entire length of the town, with the livery located at the northeast end. A walk through the pasture to the livery would be just the thing to soothe her irritation.

She hadn't covered much ground before she attracted the attention of Franks's horses. They trotted over, curious about the newcomer to their pasture. "Hello, fellas. I don't have any treats, but how 'bout some scratches?" Warm, eager bodies surrounded her, and she was kept busy for several minutes giving hearty scratches behind ears and across shoulders, backs and bellies. As the horses shifted and stretched to allow access to itchy places, Meri felt the tension begin to drain from her own body.

"Hey, Abe." She scratched a tall, rawboned black gelding. "Who's the new guy?"

A large muscular bay with a white star peeking through a long black forelock was eyeing her coolly from the edge of the herd.

"Aren't you a handsome fella?" she cooed, slowly advancing toward him. The tall horse, probably over sixteen hands high, snorted and stepped cautiously away from her. Meri mirrored his actions and backed off to take away the pressure she'd inadvertently put on him. "A little shy, are you? Okay, I'll leave you alone, but we'll be friends soon just like these other fellas. Come here, Abe. Why don't we take a ride to the barn?"

Abe, hovering just behind her shoulder in hopes of another scratch, stepped in front of Meri and dropped his nose to the ground in silent invitation. With a little jump, she landed on her stomach across his lowered neck. Raising his head calmly, he lifted Meri off her feet. Using Abe's movement, she slid down his neck toward his withers, twisting her body and swinging one riding-skirt-clad leg up and over his back to slide into riding position.

Meri rubbed his neck. "You're such a smart boy."

Settling herself and flipping her black, flat-brimmed hat off her head to hang down her back by its rawhide strap, she grabbed a hunk of mane and turned the sensitive horse in the direction of the barn using the lightest pressure from one calf muscle. "Let's go find a treat."

Abe sprang into a smooth lope that defied his rather gangly appearance, and Meri relished the feel of his muscles rippling under her and the wind across her face. This was much better than the rough buckboard ride into town and more soothing to her frayed emotions than visiting with "women friends."

Franks's land was divided into multiple pastures, and a fence was quickly coming closer. A gate provided access to the next pasture, but instead of slowing and heading toward it, Meri leaned over Abe's neck urging him into a gallop. Nearing the fence, the horse bunched his muscles and jumped, leaping up and over as if on wings, clearing the obstacle with plenty of room to spare and eliciting a delighted whoop from Meri.

Smoothly landing on the other side, she allowed Abe to gallop several more strides before sitting back and tugging on his mane to slow him to the smooth, rocking lope for the remainder of the ride. All too soon they reached the barn gate, and Abe halted, turning sideways to allow Meri to reach the latch. Meri patted Abe on the neck and leaned down to unfasten the gate.

"Hold it right there!"

Meri flinched hard at the unexpected voice, startling Abe and sending him sidestepping away from the gate. Her hand had tightened around the latch in surprise, and she was unceremoniously dumped on the ground when Abe moved, smacking her head against the gate as she fell. Shocked by the unfamiliar occurrence of falling—she hadn't come off a horse in years—Meri struggled to get her bearings and sit up, massaging the ache in her scalp. Pushing loosened strands of hair away from her face, she snapped, "What is your problem, scaring us like that?"

"I make it a point to scare rustlers."

"Rustlers? Where?" Meri scrambled to her feet, and the world spun wildly. Grabbing for the gatepost to steady herself, she closed her eyes against the dizziness blurring her vision and pulsing in her ears.

"I'm lookin' at her," replied the now-muffled voice.

"You're not making a lick of sense." Meri tried to shake off the vertigo. Moments before, she'd been flying across the pasture on Abe's back, and now she was crawling off the ground, attempting to make sense of a confusing, disembodied voice.

"I mean—" the voice slowed as if addressing a simpleton "—when you steal a horse, you deserve to be scared off of that horse."

Her whirling vision finally began to clear. Meri looked up and up again before she located the source of the voice. A tall man, boot propped on the bottom rail of the gate and arms folded along the top, stood looking down at her. He wore a tan cowboy hat that cast a deep shadow over the upper half of his face, but the lightly tanned skin around his mouth was creased in a small smirk.

"I am not stealing a horse." Meri blinked away the last vestiges of dizziness.

"That's not how it looked from here," he replied. "I watched you sneak through a fence, snatch a horse and try to ride it out of the pasture without renting it at the livery first."

"I was riding it *toward* the barn. If I were stealing it, why didn't I just jump the far fence and ride away from town?" Meri flung her hand to gesture toward the bottom end of the pasture.

"I can't begin to try to explain the workings of the criminal mind, ma'am," he said politely.

"C-criminal mind?" she sputtered. "I'm not a criminal, and I wasn't stealing that horse!" She reached for the latch and pushed on the gate. Neither it nor the man budged.

"Let me out!" Meri gritted, shoving against the gate once more. She'd controlled her tongue with Mrs. Van Deusen, but she was quickly losing any desire to do so with this infuriating stranger.

"Sorry. I'm not in the habit of releasing horse thieves, especially ones who don't have any manners." A tinge of laughter denied the validity of the apology, and a dimple winked in his left cheek.

Meri had had enough of this ridiculous conversation and turned. Abe stood behind her, head cocked, looking a little perplexed at all the commotion, but awaiting further directions. She placed her hand under his chin, gently urging him forward until he stepped up to the gate.

"Abe, open the gate." She held the latch open and pointedly ignored the stranger as she added sweetly, "Please."

The horse pushed his chest into the gate, forcing the tall man to hurriedly step out of its arching path. As the gate swung wide, Abe calmly stepped through and to one side to allow Meri to close and latch the gate behind him. Remounting in the same manner as before, she looked down at the shadowed, grinning face watching her. With tart civility she uttered two words. "Good day!"

At the touch of her legs Abe loped toward the barn and his stall. Meri ignored the chuckles coming from behind them and welcomed the protective shelter of the barn.

Wyatt Cameron watched the fiery female disappear into the shadows of the barn. She had caught his attention when she'd crawled through the fence, and as Franks had been helping another customer at the time, Wyatt had stepped outside for a closer look. The horses had blocked his view of her, however, until she'd appeared as if by magic atop the black gelding and come flying toward him.

Where had she learned to ride like that? She rode with all the skill and effortlessness of an Apache warrior. He'd commanded cavalry soldiers who hadn't ridden half so well. Wyatt leaned against the fence replaying her jump. She was clearly a capable rider, but that jump had been foolhardy. The ground in the pasture was still muddy enough that the horse could have slipped and fallen on either the takeoff or landing. At least the soft ground would have cushioned her fall. He grinned as he remembered her rubbing her head. Or maybe not.

He hadn't intended to frighten her off the horse, he'd only aimed to tease her a bit, but she'd come up fighting, again like an Apache. Reminded him a bit of his sister when he'd pushed her too far as a kid. Either that or a wet cat. Not that she resembled anything close to an Apache warrior or a wet cat. She was attractive, though not in the same overdressed style as the women he'd met around town so far. There was a fresh, carefree prettiness about her with her honey-brown hair twisted back in a windblown braid and her cheeks flushed with exercise.

Who was she? He'd not seen her before. And he'd seen every female in Little Creek. Or maybe it only felt that way because he was the newest single man in town. He certainly hadn't lacked for dinner invitations since arriving.

He was at the barn door before he realized his feet had followed her. He paused as Franks's voice rumbled in response to something the woman had said. His job as Little Creek's new marshal did not include following the first attractive woman that caught his attention. His feet stepped closer to the door. As marshal, however, it *was* his job to follow up on suspicious activity. He would just verify that Franks knew who she was before he left. *If the horses knew who she was, then surely Franks knows her.*

He ignored the logical thought, as the voices inside the barn grew more distinct.

"You is gonna spoil that hoss, missy!"

"Don't try to fool me, Franks. I know Abe is your favorite. I can't spoil him any more than you've already done."

The woman was gently running a brush over the black horse as Wyatt slid into the shadows inside the barn door. Was this the same woman who'd tried to snap his head off outside? Her prickles had disappeared, and there was a smile in her voice.

Franks chuckled. "Abe don' agree with you none. He dun say he is de mos' abused hoss on de place."

Their banter sounded like an oft-repeated ritual. Now that he knew she had told the truth, he could leave. But his feet continued to have a mind of their own and stayed put.

"You're both telling tall tales. Speaking of tall tales, some saddle tramp just made Abe dump me at the gate and accused me of being a horse thief. Have you seen any drifters hanging around? I don't think I've ever seen him before, but the way my head was spinning from bumping that gate, I could be wrong."

Franks sounded choked when he spoke. "Real tall fella?"

Wyatt had to swallow a chuckle of his own.

"Yes…" She straightened slowly, watching Franks as she exited the stall. "Do you know who he is?"

"He's helpin' out 'roun' here for a while," Franks hedged, avoiding her eyes and looking straight into Wyatt's.

Wyatt laid a warning finger over his lips and moved on cat's feet to stand behind her. He'd learned a thing or two about dealing with Apaches in his years as a cavalry soldier.

"Franks, do you know anything about this man? What if he's an outlaw on the run or something?"

Franks's dark eyes snapped. "Now, missy, I'se seen a lot of things in my time, and I knows how to read a man.

I likes what I sees in this un. Just cuz you is upset over comin' off old Abe don' mean you can go accusin' people a bein' outlaws. Yo mama dun raise you better'n that!"

Wyatt decided it was time to announce his presence before she accused him of any more crimes. "Hear, hear." The violence of her startled jump almost made up for her attack on his character.

She spun around, grabbing her head as she blinked rapidly. When she looked up at him, surprise widened her brown eyes, and she backed away. "Sneaking around, scaring a person out of their wits, doesn't speak too highly of your character, Mr.…"

The prickles were back in full force. But he hadn't become a captain in the U.S. Army Cavalry because it was easy. He could handle prickles. "Wyatt Cameron, Marshal of Little Creek, at your service." He doffed his hat and dipped his head in a small nod.

She stared then blinked like a sleepy owl. "The marshal?" Her eyes narrowed. "Where's your badge?"

He pointed to the vest he'd discarded earlier when he'd gotten warm in the barn. It lay over the edge of a stall, a five-pointed star glinting dully in the shadowy structure. "And might I add, you don't seem *too* witless to me, ma'am." He had a few prickles of his own. He also had years of military strategy and Apache fighting up his sleeve. Keeping the enemy on the run prevented them from launching a successful attack, even if the enemy was only a single diminutive female. Because a female on the run couldn't chase him.

"*Witless?* What…? What *are* you talking about?"

"You said I scared you out of your wits, but I think you're just *manner*less not witless."

"Mannerless…?"

If the confusion on her face was any indication, his

military strategy was working. But never before had he had the desire to laugh when trading fire with hostile natives. "When a gentleman introduces himself, a lady is expected to reciprocate the gesture."

There it was again! The tone that made it sound as if he was talking to a simpleton!

Meri straightened to her full height, glaring at the man towering over her. She wasn't short at five foot seven, but this man, his shoulders nearly as broad as Franks's and standing several inches taller, made her feel unusually small. Now that he'd removed his hat, she could finally see his features.

She sized up the irritating stranger. Thick wavy brown hair glinted with cinnamon highlights and framed a nicely put together face. Smiling hazel eyes were set under arched brows of the same brown hue as his hair. Sun-bronzed skin stretched over high, sculptured cheekbones and directed her eyes to a nose that looked to have been broken once. Firm lips tucked up at one corner in a lop-sided grin set off a very determined chin.

Glancing down, she noted a red neckerchief, faded blue shirt belted into dusty brown canvas duck-cloth trousers and well-broken-in boots. All of which clothed a broad shouldered, lean muscled form. Hearing a chuckle, her eyes snapped upward to find a full-blown smile show-casing pearly white teeth. Feeling a blush burning its way up her cheeks, she frantically tried to recall what had been said. Now was not the time to be distracted by a handsome face.

"I said, when a gentleman introduces himself, a lady is supposed to reciprocate." The dimple winked at her again, highlighting his smirk.

Meri was growing tired of that smirk. "Well, there's

your problem—you're not a gentleman!" Spinning around, she faced Franks who hastily straightened grinning features. "I thought you said he was 'helpin' out' around here?"

Franks hearty laugh boomed out. "He's helpin' out cuz his horse is here, but he is de new marshal shore 'nuff."

The marshal stepped into her field of vision. "And don't let me catch you trying out that stunt you pulled with Abe on my horse, or I really will run you in for horse theft. That is, after I get done pickin' you up off the ground when he tosses you on your head."

Her back stiffened at the insult. "I've never met a horse that could toss me on my head!"

He cocked his head, frowning slightly as if searching his memory. "I seem to recall you being tossed not more than a few minutes ago and by a horse, too, if my memory serves me correctly." A twinkle lit the hazel eyes, and Franks chuckled.

"Abe didn't toss me! You startled us!" Meri fought the urge to stamp her foot. She had no idea why they thought this was so funny. Gritting her teeth, she looked at Franks and scraped together the ragged remnants of her dignity. "Thank you for the use of Abe. I can see you're busy, so I'll run along."

"No need to go runnin' off in such a all-fired hurry. I was hopin' to sit an' chat a spell." Franks's eyes glinted with suppressed laughter as he glanced between Meri and the new marshal.

"I'm supposed to meet Faither at the mercantile. He's probably waiting on me." Meri planted a quick kiss on Franks's cheek and beat a hasty retreat down the aisle to the livery entrance.

"Bye, Miss Meri," said Franks.

"Good day, Miss Meri," echoed the marshal.

Meri froze momentarily before turning slowly. "A *gentleman* does not call a lady by her first name unless given express permission. The name is *Miss McIsaac* to you!"

Wyatt grinned. "See, that wasn't so hard was it?"

Meri huffed disgustedly and dropped the haughty tone. "What wasn't so hard?"

"Acting like a lady and introducing yourself."

The man was as annoying as a splinter in a wool sock. "Don't you have work to do, Marshal? Or is harassing people your only job?"

Hooking his thumbs behind his belt, he rocked back on his heels. "I've already apprehended a dangerous horse thief this mornin'. All in all I'd say not a bad day's work, *Miss McIsaac*."

Meri shot a quick glance at Franks. "I said you didn't know enough about him. When the town council learns how delusional he is, they'll fire him on the spot. He'll have so much time on his hands you can put him to work mucking out all the stalls. He should be good at it, judging by what he's shoveled out since I arrived!"

Taking advantage of the instantaneous silence, she spun on her heel and marched out of the barn, biting back a victorious smirk of her own. Finally! The last word!

But as she cleared the doorway, she heard Franks speak. "Hoo whee, Marshal, you dun riled her up sumpin' fierce! Her mamma would'a warshed her mouth out with soap for dat!"

Color flew high in her cheeks as she continued her march away from the livery stable, followed by the irritating sound of the marshal's laugh. Franks was right. Her mother wouldn't have been happy about the last comment she'd let fly. Catriona McIsaac had always admonished that just because ranch life could be crude and dirty, one's speech didn't have to be crude and dirty. Meri let out a deep breath as her shoulders slumped. She should not have lost her temper, but—honestly! The man had called her a horse thief! Between that, her lately volatile emotions and…and those unnerving eyes, it had been like waving a red flag at a bull, and she'd attacked.

Something Mrs. Van Deusen had said earlier flitted across her memory, stopping Meri in her tracks.

"…the new marshal has arrived, and you *have* to meet him. I've told him all about you."

No! Oh, no, no, no!

Mortified consternation swamped the last dregs of temper. She should have never left the ranch this morning. Faither had better be done with his business, because she wanted to slink out of this town as fast as possible. Mrs. Van Deusen could find some other unsuspecting female to throw at the new marshal. Meri wanted absolutely no part of him! Not that he'd want anything to do with her after this morning. It was going to be hard enough to come back in for church services, to say nothing of the picnic.

Dread slithered down her spine, and she groaned. Just the thought of sitting in the same church building with that man made her feel queasy enough maybe she'd just stay home from church for a while. She definitely wouldn't have to feign not feeling well! And who needed a picnic, anyway? Staying away from town was sounding better all the time.

Crack!

The sound of a gunshot slammed into her ears. Meri's heart stopped as the direction of the gunfire dawned on her.

She broke into a dead run.

Chapter Two

Wyatt examined the repaired holster before strapping it around his waist and holstering his pistol. "Looks good, Franks. I figured I'd have to replace the whole thing, but I can hardly see where you fixed it. Thanks."

Crack! The gunshot interrupted Franks's reply.

Wyatt pivoted toward the barn door, wishing for his rifle from his office.

"Wait! You might need dis." Franks tossed a rifle to Wyatt, a second rifle in his other hand.

"Thanks." Wyatt snatched the rifle out of the air and sprinted out of the barn, hearing Franks pound the ground behind him.

As they turned the corner onto the main street, Wyatt dodged the running figure of Miss McIsaac. Where did she think she was going?

"Stay back!" He barked as he passed her. He spared a split-second glance over his shoulder, pleased to see her slow down. Good. He didn't know what was going on, but the fewer spectators he had to deal with the better.

A man jumped astride a horse to ride away from the bank, throwing hot lead around and forcing curious onlookers to scurry for cover. Wyatt threw up his rifle, slamming the butt of the gun into his shoulder. As he laid his finger against the trigger, someone ran between him and the mounted gunman. He jerked the barrel of the rifle up and held his fire. He had no clear shot, but the shooting horseman needed to be stopped before someone was killed.

Wyatt pulled his pistol and fired twice in the air, aiming far above innocent heads. The bullets came nowhere near the gunman, but he sank his spurs into the horse's sides as he yanked violently on the reins and plunged down an alleyway.

The shooting stopped, and heads poked out of doorways like so many prairie dogs. "Anyone hurt?" Wyatt shouted as he ran toward the bank.

"No. But I think the bank's been robbed." An unidentified voice yelled back.

Wyatt slammed the bank doors open, Franks and several other men hot on his heels. No one was in the front room, but the door to the office stood open, and the banker was slumped on the floor just inside it. He moaned and tried to sit up as Wyatt entered. He gave the banker a quick glance then looked around the office.

"Franks, help him." He pointed to the banker and moved to a second man lying motionless and bleeding on the floor beside the massive desk.

There was blood on the floor around the white-haired man's head and more blood staining his side, but he was breathing. The wound on his side was bleeding freely, and Wyatt pulled off the red neckerchief he wore, wadding it up and pressing it against the wound to staunch the blood. "Somebody fetch the doctor!"

A commotion sounded at the office door. "Faither! No!" The piercing cry pulled Wyatt's eyes up. Miss McIsaac sank to her knees on the other side of the bleeding man, her face a mask of disbelieving horror.

"Is this your father?"

A silent nod was his only answer as her eyes frantically ran over her father's form. Her hand gripped a tiny hideout pistol. Where had that come from? More important, what had she planned to do with it? Take on the bank robber herself? *Probably.* "If you'll put that gun away, I need you to hold this while I check on the banker."

Miss McIsaac looked at the pistol as if seeing it for the first time, blinked, then tucked it away in a pocket. She looked back at him, shock darkening her eyes.

Wyatt grabbed her unresisting hand and placed it over the bloody neckerchief. "Hold this down as tight as you can. It'll slow the bleeding. The wound doesn't look too bad, but he's got a gash on the back of his head, as well. Looks like he hit it on the desk when he fell."

Her face drained of color, and he heard her breath hitch in her throat. "You're not going to faint on me, are you?" He deliberately forced a hint of scorn into the question.

It worked. The muscles along her jaw clenched as she took a deep breath, and when she spared a glance at him, some of the spark was back in her eyes if not in her voice. "I don't faint."

She might be foolhardy, but she was tough, too. He disliked leaving her with her wounded father, but he had a gunman to follow before he got any farther away. He pushed to his feet and took a last look at her lowered face as she focused determinedly on her hands. Her lips were moving soundlessly, but she was keeping steady pressure on the makeshift bandage.

"Doc's comin'," someone cried from the back of the crowd.

Relieved, Wyatt went to try to glean information from the banker.

Wyatt wondered if he smelled as rank as the men wearily riding alongside him. Then again maybe the odor came from himself alone and not his companions. Three days chasing an elusive quarry wasn't conducive to rest, much less keeping clean, and he would dearly love a bath, food and sleep; not necessarily in that order. Unfortunately it might be a while before he was able to acquire any of them. The townsfolk were going to want to know the results of the three-day chase. Returning to town with nothing to show for the posse's efforts but weary horses, weary bodies covered in trail dust and a glaring lack of a culprit and loot was not an auspicious beginning to his career as Little Creek's marshal.

In the minutes following Mr. McIsaac's removal to the doctor's office while men had scrambled for horses, Wyatt had fired questions at the assembled crowd. The banker had been too shaken up to give any helpful information, and none of the onlookers could add anything to what Wyatt had seen himself as he was running toward the bank. Armed with this pitiful lack of information, but a veritable arsenal of assorted firearms, Wyatt and the hastily assembled posse rode out of town, hot on the trail of the bank bandit.

Following the tracks of the fleeing horse and rider until night had forced a halt, they'd made a cold, dark camp lest the bandit had circled around to take a few shots at them in the glow of a campfire. Canteens of water and strips of jerky had provided their meal before they'd taken turns standing guard or grabbing a few hours of sleep. As soon as the sky had begun to lighten, they'd continued their pursuit, but had lost the trail when it had merged with a sea of tracks left by a passing cattle herd being pushed toward the Denver stockyards.

Splitting up the posse, they'd spent the rest of the day cutting for sign on both sides of the cattle trail. They'd even caught up with the herd, but the drovers had denied seeing either hide or hair of anyone but themselves and the posse.

Another day of tedious searching for sign had ended in failure when a heavy rainstorm had rolled through leaving them wet, cold, tired and discouraged. Wyatt had hated to head back empty-handed and without any idea of the whereabouts of the bandit, but washed-out sign, dwindling supplies and a dispirited posse had left no other option.

Twilight descended as they rode into town, and Wyatt thanked the men for their participation before the posse broke apart, each man heading for his own home while Wyatt continued toward the livery. His horse deserved a good feed and some rest. It had been a hard ride for them both.

Franks met him at the front doors of the livery. "From de looks ob things, I specs you dun lost dat fella."

"That about sums it up." Wyatt wearily scrubbed a hand over his face, feeling the rasp of three days' growth of beard. "How's everything here in town?"

Franks unsaddled, rubbed down and fed the weary horse as he talked. "Well, Mr. McIsaac's still out cold, and Doc is shore 'nuff worried. Miss Meri ain't left his side de whole time. De banker is okay, but he's sayin' he cain't do nuttin' 'bout the loss ob de money, and we'd better hope you foun' it. Everythin' else has been quiet like."

Wyatt gave Franks a quick rundown of the fruitless

search before adding, "I think I'll check in at Doc's office then try to find a meal and my bed, if no one needs me. Thanks for the use of that horse. He was a good fella. I appreciate you keepin' one handy for me until Charger recovers from our trip up here." Wyatt shook Franks's hand, bid the man good-night and made his way to the doctor's house.

A light was burning in the front window, and he tapped softly on the door. Dr. Kilburn opened it and, upon seeing who it was, quietly invited him in. "Did you catch him?"

"No. We lost his tracks," Wyatt ruefully admitted. He had a feeling he was just beginning to hear this question. He changed the subject. "How's McIsaac?"

Doc shook his head. "I wish I knew. I removed the bullet from his side, and it isn't such a bad wound, barring infection. It's the blow to his head that has me concerned. He hasn't shown any sign of consciousness, and I'm worried there might be swelling inside his skull due to the severity of the blow he took when he fell. It's become a waiting game, unfortunately."

"May I see him?"

"You can peek in the door, but be quiet about it. Miss Meri had just dozed off when I checked on them a few minutes ago. She hasn't slept much since it happened, and I'd like her to get some rest."

Wyatt nodded, and Dr. Kilburn led him down a short hall and quietly opened a door. A lamp glowed softly, throwing its feeble beam on the two figures occupying the room.

Mr. McIsaac, his head swathed in white bandages, was lying motionless and silent on the small bed. His face looked unnaturally pale even in the dim light of the lamp's lowered flame. Wyatt threw up a quick prayer for God's healing and turned his gaze toward the room's other occupant.

Miss McIsaac—he liked Franks's "Miss Mary" better—the woman who'd hopped on a bareback, bridleless horse to go flying across the field, snagging his attention like no gussied up, eyelash-batting, flirting female had ever done. He'd found himself distracted and thinking about her at the oddest times while tracking with the posse, remembering her reaction when she'd fallen off the horse at his feet. He'd expected tears and pouting but she'd come up fighting, and he'd kept at it just to watch her spine stiffen, her chin come up and her brown eyes spark and sizzle.

Tonight, though, the fiery spirit and ramrod-straight spine were missing. The slender young woman drooped sideways in the large rocking chair, weary distress creasing her sleeping features. Her head leaned awkwardly against her shoulder and the back of the rocker in a way that was sure to leave a crick in her neck by morning. Someone had draped a blanket over her, but her slender hands gripped the arms of the rocker. Even in sleep there was a tension about the fragile-looking figure and an obvious lack of peace that made his heart ache.

Wyatt forced his gaze back to Mr. McIsaac. He was not in Little Creek to be distracted by a female. He was here to do a job and continue to squirrel money away toward his goal. He'd seen the stress the families of army soldiers and lawmen had undergone. Long ago he'd decided not to put someone he loved through that and to avoid female entanglements until he was no longer in a dangerous profession. When he found a place to settle down and pursue his dream of raising prime horseflesh, then he would think about a family. Until that happened, however, he was riding alone. And enjoying it.

A hand on Wyatt's shoulder reminded him Doc was waiting. Stepping back, he allowed the man to softly pull the door closed and followed him to the front room.

"Now, young man, you go find yourself a meal and a bed. There's nothing you can do here tonight, and I'd like to catch some sleep myself before anyone else decides they need me."

Taking his advice, Wyatt bid the doctor good-night and left the house, praying as he walked through the dark, quiet town for God to heal Mr. McIsaac, to give Miss McIsaac strength and to help him bring the thief to justice. He reached his office and decided a meal and a bath could wait; sleep was more important. Retreating to the small rear room that held his few belongings, Wyatt wearily shed hat, boots and pistol holster. Placing his pistol and rifle within easy reach, he flopped across his bed and let out a gusty sigh. Like the doctor, he wanted rest before anyone else needed him. Dumping the questions and worry swirling through his mind at the feet of his Heavenly Father, he was sound asleep within minutes.

Please, God, don't take him, too! Please don't take him, too!

Time slowed, and the ticktock of the bank clock grew louder and slower until it was all Meri could hear as she desperately pressed the blood-soaked cloth against the bleeding wound and struggled to pray. She jerked when a second pair of hands covered hers, and she glanced up wildly.

"You can let go now." Dr. Kilburn's kind, bearded face peered into hers as he lifted her hands away. "I need to take a look."

Meri sank onto her heels, clenching bloody hands together while he examined her father. After a cursory look at the wounds, he pulled a thick cloth from his bag, folded it into a square pad and pressed it over the gunshot wound. Looking up, he motioned to two men who hurried over with a litter, and Meri scrambled to get out of their way.

"Take him to my office. Tell my wife to prepare for surgery. I'll be right behind you as soon as I examine the banker." Turning to Meri he added, "You walk alongside and keep pressure on that pad to slow the bleeding."

Unseen hands lifted Meri to her feet as she struggled to make her limbs obey her brain. Moving to her father's side, she frantically tried to keep up with the litter bearers as blood spurted over her hands. The harder she pressed, the faster the blood poured.

"Stop. Please stop!" But there was no one around to hear. She was kneeling over her father in the middle of a deserted street.

"Please, God, don't take him, too. I can't lose him. Don't take him, too!"

A rooster crowed as Meri searched for something else to staunch the bleeding. The rooster crowed again, and Meri jerked awake, a cold sweat covering her skin from the vivid dream. Aching from the rocking chair and the unaccustomed inactivity of the past few days, she slowly pushed herself to her feet and gingerly stretched protesting muscles and joints before straightening the nightgown and wrapper Mrs. Kilburn had loaned her. A tap on the door warned her, and she turned as Dr. Kilburn and his wife entered.

"Good morning, dear. I have breakfast almost ready. You have a few minutes to wash and freshen up if you like. I also washed and pressed your clothes for you. They're hanging in the spare room." Mrs. Kilburn smiled softly at Meri as she issued the invitation before hurrying back to her kitchen.

Meri delayed leaving the room, hovering over the doctor as he examined her father. "Still no change," he muttered.

"Is there *anything* we can do?" Meri asked in frustration as she looked at the pale, quiet figure of her father.

"Yes. We can pray for God's healing and wait for it to occur. Your father had a pretty big shock to his system, but so far he's holding his own." The doctor moved away from the bed and patted Meri's shoulder reassuringly. "Go freshen up and get some food in you. I'll leave the door open. We'll be close enough to hear if he stirs."

Meri allowed herself to be ushered from the room to the spare room across the hall. By the time she'd finished her morning ablutions, dressed in the neatly pressed skirt and blouse and headed for the kitchen, another voice had joined those of Dr. Kilburn and his wife.

Pastor James Willis was sitting at the table drinking coffee but stood when she entered the room. "I'm sorry for disturbing you so early, I wanted to check on Ian and see if there's any way I can be of assistance."

"Doc says all we can do now is pray and wait." The words felt like shards of glass in her throat.

"They've been keeping me apprised of Ian's condition—" he waved his hand toward Dr. and Mrs. Kilburn "—and the church family has been lifting him up in daily prayer, but what can we do to help *you?*" Pastor Willis gently asked.

"I don't know..." Meri choked as the pressure of the past three days suddenly clawed its way up her throat and overwhelmed her. The need to get away before she screamed and made a complete fool of herself robbed her of any semblance of social skills.

"I'm sorry, I... Excuse me!" Meri rushed out the door of the kitchen into the backyard.

"What about your breakfast, dear?" Meri heard Mrs. Kilburn ask as she cleared the door.

"Let her go. Food's the last thing on her mind right now."

Dr. Kilburn's voice faded as Meri left the yard, running blindly. She didn't know where she was going; she just followed her feet as they carried her away from the place where her father lay unconscious.

Adrenaline had carried her through the past couple of days, but the uncertainty of her father's health could not be ignored any longer. The doctor said wait and pray.

She'd *been* waiting.

She'd *been* praying.

Why wasn't God listening? She'd prayed and waited and waited and prayed through her mother's illness but lost her anyway. Now here she was again, in the same position with her father. She couldn't go through this again. She *couldn't!*

Fear and grief met with the fury of a mountain thunderstorm and raged in Meri's chest. Her breath came in ragged gasps, and her eyes and throat burned. She needed to get away from curious eyes. She needed to be on the range where she could run and scream. Where no one could hear and accuse the "old maid" of finally snapping.

Where could she go? For that matter, where was she?

Disoriented, Meri glanced around and realized she'd run from Pastor Willis, straight to the church building. Well, maybe praying at an altar would be more effective than the silent, incoherent pleas ricocheting around her brain the past three days.

Trying the handle of the spick-and-span little white building, she walked inside, pausing to let her eyes adjust to the dimmer light. The room that rang with preaching and singing on Sundays, and the schoolchildren's recitations the rest of the week, was unnaturally quiet and dim. The sun had just started peeking over the horizon, not yet bright enough to illumine the interior.

Collapsing onto the nearest bench, her eyes fastened on the flag at the front of the room as her mind tried to find the words to pray. Gradually her ragged breathing began to quiet.

"Heavenly Faither…" The words echoed hollowly in the empty room. "I don't know what to say that I haven't already prayed. I don't want to lose Faither. I've already lost Mither. Isn't that enough for a while?" The anger in the question surprised Meri. She was scared and sad, not angry. Meri's voice rose though she tried to temper her tone. "Please! You *have* to heal Faither!"

Unable to sit any longer with the emotions tumbling around inside her, Meri got up and paced the aisle of the little building. An open Bible lying on the edge of the desk at the corner of the platform caught her attention. It was a school day, and the teacher would soon be here to prepare for the children who would fill the benches when the bell rang. She needed to leave before she was caught yelling at God, but maybe she could find quick comfort in His word.

Grabbing the book, her eyes roamed the open pages for several seconds…

…searching… There.

Romans 8:25–28.

But if we hope for that we see not, then do we with patience wait for it.

Wait. There was that word again. She was tired of waiting. She wanted her father healed now.

Likewise the Spirit also helpeth our infirmities: for we know not what we should pray for as we ought: but the Spirit itself maketh intercession for us with groan-

ings which cannot be uttered. And he that searcheth the hearts knoweth what is *the mind of the Spirit, because he maketh intercession for the saints according to* the will *of the God.*

Pastor Willis had preached one Sunday how Jesus Christ prayed to the Father on behalf of believers. He didn't forget to pray like a person might, He always knew what and how to pray, and the Holy Spirit interpreted the muddled, incoherent prayers, which might be all a believer was capable of in times of trouble.

A hint of peace tiptoed through her heart. Someone was praying over her, and that thought brought the first comfort she'd felt in days. Her eyes continued down the page.

And we know that all things work together for good to them that love God...

She didn't know how any of the awful recent events could be good, but maybe she'd make it through them without running screaming down the main street of town.

Rereading the verses slowly, she hugged the reassurance of them to her heart before placing the Bible back on the desk. The weight on her shoulders wasn't gone, but it was more bearable, and Meri felt she could face the day and the people in it.

Hunger pangs reminded Meri of missed breakfast, so she left the little church—her return to the doctor's house much slower than her departure. Fear and worry still nibbled around the edges of her heart, but the verses she'd read seemed to be keeping the worst of it at bay.

A burst of embarrassment over her abrupt exit hit her as she slipped through the kitchen door.

"There you are. I've got your breakfast keeping warm on the back of the stove if you feel like eating." Mrs. Kilburn looked up from the bread dough she was kneading.

"I am hungry, but I need to apologize for the way I ran out so rudely," Meri said softly.

Wiping her hands off on a towel, Mrs. Kilburn walked over to where Meri was standing and wrapped her in a hug. "Oh, honey. You don't owe me an apology. I'm not upset. You've been cooped up in this house for days and have a ton of worry pressing on you. Frankly, my husband and I were beginning to worry that you hadn't let any of it out. I think that maybe you have this morning. You look like you feel better." She pulled back and peered into Meri's face.

"A little. Thank you for saving breakfast for me, and for taking the time to clean my clothes." Meri swallowed past the lump in her throat as the warmth of Mrs. Kilburn's hug sank into her heart.

"Enough of that. We keep this up, and we'll both be crying while your food spoils." Mrs. Kilburn dabbed her eyes with her apron and tugged Meri to a seat at the table before placing the plate of breakfast in front of her. "You eat while I tend to this bread, and then you can help me do the dishes. Busy hands help keep the mind off heartaches."

Meri's mouth watered as the aromas drifted up from the plate in front of her, and she bowed her head briefly. Digging into her meal, she listened to Mrs. Kilburn quietly hum the new tune "Blessed Assurance."

Mrs. Kilburn was in her late forties with curly blond hair arranged in a thick bun, and soft eyes that seemed to look at the world with a calm assurance and acceptance Meri wished she could emulate. Meri had not spent much time around the woman outside of church gatherings, but she knew Mrs. Kilburn was familiar with heartache. She'd miscarried several times and knew the grief of loss and childlessness, so her words of compassion rang with authentic empathy.

Mrs. Kilburn assisted her husband with his patients, and Doc frequently said he wouldn't be able to practice medicine without her. He bragged she was his right hand and the best nurse he'd ever worked with. Watching her over the past few days, Meri couldn't help but agree.

Finished with her meal, Meri washed and dried the dishes while Mrs. Kilburn kneaded and shaped the dough into loaves and slid them into the oven. Meri could hear Dr. Kilburn's office door open and the sound of boots getting closer.

"Come into the kitchen," Dr. Kilburn was saying to someone. "We can grab a cup of coffee while you wait for Meri to return."

Meri finished drying the dish in her hands as she glanced toward the door. Dr. Kilburn entered followed by the tall figure of Marshal Cameron. Meri stiffened her knees and spine, fighting an abnormal thudding in her heart that destroyed the measure of peace she'd found earlier.

"Ah, she's back already. Meri, the marshal stopped by to speak with you. Both of you have a seat, and I'll get us some coffee." He stepped to the stove where the coffeepot simmered.

Meri set the dish down and wiped her perspiring hands on the towel, the marshal's cool, searching eyes making her uncomfortable.

"If she can be spared for a few minutes, I need to speak to her in private." He addressed Dr. Kilburn, but his hard gaze remained on Meri, watching, waiting. He motioned toward the back door. "If you'll step outside into the garden, I have a few questions to ask you about the bank robbery."

Chapter Three

Wyatt studied Miss McIsaac, and replayed the morning's events in his mind. Questions concerning the holdup had driven him from his bed before dawn. After time spent praying and searching the Scriptures for wisdom, he set his Bible aside and pored over the wanted posters and notices filed in his desk. He had glanced through them as time permitted over the first days on the job, but early this morning, he'd studied each one carefully, looking for any descriptions that matched what he knew of the bank robber.

Sounds of an awakening town had finally caused him to push back from the desk, stretching as he stood. He needed more information about the holdup and the culprit; rushing to follow the trail of the thief hadn't left time for a comprehensive investigation. Talking with witnesses again might provide additional information to tie to the wanted posters. Buckling his holster around his waist and settling his prized Stetson on his head, Wyatt blew out the lamp on his desk and walked out the door. He'd learned the café was a favorite morning spot for many of the single tradesmen in town, and Wyatt decided to combine two chores at once: breakfast and information gathering.

The food was tasty and plentiful, but Wyatt didn't learn anything particularly useful, and he answered as many questions as he asked. Finishing his breakfast, he left the gathered diners speculating among themselves about the how and who of the robbery, and more importantly, when the marshal was going to find their missing savings.

His next stop was the bank, and though the doors were closed and locked with a sign that read Closed Until Further Notice, his knock brought Mr. Phineas Samuels to the door.

"I'd need to discuss the bank robbery if you have some time this morning."

Mr. Samuels motioned him inside and closed the door before speaking. "I see you failed to catch the scoundrel who robbed my bank, Marshal."

He ignored the accusation in the banker's voice and followed the man across the front room holding the cashier's desk to Mr. Samuels's office. As they entered, Mr. Samuels waved Wyatt toward a chair before circling his desk and taking his own seat.

"I'm sorry, Mr. Samuels, but we lost the tracks in a passing cattle drive. That's why I'd like to go over the events of that day again. I need all the information I can find. Maybe I can match him to accounts of other hold-ups and alert surrounding marshals to keep an eye out for anyone matching his description. Would you start at the beginning and tell me everything you can remember, please?" Wyatt perched his hat on his knee and pulled a small notebook and pencil from his shirt pocket.

"I don't see how that's going to help you now. Seems to me you're shutting the barn door *after* the cow has escaped." Mr. Samuels rocked back in his chair, folding his soft pudgy hands over his brocaded paisley vest.

"Humor me, if you would."

The man's tone was irksome, but Wyatt kept his demeanor passive. The balding, wire-rimmed-spectacle-wearing banker perched behind his massive desk like a king on his throne, and Wyatt felt sympathy for anyone who'd ever had to ask this banker for a loan.

Mr. Samuels grudgingly began to recite the events of the day of the bank robbery. "Mr. McIsaac and I were finishing up our business here in my office when a man walked in, pulled a gun and demanded that I open the safe. I argued, but he threatened to shoot me, so I opened the safe. When he turned his back and started grabbing money and throwing it into a bag, Mr. McIsaac pulled his own gun from beneath his jacket to stop him. Unfortunately the thief turned in time to see it and shot him. I thought he was going to shoot me next, but instead, he hit me on the head. Next thing I remember was you and Franks coming in."

"How did he get into your office without the teller seeing him?" Wyatt questioned.

"My bank teller quit a couple weeks ago to move closer to his widowed mother. I hadn't replaced him yet, so it was just Mr. McIsaac and me in the bank that morning."

"What did he look like?"

"He had a black hat pulled low over his head, a blue bandanna covered the rest of his face and he was wearing a dirty leather jacket over brown shirt and pants."

Wyatt looked up from his notes when Mr. Samuels stopped speaking. "Did you notice anything else?"

"Yes, I did. I saw the horse he rode away before I blacked out. It was wearing the McIsaac ranch brand." Mr. Samuels rocked his chair back. "If it wasn't for the fact that McIsaac was shot, I'd wonder if he had anything to do with it. Or maybe one of those derelicts he's hired as ranch hands decided the pickings were better here!"

Wyatt hid his surprise at this bit of news. "Let's not jump to conclusions just yet. If you'd been hit on the head, how did you see the horse he rode?"

"I managed to get to my feet to call for help as he left, and I saw him through the window but then I must have blacked out." The man puffed up like a little banty rooster. "I am the victim here, Marshal! Are you questioning my word?"

Wyatt hastened to smooth his feathers. "No. I'm simply trying to get the events straight in my mind. How much did he get away with?"

"Everything in the safe! You saw it that day. He cleaned me out! I've had to close the doors because I have nothing to do business with. And then you couldn't manage to catch him or get the money back! I'm beginning to have serious doubts about the town council's choice for marshal!" Mr. Samuels slammed his palms down on the desktop as he stood.

"Everything?" Wyatt let his surprise show this time. "How could one man carry everything from the safe? How much was everything?"

Mr. Samuels instantly went on the defensive. "This is a small Western bank, not a big Eastern city bank. We don't have the same amount of capital as bigger cities, and until I've contacted my investors, I'm not at liberty to divulge the dollar amount of what was stolen. Now if you'll excuse me, I need to get back to my papers. I'm explaining to my backers what's happened to their money!"

"If I'm to recover the stolen money, I need to know how much was taken, Mr. Samuels."

"*When* you have a suspect in custody, Marshal Cameron, I will divulge that information to you. Until then, I've told you everything I know. Good day, Marshal!"

"I need to know the amount that was taken, Mr. Samuels," Wyatt said implacably.

"I said good day, Marshal!" The man was sulled up tighter than a mad, wet hen.

Wyatt eyed him for a moment before reluctantly deciding to retreat from this particular battle until the man had calmed down. "Thank you for your time, Mr. Samuels. If you think of anything else that might be helpful, let me know." He picked his hat off his knee, stood, nodded to the disagreeable man and walked out the bank door.

Outside he returned his hat to his head and tucked the notebook back into his pocket.

Whew!

If other townsfolk felt the same way, it was going to be rough around here until the culprit was apprehended and the money returned. He already knew one person in particular who was definitely not going to be happy to see him when she found out the reason for his visit.

Miss McIsaac's father was still unconscious as far as he knew, but their ranch had been implicated in the bank job, and he needed answers. He really needed to talk to Mr. McIsaac, but only God knew when—or if—that would happen. Looked like Miss McIsaac would have to do.

Sending up a quick plea for help, he'd headed toward the Kilburns'.

Now Wyatt watched Miss McIsaac's reaction carefully as he motioned toward the back door. "If you'll step outside into the garden, I have a few questions I need to ask you about the bank robbery."

Her face showed the fatigue of the past several days' vigil, and there was a hint of redness around her eyes as if she'd been crying. But aside from the wariness that had appeared when he'd come in, Wyatt saw no other emotions at his words. If her ranch was somehow involved in the robbery, no hint of it showed on her face.

"Oh, goodness, there's no need for that. Sit down and enjoy your coffee." Mrs. Kilburn placed her hand on her husband's arm. "Come, dear, I'll help you straighten that mess you call a desk."

Miss McIsaac's voice halted their departure. "I'd rather you both stayed. Whatever the marshal has to say, he can say it in front of all of us. If he has a problem with that, he can leave." She enforced the last remark with a defiant look in his direction.

There was that feisty spirit he'd seen at the livery. "If having the Kilburns here makes you more comfortable, that's fine with me. I would ask, however, that you keep this conversation confidential."

Dr. Kilburn pulled out a chair for his wife. "I always protect the privacy of my patients, and as Ian and his daughter are under my care, my wife and I consider it our responsibility to protect their privacy." Mrs. Kilburn nodded her agreement.

"Very well. Miss McIsaac, would you care to have a seat, and I'll get straight to the point?" The woman still stood in the same spot, gripping the towel.

Slowly and deliberately, she turned and hung up the damp dishrag, smoothing it unnecessarily before turning back around, running her palms down her skirt and walking to the work-worn table. He saw her stiffen as he reached to hold a chair for her, sliding it in smoothly when she sat opposite of Mrs. Kilburn. Seating himself at the end, to the right of Miss McIsaac, he reached for the coffee the doctor placed in front of him. Taking a quick sip, he fired up another quick prayer that God would give him the right words. Swallowing the hot, bitter brew, he began.

"I just spoke with Mr. Samuels concerning the bank

robbery, and another detail came to light that I really need to discuss with your father, Miss McIsaac. Since that's not possible at the moment, I need you to tell me everything you know." Pausing, he watched Miss McIsaac dart a look at him from the corner of her eyes before returning her gaze to the cup wrapped in her slender hands. Was she avoiding his gaze because she knew something, or because she found his presence as unsettling as he found hers?

Her long honey-colored hair was smoothed back into a braid that fell halfway down the back of the high-necked, wheat-colored blouse and dark green riding skirt she'd worn the day of the holdup. Distractedly he wondered how she managed to look so neat and fresh after several days in the same outfit. Forcing his thoughts back to the task at hand, he pulled the notebook out of his pocket and flipped it open. "Tell me what you saw after you left the livery stable that day."

A hint of pink warmed her cheeks, and he felt a glimmer of satisfaction. So, he wasn't the only one who hadn't forgotten their first encounter.

She raised her cup slowly, took a sip and lowered it, gazing into its contents. "I heard a shot fired before I reached the street. When I rounded the corner, I saw something happening at the bank. I had just headed toward it when you and Franks passed me."

"That reminds me. I told you to stay back, yet you still showed up at the bank. You don't follow orders very well, do you?"

Miss McIsaac set her cup down into the saucer with a little more force than necessary, but still didn't look directly at him. "My…" Her voice caught, and Wyatt saw her swallow hard. "My father was in that bank. *Nothing* would have stopped me from getting to him…" The words *even you* hung in the air unspoken.

"How did you know your father would be there?"

"I didn't know for sure he was still there, but he'd told me he had business at the bank, and when he was through he'd meet me at the mercantile. When I heard the shots and saw the commotion at the bank, I was afraid he was involved."

"What do you mean, 'involved'?"

Miss McIsaac went very still then turned her head slowly and finally looked him full in the face. Wyatt felt the heat immediately.

"What exactly are you trying to imply?" Fire may have been in her eyes, but her words were encased in ice.

Wyatt softened his tone and replied calmly, "I'm not implying anything. I'm simply asking what you meant by 'involved.'"

Miss McIsaac searched his face for several moments before looking down and releasing a heavy sigh. "I mean, I was afraid he was still there when the holdup occurred. Unfortunately I was right." Her voice caught again, and he saw the muscles along her jaw clench.

"Did you see or notice anything as you ran to the bank?"

"I saw a man riding away from the bank, firing his gun." She painstakingly aligned the bottom of the cup with the ring of flowers on the saucer.

"Did you notice anything familiar about him?"

"No. Why should I?" Miss McIsaac glanced back up at him, her forehead creased in a frown.

"Did your father ride his horse to the bank?"

"No. We drove the buckboard in, parked it at the mercantile. Faither walked to the bank."

"Did any of your ranch hands ride in with you?"

"No. Are you trying to get at something, Marshal? Why don't you just ask what you want to know? Quit beating around the bush?"

Wyatt searched her eyes for a long second, ignoring the confused glare in them, and continued to watch her when he finally spoke. "When I questioned Mr. Samuels, he said the thief rode off on a horse that wore the McIsaac brand." He heard the soft exclamations of surprise from the Kilburns' lips as Miss McIsaac shoved her chair back and lunged to her feet.

"That's a lie!" She gasped, shaking her head.

Dr. Kilburn stood and placed a gentle hand on her shoulder. "Calm down, child. The marshal is just doing his job. He has to investigate what he's been told. Let's sit back down and hear the man out."

She sat with a thud. "There is no way it was one of our ranch hands. I'd trust every one of them with my life."

"The banker didn't seem to recognize the man who robbed him, but he did say the horse was a McIsaac ranch horse. Did the horse look familiar to you at all?'

She shook her head.

Wyatt wondered if she truly hadn't recognized the horse or if she merely refused to tell. He'd known this wasn't going to go well. He'd been correct. He was beginning to feel like ducking when those eyes turned toward him firing sparks. Wyatt ran a hand through his hair. It wasn't singed, yet. But the day was still young.

"I'm sorry to have to question you when your father is unconscious, but I need to gather as much information as I can to bring you father's shooter to justice."

"It's not your questions that bother me. It's the implication that our ranch was involved in the holdup. It's not true!"

"Again, I'm not implying anything. I have to follow

any and all leads I have and, unfortunately, that means asking you these questions. It also means I'm going to need directions to your ranch."

"You are not going to harass our hands with baseless accusations."

"I'm not going to accuse anyone, but you haven't been home in three days, and if it *was* one of your ranch horses, your hands might know something about it. If you won't give me directions to your place, I'll get them from someone else because I *will* follow up on this."

"Then I'm going with you. You are not questioning our hands without me there." Miss McIsaac got to her feet again, and Wyatt could feel anger radiating from her.

He could sympathize; he was beginning to feel the emotion himself. He pushed back his own chair and stood. "This is my job. I can handle it without your interference. Besides, you can't leave your father, can you?" Wyatt saw a retort die on Miss McIsaac's lips, and her shoulders slumped. His shot had found its mark.

Dr. Kilburn interrupted then. "Actually it might be a good idea for Miss McIsaac to go with you. She needs to get away for a little while. This would give her a chance to check on the ranch." Turning to Miss McIsaac, he continued, "Your father is stable, and it could be a while before he wakes up. Even when he does, it will be some time before he's ready to travel. This will give you a chance pick up anything you'll need for an extended stay."

She looked indecisive. "What if something happens while I'm gone?"

"You can make it to the ranch and back in just a few hours. I don't expect any changes with your father, good or bad, in that amount of time, and a change of scenery will do you good. If anything does happen, I'll send someone to bring you back."

Miss McIsaac looked at Wyatt. The glare was gone, replaced by a steely determination to accompany him. He doubted he'd seen the last of her temper, but the change of scene was already doing *him* some good.

His irritation cooled. "All right, you can ride along. I'll go get a buggy from Franks and be back to pick you up in about half an hour."

Grabbing his hat from the back of the chair where he'd hung it when he'd entered, he thanked Mrs. Kilburn for the coffee and headed to the front door.

Meri leaned against the edge of the livery stable doorway and worked to control her rapid breathing. She'd overheard the marshal tell Dr. Kilburn that he would ask the gunsmith to keep an eye on the town before getting a buggy from Franks. After a quick check on her father and a hurried explanation to the Kilburns, Meri had taken advantage of the marshal's plan and slipped out the back door.

Cutting through alleys at a run and keeping an eye out for a certain lawman, she'd made it to the livery unseen where Franks had helped her saddle two horses. She had no intention of riding with the man in a buggy all the way to the ranch. Horseback would be quicker, and it would allow her to keep her distance.

The intense fear and uncertainty of the past few days lifted enough to allow her to feel a tiny amount of smug satisfaction. She'd managed to regain some control of her life. Even if that control were only that she'd ride to the ranch *on* a horse instead of *behind* a horse.

The thought of sitting shoulder to shoulder with the marshal sent a funny shiver along her spine. That would be too much like courting, not that she knew anything about it. She wasn't girly enough to attract that kind of attention. When you could outride, outshoot and out rope the boys, they tended to treat you like one of the boys. And when it came time to go courtin', they went after the sweet-smelling, dainty town ladies.

Movement caught her eye, and she stepped back into the shadows of the barn as the long-legged figure of the marshal strode into view. "He's here, Franks." Meri gathered the reins of the two horses and mounted Abe in one fluid motion. "Thanks for the use of Abe. I'll have him back this afternoon. I'll also bring Sandy in with me if you can spare the room."

"I always got room for that puppy you call a hoss, honey. You be careful now, and I'll be a prayin' for yo daddy." Franks patted her knee and turned back to his forge as she rode out to meet the marshal, leading a second horse.

His eyes narrowed as Meri rode up to him and handed him a set of reins. He ignored them and shoved his hat back as he looked up at her. "Aren't you supposed to be at the Kilburns' waiting for me to return with a buggy?"

Chapter Four

"We can get to the ranch quicker this way. That is, if you'll quit standing there asking pointless questions and get on the horse." Meri tossed the ignored reins at him.

He snatched them neatly out of the air, his hazel eyes never wavering from her face. "How did you get here so fast?"

"I know a shortcut. Can we go now? Daylight's wasting." She was growing a little nervous under his scrutiny.

"Is it that you naturally don't like to follow orders…"

"You didn't issue an order. You only said you'd be back with the buggy. I decided this would be quicker." Meri's lips twitched in a nervous half grin.

"…or that you didn't want to ride in the buggy with me?" He continued as if the interruption hadn't happened.

Meri felt heat stain her cheeks at the accuracy of his guess, and a crooked grin began to spread across his face. "Standing around talking won't get us to the ranch," she blurted, and touched Abe. The horse jumped away from the grinning man into a ground-eating trot.

Glancing back, she saw him leap into his saddle without benefit of the stirrup and spring after her. Controlling the urge to race home, Meri kept the big black gelding at a respectful trot as she rode along the pasture fence to the outskirts of town and Little Creek Bridge. Maybe she *should* have stayed put and waited on the marshal and the buggy. It would have spared her the embarrassment of his accurate guess. Then again, this way she could get away from him for a minute, even if it didn't last long. She peered over her shoulder again. He was staying back, though he'd probably catch up to her once they were on the trail out of town, but it would be enough time for her cheeks to cool.

Abe's hooves thudded across the planks of the bridge spanning Little Creek, the clear-running stream that lent the town its name and marked its western boundary. Meri drew a deep breath. Dr. Kilburn was right. She *had* needed to get away and clear her head, and a horseback ride to her beloved home was the perfect way to do that even if she did have to put up with the meddlesome marshal.

"I thought I had a squirrel in that hole." Apparently he wasn't going to let her ignore the fact he'd guessed her real reason for riding horseback.

She felt her cheeks heat again at his satisfied tone. So much for having time for her blush to fade. If this kept up, she'd just have to get used to the sensation of her face being on fire.

Or…she could…

Meri flexed her heels against Abe's ribs, and the gelding switched to the rocking-chair lope that temporarily carried her away from her tormentor. The escape didn't last long. Franks had provided the marshal with a horse every bit Abe's equal, and in minutes the horses were side by side. The road wasn't in good enough shape from the recent deep mud to indulge in a full-out gallop, so Meri contented herself with the current pace and the wind in her face, thankful when the marshal remained silent.

The fresh pine-and-cedar-scented breeze began to weave calming fingers through Meri's hair as the beautiful scenery slipped past. Some of the tension melted from her shoulders, and the silence grew less uncomfortable in spite of feeling his eyes on her from time to time.

When he spoke, his comment caught her off guard. "I was sorry to hear about your mother."

Meri looked at him, but for a change, he wasn't looking at her. Somehow that made it easier to answer him. "How did you know?"

"Some of the men on the posse mentioned it—said it hadn't quite been a year since her death?"

Meri felt the weight of guilt and grief crash back down as she nodded. Her father had teased her on the way to Little Creek that her mother would have scolded her for wearing riding attire instead of a dress since she was going into town in a buggy. The words had reminded Meri of their loss, and she'd snapped that her mother wasn't around anymore.

She'd immediately regretted it. Instead of apologizing, however, she'd sulked, not understanding how less than a year after her mother's death, her father could tease about her mother's memory and seem to be handling her death so much better than Meri was. How she wished she'd guarded her tongue that day. She'd not apologized, and now it might be too late.

"What was her name?"

Meri welcomed his interruption of her depressing thoughts. "Catriona."

"So, both of your parents were from Scotland?" He

was watching the passing landscape as if memorizing every detail.

"Why did you say Scotland? Most people guess Ireland."

He looked at her then. "My name *is* Cameron. My grandparents came from Scotland. I recognize the brogue."

"I don't have a brogue."

"You do when you say *faither,* and I'd be willing to guess you used the Gaelic *mither* instead of *mother.*"

Meri nodded. "They came to America before I was born so their accent had softened, but when I was little they used a lot of Gaelic." A memory surfaced. "I did have a brogue by the time there was an actual school to attend. I remember the kids teasing me because they thought I was hard to understand. I worked hard to sound more like them, but I never quit using *mither* and *faither* to address my parents." She cocked her head. "I had forgotten about that."

Their horses topped a rise, and below them lay the McIsaac ranch nestled among the foothills of the Rockies. Marshal Cameron pulled his mount up, and Meri followed suit as they gave their horses a breather from the hour-long, gradually climbing ride and surveyed the property below them.

A large log ranch house was surrounded by orderly, well-kept outbuildings that included a couple of barns, a bunkhouse, a summer kitchen, a smokehouse and sundry smaller buildings. White fencing encircled a pretty garden already showing the effects of early springtime planting, and corrals housed horses and a few cattle. Empty pastures and hay fields radiated out from the ranch buildings and disappeared into trees and over foothills.

"So, this is home."

Meri nodded. "Beautiful, isn't it?"

"Absolutely." Silence reigned a few moments as both riders drank in the scene below them. "I do have a question, though." A puzzled look sat on his face.

Meri was becoming wary of his questions but was curious about the cause of the expression. "What?"

Marshal Cameron pointed toward the barn corrals. "What in the world is that…critter?"

A spontaneous laugh burst from Meri's lips when she looked in the direction he indicated. "Those are Highland cattle from Scotland. Faither imported them several years ago. They come from the mountainous region, and their thick wooly coats make them quite hardy in our cold snowy winters. Several ranches around Colorado raise them. There's even talk about starting a breed association. They're very self-sufficient cattle and thrive on the grazing that we have here. They're also easy to work with because they're so friendly."

"Well, it certainly is the hairiest beast I've ever seen, outside of a buffalo." He was watching Meri closely, a peculiar, distracted look on his face.

"And what have you ever seen *inside* a buffalo?" Meri kept a straight face but couldn't resist the question.

"What?"

A chuckle escaped her. "Never mind."

The dreaded smirk reappeared, and his searching gaze never left her face. "Oh, I got it. You…just surprised me. I didn't realize you were—"

He broke off abruptly. Meri wondered what he'd intended to say, but a distant shout prevented her from asking. Meri waved at a figure standing in front of the biggest barn.

"Come on. I'll introduce you to our foreman. He can answer any questions you have about the men and our horses."

* * *

Wyatt followed Miss McIsaac the rest of the way down to the ranch yard, enjoying his view of the spunky lady. So, this was the woman Mrs. Van Deusen wanted to introduce him to at the church picnic. Her full rich laugh and the way her face had lit up as she'd explained the cattle had nearly made him blurt the realization aloud. He had managed to catch himself, thankful for the distraction of the ranch hand's shout that had prevented Miss McIsaac from asking the question he'd seen on her face.

When he'd arrived in town, his bachelor status instantly made him the most popular person for invitations to a meal to meet someone's daughter, or niece, or sister or granddaughter. He'd quickly started turning a politely deaf ear when the conversation changed to, "Oh, I have someone you just have to meet…"

Mrs. Van Deusen had been somewhat more subtle but just as persistent. She never mentioned names or invited him to a meal to meet some female, but she'd mentioned her dear departed friend's lovely daughter every time Wyatt happened to cross her path. He'd let the hints go in one ear and out the other, but as he'd looked down at the ranch a moment ago, Mrs. Van Deusen's voice had echoed through his memory.

"If they can get in from their ranch," Mrs. Van Deusen had said, "they raise those strange cattle from Ireland or Scotland or someplace foreign like that, you know— I'll finally be able to introduce you to her at the church picnic."

That tidbit had snagged his attention since his own family tree originated in Scotland, but that was the extent of the notice he'd taken of it at the time. With the disturbance of the holdup, he'd not had time to realize Mrs. Van Deusen's hints added up to the spirited, rides-like-the-wind Meri McIsaac. After the onslaught of gushing, flirting females breathing down his neck the past few weeks, Miss McIsaac's prickly reaction had been a fresh change and had actually snagged his attention. Not that he planned to do anything about it; he still had a dangerous job and no home to offer a woman.

Wyatt mentally scoffed at himself. Even if *he* were willing to think about going along with Mrs. Van Deusen's schemes, he was quite sure her quarry had no intention of being caught. Besides, he had enough trouble on his hands trying to catch a bank robber and find the missing money.

"Howdy, miss, how's the Boss man?" A familiar voice cut through Wyatt's musings.

"Still unconscious. I came to pick up a few things and get an update on the ranch. Faither will want to know when he wakes up. Where's Barnaby?" Miss McIsaac kept her voice brisk and businesslike, but Wyatt heard the underlying fear.

"He's riding range with a couple of the boys, said he might be back for lunch."

"This is the new marshal. He needs to ask Barnaby some questions. He seems to think the horse the bank robber rode was one of ours." Miss McIsaac and Wyatt dismounted simultaneously. "Marshal Cameron, our top hand, Jonah Chacksfield."

"There's no need to introduce us, miss. I've known Captain Cameron since he was a lowly shavetail lieutenant fresh from the East." Jonah snapped a sharp salute.

"At ease, Sergeant." Wyatt put out his hand and grabbed the man's burly paw in a hearty handshake. "It's good to see you. What are you doing out of the army? You were one of the best sergeants I ever served with, figured you'd be in uniform until you got too old to climb into a saddle."

The stocky barrel-chested ranch hand looked away momentarily. When he looked back, Wyatt thought he saw a sheen of wetness in the man's eyes. "I just didn't have the heart to reenlist after my Sally passed."

Wyatt gripped the sergeant's shoulder and cleared his throat against a sudden hoarseness. "I wondered why I quit getting letters from her. I assumed you'd been transferred, and they were getting lost." He stopped and swallowed hard. "She was a quite a lady. I'll miss her."

Jonah was the first to break the silence that shrouded the little group, saying gruffly, "Now, sir, what's this about one of our horses being used in the bank job?"

"Drop that 'sir' stuff, and call me Wyatt. When I questioned the banker this morning, he said the horse the thief used wore the McIsaac brand. None of the other witnesses I talked to mentioned that. Maybe they assumed Mr. McIsaac had ridden in on that horse and the thief stole it. However, since that wasn't the case, I need to know if you've noticed any horses missing and where all the ranch hands were that day."

"I told you before, none of our hands would be involved in anything criminal." Miss McIsaac flared up again.

Jonah wrapped a beefy arm around Miss McIsaac's shoulders and gently squeezed. "He's just doing his job, Miss Meri. No need to get upset about it. You've got enough on your plate. Let me and Barnaby handle the captain and his questions. You go in and chat with Ms. Maggie. That housekeeper's been frettin' around here for days like a hen that's lost her chicks."

Wyatt waited for the inevitable argument, but her shoulders drooped as she exhaled noisily. "You'll let me know if anything's wrong, and send Barnaby to see me when he comes in." It wasn't a question.

"I will. Now go let Ms. Maggie fuss over you for a bit." Jonah gently turned Miss McIsaac toward the house and gave her a gentle push. "Scat."

Wyatt watched in amazement as Miss McIsaac meekly walked to the house and disappeared inside. "I've seen you wrangle raw, rowdy recruits and turn them into well-disciplined troops, but until today I never fully appreciated the extent of your skill." Wyatt looked at Jonah with newfound respect. "How exactly did you manage that?"

Jonah's hearty laugh thundered out. "She's a handful, but I'll take a strong, opinionated female over a silly, pampered flibbertigibbet any day of the week."

"As will I, but that doesn't explain how you managed to get her to go so quietly."

"A good sergeant never reveals his secrets, Captain. Besides, I have a hunch you'll figure out how to handle her. Half the fun of courting my Sally was figuring out how to deal with her strong temperament."

"Sorry to disappoint you, but a lawman's life doesn't leave room for courtin'."

"Are you still stuck on the notion you have to have a 'safe' job before you can have a wife?"

"It's not a notion. I saw more than one bride-to-be hightail it back East when she saw her future living quarters. I saw wives leave their husbands because they couldn't handle the long absences, and I saw women devastated when their husband rode in draped over the back of a horse. I won't do that to a woman."

"You saw a couple of bad examples and focused on them instead of the good ones. What about my Sally?" Jonah sounded a bit offended.

Wyatt hurried to soften his remarks. "You were the exemption to the rule. Sally was special."

Memories glistened in the tough old sergeant's eyes. "That she was, that she was."

Wyatt changed the subject. "Back to the reason I rode out here—what do you have to tell me that you didn't want Miss McIsaac to hear?"

"You always were one of the sharper knives among that lot of army brass. We *did* have a horse go missing for several days before showing up among some of our cattle all covered in dried sweat. I don't want Miss Meri to be worryin' about it just now since there's nothing she can do. I've questioned all our hands, but no one noticed anything unusual, and I trust our men. We've got a few who can be a little wild occasionally, but they're all honest fellows. Mr. McIsaac has given all of us a hand up when we were down on our luck, and not a one of us would do anything to hurt him or Miss Meri."

"Are any of the men available that I can talk with them?"

"Barnaby, our foreman, and most of the hands are out doing various chores. If you're hungry, we can grab a sandwich from our cook, and I'll introduce you to the ones in for lunch. Barnaby should be back in as well, and you can ask 'em any questions you have. Afterward, I'll take you out and show you where we found that horse."

"I'd appreciate that."

Over lunch Wyatt met the handful of cowboys that assembled for food. None of them knew anything more than what Jonah had already told him, and to a man, they had nothing but concern and well wishes for their wounded "Boss man."

When everyone drifted back to their various tasks, Jonah brought up a couple of fresh, saddled horses.

"Ready to ride, Captain? Barnaby hasn't made it back, but I'll wager we'll run across him before we return to the ranch."

Wyatt mounted the horse. "You've probably told me as much as he can, but I'd appreciate getting a chance to meet him. And I thought I told you to call me Wyatt?"

"Too many years in the army. Captain comes easier to the tongue."

Jonah led the way across the ranch yard, and as they passed the main house Miss McIsaac stepped out on the porch. "Hold up! I'm going with you," she called out.

"No. Stay put. Jonah's going to show me around, let me get a feel for the land out this way and maybe catch up with your foreman. I'll be back to escort you to town before it gets dark." Wyatt lifted his hat and loped his horse away, ignoring the protests from the woman on the porch and Jonah's sardonic snort.

Chapter Five

Jonah waved a hand toward the land in front of them. "This is where we found that horse day before yesterday. He'd been ridden hard and still had the dried sweat, saddle and spur marks to show for it. Made the boys livid. Not only had someone stolen one of our remuda from under our noses, they also used it badly in the process. Our hands pride themselves that when they *do* use their spurs they do it with such gentle finesse they never leave a mark or a sore spot on the horse.

"I backtracked the rider and found where he'd had a fresh mount waiting. After he'd swapped, he set ours loose. Both sets of tracks led into and out of that churned-up ground where the trail herd circled town a few days ago."

Wyatt nodded. "That's where we lost him when we were tracking him. We caught up with the drovers, but they said they hadn't seen anybody, and we couldn't find where he'd turned off before it started raining."

"He was pretty slick about it. I might not have found it if he hadn't used the same route coming and going from the cattle trail. He used an offshoot of Little Creek to hide his tracks, but he was a little less careful after he swapped horses. I was able spot the signs of his previous trip when I trailed the new horse back. I didn't follow him any farther after he hit that trail—figured we had our horse back and that was the end of it. We let the surrounding ranchers know to keep an eye on their own remudas and left it at that. Never thought about it being connected with what had happened in town."

"The tracks'll be washed out, but show me where you trailed him so I can get an idea of where he was and where we lost him."

"Sure 'nuff. We'll go right through the area Barnaby was plannin' on workin' when he left this morning. If he's still there, we'll stop and chat."

They did meet up with Barnaby and several other hands moving cattle to another area for fresh grazing. Wyatt was impressed with the graying, quiet-spoken man, but again didn't learn anything new. Barnaby promised to keep his men alert to anything that might be of interest to the marshal. He also told Jonah to ride in with Wyatt and stay in town where he could keep an eye on the Boss man and Miss Meri.

The rest of the afternoon passed quickly, and Wyatt got a feel for the land. It was beautiful mountain-valley country, and he was impressed with the way the land was being utilized to its fullest potential. Every time he saw the strange-looking woolly red cattle, the memory of a laugh rang through his thoughts.

The McIsaac ranch lay west and slightly north of Little Creek and the bandit had ridden out of town heading east. The trail herd had bypassed the town on the west before veering northeast toward Denver.

"Do the trail herds always go this direction?" Wyatt asked. "Seems like it'd be shorter to go around the east side of town."

"We don't have as many now that the railroads are getting more accessible, but a few still come around the west side and across a portion of our range because McIsaac allows them access. There are more farmers on the east side now, and they don't appreciate their crops getting torn up. Most of the trail bosses do their best to ensure they do the least amount of damage possible," Jonah replied.

Wyatt studied the land. "When we first lost the tracks, we continued east in the direction he'd been traveling. We followed the trail herd until we caught up to the drovers, then we backtracked and had almost made it to where you're showing me he cut out before it began to rain. If we'd come this direction first, we might have found his trail before it rained and been closer to catching him." Wyatt was frustrated. "Why did he circle back around the town and stay in the area when he knew a posse was after him? Why didn't he get as far away as he could, as fast as he could?"

"Maybe he did. By coming this way, he did the unexpected and bought himself more time," Jonah mused.

"This is *definitely* not an auspicious beginning to my job as Little Creek's marshal, and if I don't catch him and get the bank's money back, it'll be a very short-lived job. The good citizens are understandably nervous about that money," Wyatt groaned.

"Well, there is someone we can talk to who'll be able to point us in the direction we need to go for you to catch him," Jonah said, turning his horse to face Wyatt.

"Who?" Curiosity filled Wyatt's voice.

"Him." Jonah glanced up briefly before bowing his head, and Wyatt felt peace descend and frustration melt away as he listened to the former master sergeant bend his knee before the Master of Heaven, asking for God's wisdom and guidance in the task before the marshal.

He echoed the prayer in his heart and uttered a hearty Amen when Jonah finished. "Thank you for realigning my perspective, Sergeant. You were always good at that, if I recall."

"I did straighten out a few smart-mouthed lieutenants in my time. Although I must say, I had less polishing to do on you then some I ran across. Your mother'd done a pretty good job already." Both men chuckled as they headed back.

Riding into the ranch yard, Wyatt cast a glance at the lowering sun. "Miss McIsaac is going to be champing at the bit to get back into town."

"If she hasn't already left." Jonah grinned.

"I told her to wait—that I'd ride back with her. I don't want her, any woman, out on these roads alone, at least until we catch this fella."

Jonah snorted. "I'll be much surprised if she waited around more than a few minutes after you threw that order at her."

"Why didn't you say something earlier? Stop her from going in alone?"

"Figured it was about time you learned you can't bark orders at a woman as if she's a soldier. It just don't work. Besides, Boss man has a standing order. When someone sees her ride out, which is frequently, they are to let the bunkhouse cook or Ms. Maggie know and then follow Meri to make sure no one bothers her. Boss man couldn't cure her of riding alone, something he loves to do himself, so he makes sure someone is always keeping an eye on her. I think she figured out his little scheme a long time ago, but as long as they stay out of her way, she tolerates it."

The men stopped their horses in front of the main house and a sturdy, dusky-skinned woman, black braids wound in bands around her head, stepped onto the porch carrying a tray with a pitcher and several glasses. "Thirsty? I have fresh lemonade here," she said in a lightly accented voice.

"Yes'm, Ms. Maggie! Sounds great! Captain Cameron, meet the real ramrod of the McIsaac ranch, Maggie Running Deer, the McIsaac's housekeeper." Jonah took the tray and set it on a table between several comfortable-looking rocking chairs. "Ms. Maggie, the new marshal of Little Creek."

Wyatt doffed his hat and bowed slightly to the woman. "Nice to meet you, ma'am. Is Miss McIsaac ready to head back to town?" He took the glass of lemonade Jonah handed him and swallowed half of it in a single swallow, choking when he heard the woman's answer.

"She left a couple of hours after you rode out. Barnaby rode in, and after talking with him, she tossed a bag on Abe and took him and Sandy back to town."

A sly grin appeared on Jonah's face, but he refrained from saying *I told you so*.

Wyatt hastily swallowed the last of the tangy drink before setting the glass down. "Thank you, Ms. Maggie. That hit the spot."

"Sit down, Captain, and take a load off." Jonah disposed of his own glass. "I've got to put a few things in my saddlebags before we head to town." Thanking Ms. Maggie, he headed for the barn leading the two horses.

Wyatt quelled the urge to rush back to town and slowly sat down. Miss McIsaac had, by now, probably already arrived back in town, but his hands itched to give her a good shaking—the little scamp. Instead he controlled his impatience and accepted the refilled glass Ms. Maggie handed him before heading back to her baking.

One of the cowhands he had met earlier ambled up leading the horse he'd ridden from town, along with another saddled horse, and tied them to the rail in front of the house. "Jonah'll be 'long direc'ly." The man sauntered away.

The minutes dragged by as he gazed unseeingly at the tidy ranch yard, fingers drumming on the arm of the rocker. Flower beds sported a few early delicate blooms, a kitchen garden boasted rows of emerging greenery, and neat fences spread out and away, delineating pasturage. All lent a well-cared-for air to the place, yet they failed to register beyond a vague awareness as Wyatt turned the day over in his mind. He needed to separate the few pieces he'd found and examine them thoroughly; see if, and where, each piece fit into the puzzle of the bank robbery.

"You gonna sit staring into space all day, or do you want to ride in with me?" Jonah laughed at his blink of surprise when he looked up to see the sergeant already mounted.

Wyatt hurried off the porch and swung into the saddle. "Don't get uppity, Sergeant, or I'll put you on report!"

Jonah's laugh rang as they turned their horses toward town.

Meri imagined the look on the marshal's face when he realized she was gone, and grinned. She'd eaten lunch while Ms. Maggie fussed about the holdup and Boss man's injury and had just finished packing a bag when she'd seen the marshal and Jonah riding out. Planning to ride with them and speak to Barnaby herself, she'd instead been ordered to stay put. She'd tried to argue they could get back to town quicker if they combined their tasks but had been completely ignored as the overbearing man had ridden away at a lope. She'd nearly gone back to town then and there but had curtailed the impulse. The job she'd left her wounded father's side to do wouldn't be completed to her satisfaction until she'd spoken with Barnaby.

Time had crawled as she'd prowled the barns and grounds, repeatedly answering the question, "How's Boss man?" from worried ranch hands who wanted the information straight from her. Impatience had finally gotten the best of her, and she'd been saddling Sandy to go find the foreman herself when he'd ridden in. Having already heard the latest update on McIsaac from Jonah and the marshal, Barnaby had quickly filled her in on ranch happenings. He had things well in hand and had promised to send a rider in frequently with news of the ranch and to check on Boss man. Faither would be pleased, but not surprised, at Barnaby's capable management in their absence.

Thanking him for his diligent care of the ranch, she'd tied her bag to Abe's saddle, shoved her .44-40 Winchester carbine into the rifle boot, mounted Sandy and left the annoying marshal to fend for himself. The nerve-rattling tension was absent on this leg of the journey, and Meri smugly congratulated herself on getting back to town on her own terms. She shoved away the ridiculous notion that the trip seemed rather dull in comparison to the ride to the ranch.

Heavenly Father, please heal Faither so we can return home and life can get back to normal...without that bossy marshal.

The silent prayer evaporated before she finished, and the peace she'd tasted earlier was nowhere to be found. All the joy she normally experienced when riding her lovely palomino failed to materialize, and even the satisfaction at having outsmarted a certain lawman tasted stale.

The unexpectedly disappointing ride finally neared the end, and Meri breathed a sigh of relief as she approached the edge of town. Pausing, she heard echoing hoofbeats behind her. Spying a suitable hiding place in the brush alongside the road, she situated herself and Sandy, tied Abe's lead rope around his neck and tapped his hip to send him on down the road. She was rewarded shortly when the cowboy who'd been surreptitiously following her rode into view. He pulled his horse up short when he saw Abe grazing along the roadside alone. He glanced around suspiciously.

"You can head home now, Shorty. Tell Barnaby and Ms. Maggie I made it to town in one piece," she said dryly, nudging Sandy out of hiding.

Shorty touched the brim of his hat and turned his horse, a sheepish smile at being caught on his face.

Meri grinned at him. It had become a game to see if she could spot the rider tailing her. Some were better at staying hidden then others, but she knew someone was always within earshot on her "solitary" rides.

There had been Indian trouble in several areas of the newly formed state, but they hadn't had a problem in this area for many years. She felt so safe on the ranch, she often forgot she lived in what Easterners called the "Wild" West and took off alone on Sandy. Her father allowed this, as she was always armed, but quietly arranged for additional protection. Meri suspected her father, himself, followed her from time to time and was one of the riders she felt but never saw or caught.

Faither.

Her throat ached with a sudden tightness as she remembered him lying so still, blood pooling on the bank floor. She couldn't handle losing him, too.

Meri turned her head in the direction of the cemetery where her mother's body lay. The burial ground sprawled along a high slope a little over a half a mile from the western edge of town, out of danger of any floodwaters from Little Creek.

Retrieving the happily grazing Abe, Meri detoured and headed that direction. She'd not been back to her mother's grave since the funeral. She knew only the shell of the loving wife and mother was there, but the loss seemed so bitterly final there that Meri only wanted to avoid it. The cemetery represented nothing but death and heart-ache to her.

She missed her mother so much she physically ached sometimes. She missed her hugs, her laugh. She missed the way her mother would lovingly call her by her full name—America Catriona. She didn't need a cold gray headstone to reinforce her loss.

Today, however, she forced herself to keep riding to-ward it. She should at least check on her mother's plot. Then when Faither awoke, she'd be able to tell him she'd checked on the ranch *and* Mother.

Nearing the graveyard, she noticed movement between the tree line bordering the top edge of the cemetery and a ridiculously ornate crypt. Meri halted Sandy. The crypt was the local oddity, having been built by an eccentric miner who'd struck it rich. He'd resided around Little Creek long enough to see it completed before moving on to follow rumors of another gold strike and leaving the empty, imported-marble monstrosity looking disdain-fully down upon meager creek-stone or wooden markers. Two marble lions guarded the door of the vault, but they proved inadequate protection against curiosity seekers and mischievous boys.

Meri fully expected to see a couple of those boys now, but instead, Mr. Samuels appeared around the side of it, head down, walking slowly. She felt her eyes widen in surprise. He hadn't been out and about much since the theft at the bank, owing to his own head injury, and he must have walked because she didn't see his buggy anywhere. Why was he wandering around up there anyway? His wife's grave plot was down near the front of the cemetery not far from her mother's plot. Had the blow to his head left him a little confused?

He glanced up, saw her and flinched as if startled. Meri lifted her hand to wave, but he ducked his head and scurried down the slope of the graveyard. Reaching his wife's grave, he knelt, turning his back to her.

Meri felt for him. She understood how it was when someone intruded on your private grief and quietly turned the horses away from the cemetery with a sense of relief for the reprieve. She could always come back later when she wouldn't be interrupting anyone, and she really needed to get the horses tended to and return to Faither. She'd been gone far too long already.

Several minutes later Meri dismounted in front of Dr. Kilburn's and looped the reins around the hitching post. Taking her satchel off Abe, she saw a tall boy walking toward her. "Billy?"

"Yes, ma'am?"

"Are you available to run an errand for me?"

"Yup, I was keepin' a lookout for ya. I'm to let Mrs. Van Deusen know when you get back here 'cause she's gonna bring you a plate of supper, and she'll give me my choice of candy next time I'm in the store." Billy nodded, grinning. "I reckon I kin do that when I run your errand."

Meri grinned in response to Billy's freckled, friendly one. "Yes, I reckon you can. I'll give you a nickel if you'll walk Sandy and Abe over to Franks's, and tell him I'll come see him as soon as I can."

"Yes, ma'am! I'll take real good care of 'em! And Mrs. Van Deusen'll bring you a real nice supper when

I tell 'er you're back." Billy's grin stretched even wider as Meri placed the promised nickel in the grimy outstretched hand.

"By the way, why is Mrs. Van Deusen bringing me supper?" Meri asked.

"On account a Mrs. Kilburn havin' to sit with somebody who's sick, I guess. Mrs. Van Deusen said she'd take care of you and Doc this evenin'." Billy carefully untied Abe and Sandy.

Meri took her bag and slid her carbine out of the saddle scabbard, stepped back and watched as the lanky adolescent proudly led the two steeds down the middle of the road, whistling and calculating whether to spend or save the precious nickel.

"I'm glad you're back so soon, Meri," Dr. Kilburn said gravely as he opened the front door and waved Meri inside.

Meri's heart lurched in fear. "Faither?"

"He's taken a turn for the worse." His tone was sober and regretful.

If Dr. Kilburn was worried, it must be bad. Fear swallowed Meri. This couldn't be happening. Not again!

She ran for the room where her father lay. Reaching for the door handle, she stared at her full hands. She'd forgotten she was still carrying her bag and carbine. Her frantic brain wasn't able to coordinate the task of setting down the items to turn the knob.

Doc reached around her and opened the door before gently relieving her of the items. Meri hastened over and collapsed to her knees at the edge of the bed. Her father looked so much worse since just this morning. His breathing was labored, his skin flushed and damp with perspiration and creases slashed across his drawn face in cruel lines.

It was only a bump on the head and a slight wound! People recovered from worse. Why wasn't her father recovering? Looking up at Doc, she croaked, "Why...?"

Doc seemed to understand what she couldn't voice. "He's fighting infection in that bullet wound, and his fever is rising. He's not responding to anything I've given him."

A soft tap sounded on the door frame, and Pastor Willis stepped into the room. "I stopped to check on Ian."

Doc repeated what he'd told Meri. As he finished speaking, Pastor Willis dropped to his knees alongside Meri and placed his hand on McIsaac's shoulder. Speaking quietly, he prayed aloud for healing and restoration, wisdom for Doc and peace for Meri. When he finished, he turned to her. "Is there anything I or the church members can do for you besides keeping people informed and praying?"

Meri shook her head then stopped as an idea pierced through the fog in her brain. "Uh, maybe. Do you remember the sermon you preached once about calling for the elders of the church?"

"Yes, I do—James 5:14 and 15. 'Is any sick among you? let him call for the elders of the church; and let them pray over him, anointing him with oil in the name of the Lord: And the prayer of faith shall save the sick, and the Lord shall raise him up...'"

"That's the one. Would you do that for Faither?"

"Of course, dear. All you had to do was ask. I'll go notify the men of the church and bring them back here as quickly as possible." Pastor Willis patted Meri on the hand, pushed himself to his feet and left the room.

"Is there anything I can do to help Faither while we wait?"

"I'll get some fresh water, and you can sponge his face and neck to give him some relief from the fever.

That's what I was doing when I heard you arrive." Picking up a basin and wet cloth from the bedside stand, he left the room.

Meri dropped her face into her hands. Fear sat so heavy on her chest it was difficult to draw a breath, and she trembled all over. Her heart labored with hard, painful thuds. She couldn't have stood to her feet if she were forced at the point of a gun.

A gun.

The nasty urge to find the man who'd injured her father swept over Meri in a black rage. Oh, how she wanted to hurt the man who'd done this! Do to him what he'd done to her father! Anger surged through her temporarily replacing fear, and Meri shot to her feet as Dr. Kilburn reentered the room carrying a fresh cloth and basin of water.

"Here, keep your hands busy and your father a little cooler."

Meri moved to do his bidding, tenderly wiping her father's face repeatedly with the cool wet cloth while chewing on the anger raging through her and envisioning what she would do when she got her hands on the person who had caused her father's injury.

It was some time before she paid any attention to the quiet nudging in her spirit to pray, to forgive, and when she did, she couldn't push any words past her clenched teeth or her even tighter heart. The man who did this didn't deserve to be forgiven, her emotions argued.

Giving up the halfhearted struggle, anger and fear once again vied for dominance, and the bitter ache that had resided in her heart since her mother's death shaped itself into a hard, defiant, angry knot.

Meri lost track of time and jumped when she heard subdued voices and multiple feet entering the house. Laying aside the wet cloth and grabbing a nearby towel, she hastily dried her hands, smoothed back her hair and straightened her clothes. She wished she'd taken a moment to change into fresh attire, but she was out of time. A knock sounded, and she stiffened her spine and took a deep breath before stepping to the door to open it.

Pastor Willis entered the room followed by six more men, all showing signs of having recently and hastily washed up from their day's labors. The men included Mr. Benhard, the Western Union agent; Mr. Allen, the surveyor; Mr. Gumperston, owner of the café; Mr. Hubert, the barber; Mr. Van Deusen and Franks. All were members and elders of Little Creek Baptist Church, and hearing the clock chime from the parlor, Meri realized that these men, in all probability, had delayed their supper by coming to pray for her father. The knot in her chest softened just a bit at this display of concern and care for him, and she struggled to swallow past the lump that blocked her throat.

Dr. Kilburn was last through the door, behind the solemn little troop, and ushered Meri through the now-crowded room to seat her in the rocker. Pastor Willis stood at the end of the bed and pulled a small Bible out of the pocket of his black frock coat. After flipping through the pages, he stopped and read aloud the passage from James 5 before asking the assembled men to take turns praying.

Closing her eyes, Meri listened to the humble prayers. Men she had been acquainted with only in a cursory way through church and town activities now knelt at the Throne of Grace asking for healing for their Brother in Christ. Men like Mr. Van Deusen who never spoke more than a few words at a time poured out their hearts to God as they prayed for her father. Their fervent requests made the small room ring, and the simple eloquence of their prayers further loosened the knot that had formed in her chest.

When Franks stepped up to pray, Meri's eyes startled open, and her gaze flew to his face when he mentioned her. "Father God, I ask in faith, dat you heal Brother Ian, dat you raise 'im up from dis bed a sickness. And Father, I ask dat you heal Miss Meri from de hurt a losin' her Mama, and dat you give her de abil'ty to forgive de man dat did dis crime. I ask dis in de precious, holy name ob Jesus!"

How had Franks known she was struggling with forgiveness? She hadn't realized it herself until moments before the men had arrived. Meri forced her eyes shut as Pastor Willis began to pray and wrap up the solemn little service. He reiterated the requests for the full recovery of Mr. McIsaac and for peace, grace and the ability to forgive for Meri, and finished by thanking God for his promise of healing and for the willingness of the gathered men to humble themselves in prayer for Ian McIsaac.

Meri stood and moved around the end of the bed at the gruffly chorused Amen and watched as the men surreptitiously wiped at their eyes. Her own eyes were dry, but her throat was painfully tight as she tried to express her thanks to men who, one by one, came up to her, shook her hand and thanked *her* for the opportunity to help, to pray.

Pastor Willis urged Meri to let him know when there was any change or any further way he could be of service, and then he exited the room behind the men, leaving Doc and Franks with Meri. Doc leaned over and checked on Ian, and Franks reached down to draw Meri into a gentle hug. How she wished she could give in to the desperate urge to cry. Her eyes and throat burned but no relief of tears came. She heaved a dry, sobbing sigh.

"Hush now, chil'. I know you is hurtin', maybe wurse

den yo' pa, but our God'll heal you, if you let 'im. Jis as surely as de sun rise in de mornin'. You jis place yo' faith in His promise!"

Chapter Six

Meri forced her aching eyes open. It had been a long night of no rest as she'd kept vigil, bathing her father's feverish face repeatedly. Mrs. Van Deusen had delivered supper and given Meri a chance to wash up, change clothes and eat, and then had insisted on staying the rest of the night. Meri had tried to dissuade her, dreading the woman's chatter, but Mrs. Van Deusen had refused to leave. To Meri's grateful surprise, however, the shopkeeper had seemed to realize Meri was near the end of her rope and had merely added her quiet prayer to those still echoing in the room before pulling out her knitting.

In the early-morning hours her father's fever had broken, his breathing had grown easier and Dr. Kilburn had declared the immediate crisis over. Mrs. Van Deusen had dozed off and on during the long night and had ordered Meri and Doc to their rooms for some rest, promising to wake them if there were any changes. Stumbling to a spare room, Meri had collapsed on the bed fully clothed, asleep as soon as her head hit the pillow.

Now, trying to focus her weary eyes on the small clock on the bedside table, she was surprised to see it was after nine o'clock. She'd slept the morning away. Sitting up, she tossed aside the blanket someone had laid over her and moved to the dressing table. Fresh water was in the pitcher, and she gratefully splashed the cool liquid on her face before brushing her hair and pulling it off her face in a hasty braid. Changing into a fresh skirt and blouse, she hurried to her father's room.

Dr. Kilburn looked up from his examination of her father as she came in.

"Has his fever come back?" she asked fearfully.

"No." Doc's voice was hushed and held a strange note. "In fact, if I hadn't seen it yesterday, I wouldn't believe he ever had a crisis."

"What do you mean?" Meri asked in confusion.

"I mean there is absolutely no sign of infection, the wound is clear and healing well, there's no hint of fever, his color has improved and his breathing and pulse are all normal for someone who's just asleep." Doc moved to the nearby basin and washed his hands, muttering under his breath. "We asked God to intervene yesterday, but I guess I didn't expect it to happen so fast. I claim to have faith, but…" Doc shook his head, a rueful expression on his face.

"I don't understand. If he's better, why is he still unconscious?"

"Your father was in a coma from the head injury and then had complications from the infection. Today the infection is gone, the lump from the blow to the head is nearly gone, the symptoms that indicate a coma are gone, and he's responding to stimuli. Your father exhibits all the signs of a man who is simply sleeping."

"Then why don't you wake him up?" Meri whispered in frustration.

"He stirred some during my examination but didn't

wake completely. Sleep is healing to the body, and I'd like him to wake on his own."

Taking her by the arm, he ushered her out of the room, gently closing the door. In the kitchen he poured two cups of coffee. Handing one to Meri, he sat down, took a sip of the steaming brew and heaved a huge sigh of satisfaction. "My wife should be home shortly since the patient she was watching last night is on the mend, and with your father looking so much better, I'm feeling quite the successful practitioner this morning." He chuckled. "I don't think I had all that much to do with any of it, though. A greater Physician than I has been at work this morning."

Meri tentatively sipped the bitter drink and hid a grimace. She really didn't like the stuff, but maybe it would wake her up since she seemed to be walking through a dream. As the liquid hit her empty stomach, it growled loudly in protest. "Excuse me!"

"No. Excuse me. I forgot to tell you breakfast is waiting for you at Naoma's. She left early this morning after I returned from checking on my other patients. We let you sleep as long as you wanted. You are under doctor's orders to get some fresh air, stretch your legs and have a hearty breakfast."

"What about your breakfast, and Faither—I need to be here when he wakes up."

"I had a lovely breakfast with my wife when I checked on her and her patient, and you sitting around waiting for your father to wake up won't change things or hurry them along. I don't want you as a patient, too, so follow my prescription and go get some hot breakfast."

"But what if he wakes up while I'm gone?"

"I'll be right here, and he'll still be here when you return. You're only going to Naoma's, not around the world.

You'll be back before you know it. But don't run there and back. Walk."

Feeling her stomach rumble again, Meri took his advice, and after checking to see that her father was still asleep, she walked toward Thomas and Naoma Van Deusen's home.

"Well, good morning. I wondered where you were hiding." The marshal's voice rang out, startling her and causing a couple of passersby to turn and look at the man walking toward her.

"I wasn't hiding, but maybe I should have." A grin lit the marshal's face at her feisty reply, and she fought the unexpected urge to grin right back. *No,* she warned herself. *Don't encourage him.*

"I saw Doc when he did his rounds earlier. He said your father was doing better. Is he awake yet?" He fell into step alongside her.

She shook her head. "Doc *says* Faither is better, but he hasn't woken up." She winced at the childish whine in her voice, but the fear that Dr. Kilburn might be shielding her… Meri turned to head back. She should not have left her father.

Fingers touched her arm, halting her steps. Almost as soon as she registered the contact, his hand withdrew, and he shoved it into his pocket. "Is Dr. Kilburn a liar?"

"What? No! Of course not." The worry whirling inside her dissipated at the unexpected question.

He parked his free hand on the butt of his pistol. "Because I'm the man to see if you want to file a complaint against him."

The absolute ridiculousness of filing a complaint against Dr. Kilburn caused a rueful grin to tug at her mouth. "And who do I see if I want to file a complaint against you?"

He rubbed at his chin thoughtfully. "Now, I don't rightly know. I've never had anyone complain about me before."

The grin tugged harder, turning up the corners of her mouth as she forced her feet to continue to Mrs. Van Deusen's house. "You are incorrigible."

"Well, thank you, but that's not exactly what I'd call a complaint." His long, easy stride brought him alongside her again as she neared the little cottage tucked behind the mercantile.

Mrs. Van Deusen stepped onto the porch and waved. "Good morning, Marshal. Come in and have some breakfast with Meri."

"No, thank you. I ate at the café this morning."

Meri hid a relieved sigh. The thought of sharing breakfast with him did funny things to her insides.

"That was hours ago. I know because I saw you leaving when I headed home. I have plenty of hot biscuits, sausage and gravy, and I won't take no for an answer."

He shrugged. "Who can refuse an offer like that?" He stepped onto the porch and held the door open for her. "After you."

"Thank you," she said to the marshal. As they entered the kitchen, she turned to Mrs. Van Deusen. "I'm sorry you had to go to all this trouble after being up all night."

"Fiddle-faddle. I left early enough this morning that I had a chance to take a nap after Thomas opened the store. I had just gotten up when I looked out and saw you coming. Now quit apologizing and dig in." She set two steaming plates of food in front of them. "You two keep yourselves company. I, ah, I need to take something to Thomas. He's so absentminded you know."

Meri knew nothing of the kind. Thomas might be quiet and reserved, compared to his voluble wife, but absentminded he was not. Naoma scurried out the door leaving a painful silence behind her.

"Shall I ask the blessing?" At her nod Wyatt bowed his head and prayed a quick prayer before picking up his fork and digging into the fragrant food on his plate. He ignored the bowed head and pink cheeks on the woman across the table.

She took a halfhearted bite of food, keeping her head down. The food must have sparked her appetite, because after the second bite, she dug in eagerly. When her plate was almost empty, she laid her fork down and leaned back, still avoiding his gaze.

Wyatt stood and gathered his dishes. Since she didn't seem inclined to break the silence, military strategy called for a diversion to end the standoff. "Why did your parents leave Scotland?"

Miss McIsaac dabbed her mouth with her napkin, a feminine move that might have distracted a less disciplined soldier. "They were evicted off the land and put on a boat to Canada during the potato famine."

"How'd they wind up in Colorado?" He placed his dishes in the tub of soapy water and began to wash them. He didn't want Miss McIsaac to think he was going along with Mrs. Van Deusen's matchmaking scheme, but it was only polite to do the dishes in return for such a fine meal.

"They worked their way down to the States, where I was born, and saved every penny they could. Faither worked as a hired hand, and Mither took in laundry. When they heard about the gold rush, they followed it out here."

"Did they strike it rich?"

"Not in gold. Faither tried panning for gold, but he found he could make more money driving freight wagons of supplies to the miners." She grinned slightly, remembering. "Mither panned more gold dust than Faither ever did."

She should smile more often. Then again, it might be safer for him if she didn't. "What do you mean?"

"Mither took in washing and mending from miners who couldn't or wouldn't do their own. She said she would pan her wash water before dumping it out to collect the gold dust she'd washed from their pockets."

Wyatt chuckled. "Smart woman."

Her smile disappeared. "She was." Her eyes took on a distant look. "I was little, but I remember how tough those years were. They scrimped and saved, and when the Homestead Act was passed, Faither staked his claim on a piece of land he'd seen while hauling freight. For the first time in his life, Faither owned his own piece of ground. He kept driving freight wagons for a while to bring in money, buying a couple head of cattle at a time to stock his ranch. It was slow, but he built a home and solid herd without going into debt. Later when they modified the Homestead Act, Faither was able to acquire more land. The ranch is nearly a thousand acres now—bigger than the estate their landlord owned in Scotland."

"And stocked with the furriest cows I've ever seen."

Mrs. Van Deusen's return interrupted whatever reply Miss McIsaac might have made. "Aren't you the sweetest man? A marshal who does dishes. I knew I liked you. Our town is so blessed to have been able to get you to fill the position of our marshal."

She picked the remaining dishes off the table and handed them to him to wash, never taking a breath as she turned toward Miss McIsaac. "He resigned his commission in the army and moved back to Virginia when his father died and his mother grew ill. When she died, he came back West and was working down in Texas as a deputy. The first Sunday he was here after arriving to meet with the town council about the position, he came to church services. He has such a lovely voice and sings right out on the hymns. We had him over for lunch that very day. Thomas is on the town council you know. Marshal Cameron won my husband over right away! Now Thomas isn't easily impressed. He reserves judgment on people 'til he's known them awhile. Why, he still hasn't warmed up to Banker Samuels, and we've known him for nearly ten years!"

If he hadn't been so anxious to get out of the kitchen, Wyatt might have been impressed at how long the woman could talk without stopping for air.

"Thank you for the wonderful breakfast, but I really should get back to Faither." Without waiting for an answer, Miss McIsaac hurried to the kitchen door and through the house to the front door. Mrs. Van Deusen followed hot on her heels.

Wyatt took a deep breath and exhaled noisily. Much more of that and he would have been the one blushing.

Mrs. Van Deusen's voice carried through the house. "He's thirty-three, you know."

"Mr. Samuels?" Miss McIsaac sounded as confused as Wyatt felt. He swiped his rag over the last dish. He had better make good his own escape before the woman returned.

"No, dear. Marshal Cameron. He's never been married, and you two are so close in age."

"I'm not thirty yet, Mrs. Van Deusen!" Miss McIsaac's voice was growing fainter.

"You're not? Hmm…I thought you were. Oh, well, you're not very far from it. Goodbye, dear."

Wyatt dried his hands on a towel. Dishes or no dishes, it was time to retreat before the matchmaker returned and trained her guns on him. He strode to the open front door. Miss McIsaac was nearly running in her attempt to put distance between her and Mrs. Van Deusen. He would have laughed if he hadn't been so impatient to escape himself.

"Marshal?" Mrs. Van Deusen turned to reenter the house and nearly ran him over. "Oh, there you are. You aren't going to let her traipse all the way back to Doc's by herself, are you?"

"No, ma'am. Thanks for the meal." He sidestepped her and hurried down the steps to follow the other fleeing victim of the matchmaker's ambush.

He tried to keep his retreat dignified but quickly realized he would have to hustle to catch Miss McIsaac. She might be shorter by almost half a foot, but she could sure cover some distance when she wanted. She had passed the mercantile, the newspaper office and the hotel, and was nearing the barbershop when Jonah exited it and called out to her.

She stopped, giving Jonah and Wyatt a chance to catch her. "What are you doing in town?" Wyatt noticed she wasn't even breathing hard.

"I rode in yesterday evening with the captain. Barnaby sent me in to check on you and Boss man and be available when you needed me. I caught Doc this morning as he headed out to check on patients. He said Boss man was doing better, and you were finally getting some sleep. I was just headin' back there to check on you both."

Several townsfolk had wandered over while Jonah was speaking and now voiced their desire to hear how Mr. McIsaac was faring. When Miss McIsaac repeated Doc's assessment from this morning, there were replies of surprise and amazement peppered with an occasional Praise the Lord here and there. The gathering crowd then turned its focus on Wyatt.

He willingly answered the pointed, sometimes accusing questions concerning the still-at-large thief and their missing savings. However, after a few minutes he subtly turned the inquisition into an opportunity to interrogate the crowd about what they had seen that day or whether they had noticed anyone matching the description of the holdup man since. The crowd began volunteering to contact friends or family in neighboring towns as to whether or not they knew anything that might lead to the discovery of the bank robber's identity.

As the impromptu meeting began to discuss the ramifications of the theft, Wyatt noticed Miss McIsaac surreptitiously edging to the side of the crowd and slipping down a side street. Catching Jonah's attention, he motioned with his head to indicate he was following her and made his own way through the dispersing crowd.

She had her head down when his longer strides overtook her and didn't notice him at first. Remembering the spark that had shocked his hand when he'd touched her arm earlier, Wyatt kept his hands firmly at his sides, denying the itch to find out whether it had just been a chance occurrence. He cleared his throat to get her attention.

She visibly flinched as her head flew up and swiveled toward him. "I do wish you'd quit sneaking up on me, Marshal!"

"I wouldn't have to sneak up on you if you stayed still once in a while." He lengthened his stride to keep up with her quickening pace. "Speaking of which, I seem to recall telling a certain young lady to stay put yesterday, but she flagrantly disobeyed that order. You wouldn't know anything about that, would you?"

She avoided his eyes. "I seem to recall a slightly out-of-his-jurisdiction marshal hollering something over his shoulder as he rode away from the ranch yesterday, but as he couldn't be bothered to wait for me, I came back."

"I can see how a would-be horse thief might have trouble following orders from a marshal and worrying about where his 'jurisdiction' is or isn't."

They reached the doctor's house, and she paused, turning to face him. She tilted her head slightly. "Now that's just a bit of the pot calling the kettle black, don't you think, Marshal?"

The innocent confusion on her face tempted Wyatt like a mouse to cheese, but her sugary-sweet tone warned him of the trap. "How so?"

Opening the front door, she stepped across the threshold and turned to face him, saying quietly, "I seem to recall you riding out of my ranch yard yesterday...on a horse that did not belong to you!" She firmly shut the door in his face.

Wyatt grinned in spite of himself at Miss McIsaac's verbal riposte.

"I'm beginning to think you provoke that woman on purpose just to watch her reaction." Jonah had caught up with them and now made his presence known.

Wyatt shot a grin at him, but didn't reply as he reached for the door that had so recently been shut in his face. He did enjoy getting a reaction out of her and liked the fact she didn't back down from him even when rattled or frustrated. If he were in a safer occupation, had a place of his own... Wyatt broke off the thought. But he wasn't, and he didn't. He might enjoy sparring with the pretty female, but that's all there was to it.

He ignored the little voice that whispered, *for now.*

There was no one in the front office when they walked in, but the far door stood ajar, and Wyatt heard Miss

McIsaac speaking. She sounded pleased, but he couldn't make out what she said before a second unknown voice responded.

"That's Boss man. He's awake!" Jonah exclaimed.

Chapter Seven

They hurried to Mr. McIsaac's room, and coming to a standstill in the doorway, watched as Miss McIsaac gingerly hugged the man sitting propped up in the bed. Dr. Kilburn leaned against the opposite wall, hands tucked into his vest pockets, a beaming smile lighting his usually earnest expression.

The little tableau brought a sting of moisture to Wyatt's eyes, and he quietly thanked God for sparing this woman more grief by restoring her father to her. Only the soft crooning of Mr. McIsaac broke the silence, and Wyatt recognized the quiet words as Gaelic. As a child he'd heard his grandfather use the language of the Old Country when his emotions got the better of him. Jonah's noisy sniff brought Mr. McIsaac's attention to them, and Meri quickly pulled away, busily straightening the coverlet.

Mr. McIsaac batted away her hands. "Quit fussin', darlin' girl. Ye'll make these gentlemen think yer faither's a feeble auld man."

Miss McIsaac gave a very unladylike snort. "You are feeble, and while you may not be old, you've definitely aged me the past several days, so I can fuss if I feel like it."

Mr. McIsaac gave her a glare that Wyatt recognized. He'd earned that same look from the man's daughter. He grinned. It was rather fun to see her on the receiving end of it for a change.

"Watch your sass, lassie! Ye're not too big to turn over me knee." Laugh lines radiated away from dark eyes twinkling in response to Miss McIsaac's growl.

"Faither…"

"Excuse me, darlin'," he interrupted her, "Jonah, don't just stand there. Come in and introduce the fellow with ye."

As the two men moved farther into the room, Dr. Kilburn left with the admonishment that he'd let them talk for a few minutes, but when he returned, they'd need to leave and allow Mr. McIsaac to rest.

Jonah introduced Wyatt and was summarily ordered by Mr. McIsaac to bring a couple more chairs so he wouldn't have to break his neck looking up at them.

"It's nice to finally talk with you, Mr. McIsaac. It's a privilege to meet the answer to so many prayers." Wyatt shook hands with the man as Jonah left the room in search of chairs.

"I'm pleased to meet ye, Marshal Cameron, but call me Ian. Now, I want to know what happened after I was shot. Did ye get the man?"

"No, sir, and call me Wyatt. We were unable to catch him that day, and I haven't tracked him down yet. I've got a few questions I'd like to ask you if you feel up to it."

"I think you should wait, Marshal, 'til Faither's a little stronger before you bother him with your questions," Miss McIsaac interjected.

"America Catriona McIsaac! A measly scratch does not make me senile. I can certainly handle a few questions. Now stop interrupting, and let's hear what the man has to ask."

Mr. McIsaac gave a stern glance at his daughter, and Wyatt cleared his throat to hide his chuckle at her look of chagrin. He'd certainly learned the source of her fiery spirit. From his vantage point it looked like she'd inherited her mother's features and her father's temperament.

Ian McIsaac had an unruly thatch of white hair above snapping dark eyes and thick, white brows. Meri's eyes held the same snap but were a light brown with delicately arched brows, and her head was crowned with thick wavy light brown hair that reminded Wyatt of honey when it was held up to the sun. McIsaac had broad, weathered features that were in contrast to Meri's refined features of high cheekbones and straight delicate nose, full, rosy lips and a neatly rounded, but decidedly determined chin.

The pale yellow shirtwaist she was wearing made her lightly bronzed skin glow, and the way it skimmed her figure down to the waist of her full blue skirt highlighted the curves of her slender frame. She was beautiful. And her name was America, Meri for short. The two words sounded alike, but he'd assumed Franks was saying "Miss Mary" when he addressed her.

"Marshal?"

His thoughts snapped back to attention. "Yes?"

"Ye had some questions for me?" Mr. McIsaac's eyes bounced between his daughter and Wyatt with a speculating gleam that disappeared so quickly Wyatt almost missed it.

Wyatt sat in the chair Jonah shoved toward him and cleared his throat. Pulling the little notebook from his pocket, he prepared to take notes and asked Mr. McIsaac to recount the events on the day of the robbery.

"I left Meri at the mercantile and stopped in to the bank to discuss some business with Mr. Samuels. I was just finishing up with him when someone entered the bank. Mr. Samuels left me in the office to see who it was. After a minute or two he walked back in at the point of a gun."

"Do you remember what the man was wearing?" Wyatt asked.

"I do. He'd changed clothes since he'd drifted through the ranch a week or so before, but I remember what he was wearing both times."

"What?" Wyatt voiced the startled question in chorus with Miss McIsaac.

"He came through our ranch?" she asked incredulously.

"Yes. Ye were out riding at the time. He drifted in about lunchtime. I didn't like his looks or his attitude. He seemed to be up to no good. I caught him prowling about the barn. When I confronted him, he gave me a hard-up story. Our policy is to feed strangers, so I had Cookie, our bunkhouse cook, fix him a plate, but the man kept trying to get information about the ranch, the surrounding neighbors and the town. Most drifters are more interested in who might be hiring, not how many head I run, how big the spread is or how big me neighbors' spreads are. When he'd finished his meal, I suggested he keep riding."

"How long ago was this?" Wyatt questioned.

"What day is it?"

"It's Saturday. The holdup happened on Tuesday, and you've been unconscious ever since." Miss McIsaac reached to touch her father's hand from her place on the other side of his bed as if to reassure herself he was truly awake.

"Then it was two weeks last Wednesday that he rode through the ranch," McIsaac said after a quick calculation.

Wyatt made a note of that. "You said he was wearing

something different at the bank. Are you sure it was the same man?"

"Aye. He was wearing a black hat, a blue shirt, brown pants and a yellow bandanna when I first met him. He was still wearing the black hat when he robbed the bank, but this time he had a leather coat covering a brown shirt and pants and had a blue bandanna pulled up over his face. Most of his face was covered by the hat and cloth, but I recognized his voice and the way he carried himself."

"Did you learn his name when he was at your ranch?"

"No. That was another thing that made me suspicious of him at the time. Every time I asked his name, he'd pretend not to hear me and ask another question or change the subject."

"What happened after he came into the office with Mr. Samuels?"

"He waved the gun at Mr. Samuels and ordered him to open the safe there. Mr. Samuels refused, but the man grabbed him and shoved him toward it, put the gun to Mr. Samuels head and again ordered him to open it or he'd shoot him. Mr. Samuels obeyed him, and then the scoundrel shoved him out of the way, pulled a cloth bag out of his pocket and started filling it. I had been sitting by the desk, but when they came in, I stood up. He ordered me not to move, but didn't search me and didn't realize I was carrying a gun under me coat. I was slipping it out when Mr. Samuels looked me way and shouted…something. I can't remember exactly what. At his shout the man turned and fired. I remember falling, and I think I heard both men yell something again before I passed out."

Wyatt finished writing and flipped back a couple of pages to read some earlier notes. "Samuels said you tried to stop it by pulling your gun, but he didn't mention shouting. He said the man turned, saw you pulling your gun and fired."

McIsaac thought for a moment. "No. I definitely remember he didn't turn until Samuels shouted."

Wyatt scratched a few more words in his notebook.

"What did Samuels say happened after I was shot?" Ian McIsaac leaned forward intently, winced a little and sank back against his pillows.

"Mr. Samuels said the bandit hit him over the head after shooting you and left after grabbing the rest of the money out of the safe. He doesn't remember much after that because of the blow to his head."

"I definitely remember voices right after I fell." McIsaac muttered. He was quiet for a moment, thinking. "By the way, what happened to me gun?"

"I didn't see it when we got there. Do you have it, Miss McIsaac?"

"No. I didn't even think to look for it although I know he usually carries one. I haven't even thought about it since."

"That was me favorite pistol," McIsaac grumbled. "I sure would like it back."

"I'll ask around," Wyatt said. "Maybe someone else picked it up that day and forgot to mention it."

"You said the thief cleaned out the safe?" McIsaac asked.

"Yes. Mr. Samuels said he got everything."

"That must have been a lot of money to carry if he took everything."

"How much do you think he got away with?" Wyatt looked from his notes.

"I have no idea, but Samuels had just been bragging how well the bank was doing. I assumed there was quite a bit of money in that safe."

Dr. Kilburn walked in and cleared his throat. "It's time to let Mr. McIsaac get some rest. I don't want him to overdo things on his first day awake, even if he has made a remarkable recovery from yesterday."

"Now, Doc, I haven't had a chance to speak to Jonah about the ranch," McIsaac protested.

"Jonah can drop back by after you've had some rest. Your ranch will still be there." Doc's stern tone brooked no argument.

Getting up from his chair where he'd been quietly listening, Jonah hastily assured McIsaac that the ranch was fine and not to worry his head about it as Barnaby had things well in hand.

Wyatt asked Mr. McIsaac to describe the physical characteristics of the man who'd visited his ranch, and after writing down the information, he closed his little book and slipped it and the pencil back into his pocket. "If you think of anything else, let me know. Until then you have my word that I'll do whatever it takes to track down the culprit."

Doc shooed them out, ordering Miss McIsaac along with them. "I want to examine your father, and then he needs to rest. You go get some fresh air or take a nap, but run along."

Wyatt was mulling over what he'd learned from Meri's father as he and Jonah walked to the front door, aware that Miss McIsaac had followed them. Stepping aside to allow her to precede him, he watched her blindly walk through the door Jonah held open. She looked a little lost and unsure what to do with herself. He followed her into the brightly lit outdoors, admiring the glints of gold that danced to life in the honey-colored thick braid as sunlight touched her uncovered head.

"What are you going to do, Miss Meri?" Jonah asked.

Meri glanced around, seeming to search for an answer

before replying with forced cheerfulness, "I think I'll enjoy Mrs. Kilburn's garden for a bit, and then I might take that nap Doc suggested."

Jonah patted her on the shoulder. "You do that, miss. I'll come back by later this afternoon, and if your pa's feeling up to it, I'll give him the details he wants about the ranch." Turning, he walked down the street.

Her gaze followed him for a moment before she looked at Wyatt. "Good day, Marshal." She walked toward the corner of the house where Mrs. Kilburn's well-nurtured flower garden began.

"My name is Wyatt. Do you think you could use it instead of Marshal?"

As soon as he uttered the words, he wondered why it even mattered and half wished he'd left well enough alone. When she continued to walk away without responding, though, the silent challenge was too strong to ignore. "I could order you to use my name."

She paused and glanced over her shoulder at him. Was she trying not to smile?

"You could try—" she started walking away again "—but it wouldn't work."

"Hmm… Then I'll have to come up with something else. But…Miss McIsaac?"

This time when she stopped, she turned to face him squarely. "Yes, *Marshal?*" She threw the gauntlet with a bland inquisitiveness that failed to mask completely the glint in her darkened eyes.

Wyatt accepted the challenge, throwing down his own gauntlet. "I won't *order* you to use my name, but make no doubt about it…you *will* use my name!"

Meri never made it back to her room for a nap after Jonah and the marshal departed. All vestiges of weariness had vanished as swiftly as the lawman after his self-confident pronouncement. She prowled the garden oblivious to the beauty of new green leaves and tender buds, arguing with the man in her thoughts.

Of all the egotistical… If he thinks he can make me call him by his first name, he's got a disappointment coming. I refuse to give the gossips of this town one more reason to discuss me. I will not give them the satisfaction!

She ruthlessly quashed the little thrill of longing that accompanied the thought of having her name coupled with his.

*The only reason he's interested in you, Meri McIsaac, is because Faither was involved in the holdup and because—*she groaned, remembering—*because you probably pricked at his ego with your refusal to use his name.*

It wasn't that she didn't like his name. She did—there, she'd admitted it—but using his name felt too informal, too…intimate, as if she was letting him get too close. She needed to keep him at arm's length, so when he lost his interest in her and moved on to someone prettier and more feminine, it wouldn't matter.

Before long someone would kindly inform him that Miss McIsaac was more interested in working cattle and riding her horse, Sandy, than in sewing a fine stitch and filling her hope chest. They'd shake their heads in laughing pity and observe that at the ripe old age of nearly thirty, she had never entertained any serious suitors and likely never would.

All of which was true, but anytime Meri overheard such comments, they made her feel like the local oddity. She could only imagine how those remarks, coming from a smiling, eyelash-batting, oh-so-willing-to-please female, would sound to the handsome marshal. Meri shook her head. No. She *wouldn't* imagine it.

Besides, the only *interest I have in him is whether he finds the man that tried to kill my father or not. And I hope Faither heals quickly so we can go home. Once we're back on the ranch, life will get back to normal, and I'll stop worrying about what everyone else thinks.*

"That's a fierce look. Do you not like roses?" Mrs. Kilburn's amused tone interrupted Meri's mental rant.

She turned away from the glossy bush just erupting in tiny buds she'd apparently been glaring at. "I *do* like roses, but I'm afraid I was quite lost in my thoughts."

"From the look on your face, they weren't pleasant. Are you worried about your father? He's doing remarkably well today, and Doc says he doesn't see any reason he won't have a full recovery."

"I think the week is just catching up to me." Meri evaded the question.

Mrs. Kilburn laced her arm through Meri's and led her through the back door into the kitchen. "What you need is some food. Come on in, I have lunch ready."

Inside Meri found a tray prepared for herself and her father. Mr. McIsaac was less than impressed, however, when he realized his lunch consisted of a light broth, toast and glass of milk.

"Dr. Kilburn says you can have something a little more substantial tomorrow if your stomach handles this okay. It has been empty for several days, and it'll be best not to overwhelm it just when you're starting to feel better. Now, do you want me to feed you?"

"Allow me the dignity of feeding meself, even if it is a paltry excuse of a meal," Ian said scornfully, carefully spooning broth into his mouth. "Oh, what I wouldn't give for a thick steak!" he moaned, eyeing Meri's thick sandwich.

Meri grinned at his antics but quickly sobered. "Did we lose an awful lot in the robbery, Faither?"

"We lost some, but ye know I never trusted all me money to the bank. I only kept a small amount there to stay on good terms with Mr. Samuels. I've never let anyone except yer mither know how much we managed to save back and that includes the banker. I'm sorry the bank was robbed at all, but it didn't surprise our Heavenly Father. Savings or no savings, He's always taken care of us and always will, so don't worry over what we did or didn't lose. Our treasure is in Heaven, not some safe or bank down here."

They discussed the ranch and what had happened while he was unconscious as they ate. Gathering up the dishes when they'd finished, Meri noticed her father was drooping a little. "Why don't you close your eyes and rest so you'll be ready when Jonah drops in. I think I'll go check on Sandy."

He argued, but there wasn't much effort in the argument, and she left the room carrying the tray of dishes. After washing up the lunch things, she went into her room and changed from the blue skirt she'd donned earlier into her tan split riding skirt. Slipping a dark, buttery-soft leather vest over the yellow calico blouse, she grabbed her hat and hurried to Franks's Livery.

As she neared the stables, she heard Franks's rich, deep voice raised in song, the sound rumbling pleasingly through the air.

His singing halted as he greeted her warmly. "Miss Meri! I hear de Lawd has answered our prayers!" Sitting down on a bench against the wall, Meri filled him in on the doctor's prognosis and Franks's wide grin split his face. "It be a day ta praise de Lawd for his mah'vlous goodness ta man!"

A weak smile and nod was Meri's only reply.

"You is mighty quiet for someone who should be rejoicin'. Is yo thankful bone broke?"

"I am very thankful God heard the prayers of you and the men who prayed for my father and that he's doing so much better." Meri squirmed under Franks's penetrating gaze.

"What 'bout yo prayers?"

Meri shrugged her shoulders. "It feels like my prayers aren't heard anymore, like there's something in the way."

"Honey chil'! Yo Heavenly Father promised never ta leave or fo'sake you! If dere's sumpin' in de way, it ain't on his end!"

Meri felt the familiar ache in her throat return. "I feel like I've been forsaken."

"Mmm-hmm, evah since yo momma died, I reckon. You put on a good show and mos' likely fooled ever'one, but I'se noticed the joy and peace in yo eyes been missin' fo' some time now."

Meri fired up at the gentle rebuke. "How am I supposed to have joy and peace when Mither died so suddenly, and then I almost lose Faither?"

Franks shook his head sadly. "Joy and peace ain't foun' in yo circumstances, they is foun' in God's promises." Franks bowed his head all of a sudden, leaving Meri staring at him. "Lawd, You know dis chil' is hurtin'. Open her eyes ta what needs fixin' so You can heal de hurt. Amen." He stood abruptly. "Now go see dat spoiled pony. He been a hollerin' for you all day."

Meri frowned as he returned to his forge and stirred the coals. She loved the man dearly, but she was a little miffed at his scolding. *I'm hurting and somehow it's my fault?*

She drew a deep breath to calm herself. She'd never

been angry with Franks before. *You do have a problem if you're getting upset with Franks!*

She stood and went outside to Sandy. The palomino saw her coming, whinnied deeply and ran for the gate. At least someone was glad to see her. She slid through the fence and wrapped her arms around his neck, burying her face in his mane and breathing deeply of his horsey scent, of fresh air, sweet grass and hay. After several moments she led him to the barn and saddled him, feeling some of the tension leave her shoulders. Scolding herself for her poor attitude, she mounted Sandy and called over her shoulder to Franks, "We'll be back later."

"Be careful."

With a short nod she rode out of the barn. Detouring to Doc's place and finding her father still asleep, she retrieved her guns. Sheathing the carbine in the saddle scabbard, she strapped the cartridge belt and pistol she'd brought back from the ranch around her slim waist. She'd lived in the West long enough to know it was wise to have protection from four-legged and two-legged varmints even if she was only going to be on the outskirts of town.

Her father had long ago ensured she was proficient with firearms, giving her the .44-40 Winchester carbine, sometimes called the Saddle carbine, several years ago for her birthday. It was four inches shorter than the regular .44-40 Winchester rifle and made for a lighter, more compact gun for her to handle. The rifle and the pistol Meri carried on her hip were chambered for the same rounds, therefore the extra cartridges she carried in her belt would fit either gun. Altogether, Meri felt very capable of protecting herself from any threat.

Swinging up aboard the pretty palomino, she took the long way to the cemetery, circling the outside edge of town. Maybe by the time she reached it she would have worked up the nerve to go in. Meri kept Sandy at a sedate walk, waving at a few townsfolk who called out as she passed. All too soon, she reached the waist-high wrought-iron gate in the fence that lined the front edge of the burial grounds. Dismounting, she reached for the latch then let her hand fall back to her side.

She'd put this off so long it had become a monster she couldn't face. She should've made herself come with Faither when the headstone was set, but at the time, her cold was too convenient an excuse.

Sandy shoved his nose against her back, giving her a hard nudge. "I just can't do it, Sandy." The horse snorted and shook his head, setting his bridle to jingling. "I know. I'm a coward, but let's get out of here."

Remounting, she escaped into the hills behind the cemetery. There was a place nearby conducive to a full-out gallop without danger of running over someone on the road or running her horse into a hole and Meri took full advantage it. After an hour of riding, though, she felt only marginally better. A long, solitary ride, the joy of a smooth-moving horse, the wind in her hair and the beautiful countryside had always been the cure-all for anything bothering her, but the remedy was sorely lacking today.

Meri berated herself. She should be feeling at least a small portion of the joy and peace Franks mentioned earlier, if only for the fact that her father was now on the mend. Why was she still feeling completely out of sorts? And why did her thoughts keep straying to a certain star-toting man? Maybe when she got out of town and back to normal ranch life, her unsettled emotions would straighten out. For now she'd just have to live with them.

Reluctantly she turned Sandy toward town. They'd ridden east through the foothills bordering the northern edge of Little Creek and were only a couple of miles from town if they dropped down and took the road in. Riding through the thickly forested area that lined the road, Sandy slowed, pricked his ears and lifted his nose, scenting the air.

"Someone else around, fella?" Meri asked quietly, letting him have his head. She hadn't expected to be followed like she always was on her ranch, but her horse had heard something. Maybe Franks had sent someone after her.

Sandy slowly stepped to the edge of the trees, pausing to peer intently down the road away from town.

Two men were standing between their horses in the bend of the road about one hundred and fifty yards away from Meri. Both men had their hats pulled low, shading their faces, and from their body language they seemed to be arguing. Meri could hear their raised voices but was unable to understand what they were saying.

"So that's what you heard. I wonder what their problem is?" As Meri whispered this to Sandy, the taller of the two men grabbed the other man by the collar, yanking him off his feet and shaking him as he yelled and shook his other fist in the poor man's face.

"Hey!" Meri shouted, simultaneously pulling her rifle and nudging Sandy toward the men.

The smaller man, his back to Meri, nearly fell as the larger man dropped him and shoved him away roughly. He recovered his balance, and both men ducked their heads and scrambled onto their horses. Wheeling their mounts away, the smaller man glanced over his shoulder as he spurred his horse.

Meri saw a flash and something whistled past her ear.

Chapter Eight

Crack!

Sandy flinched at the loud report and sidestepped, saving them from the second bullet that whizzed past. Meri dropped the reins and jerked her own rifle to her shoulder, snapping off a quick shot before the men disappeared around the bend.

"Get 'em, Sandy!"

Scooping up the reins in one hand, she held her rifle ready in the other as Sandy leaped forward into a full run after the men. They had a good head start on her, and as she rounded the bend, they were already rounding the next curve in the road. Meri knew a straight stretch was around that corner and thought she could gain on them by then for a better look, but when she reached it, they were nowhere in sight. Sandy slid to a halt at Meri's signal, snorting impatiently.

"I know, I wanted to catch them, too, but they must have left the road and could be lying in wait for us now. I'll be in plenty of hot water if Faither finds out I followed them at all!"

Suddenly uneasy over the whereabouts of the two men, Meri turned Sandy and they flew back toward town. They were within a half mile of the edge of town when Meri saw two riders racing toward her. Wheeling the palomino sharply, she dived off the edge of the road into the trees. Flinging herself out of the saddle almost before Sandy had stopped moving, Meri flipped his reins over a limb and ducked down behind a tree. Heart racing, she steadied her rifle, waiting as the two riders neared the spot where she'd flown off the road.

She heard the horses slide to a halt and a familiar voice spoke. "Miss Meri, is that you?"

Meri closed her eyes, resting her forehead against the tree trunk as she drew a much-needed breath into grateful lungs. *Jonah.* Her pulse began to slow its frantic pounding.

A second voice commanded, "Come out where we can see you, but be careful about it!"

Wyatt.

Meri groaned quietly as her pulse surged into panic mode again. *No! He's the marshal.* She corrected herself. *I will not call him Wyatt.*

Willing her racing heart to cease with the acrobatics, she retrieved Sandy. Mounting, she gulped another steadying breath then ducked back through the brush to the road.

Two guns were hastily reholstered as Jonah spoke. "I thought that looked like you an' Sandy. Are you all right?"

"I'm fine." Something brushed Meri's ear, and she flinched at the unexpected sensation. Trying to recover a facade of unconcern, she felt around her ear and discovered a twig snagged in her hair.

"If you're fine, would you care to explain why we heard gunshots, and why you're running and hiding?" All warmth had disappeared from the marshal's hazel eyes, leaving only cold steel behind.

"I am not running and hiding!" Steely eyes bored into her as she untangled the stubborn twig and tossed it aside. "Okay, fine! I was hiding. Now, will you quit glaring at me?"

"I'll decide whether to quit glaring when you finish answering my question." His eyes never wavered from hers.

"I was headed back to town when I saw two men on the road having an argument. When they started fighting, I yelled at them. When they saw me, they took off. One, or both of them, fired a couple of shots."

Both men inhaled sharply.

"I fired back and chased them..."

"You *chased* them! After they *shot* at you? Have you lost what little sense you may have ever had?" The marshal's glare sizzled as he growled in her face.

Meri blinked. When had he gotten so close? And how was it possible for him to be so close when they were both still on horseback? She fought the impulse to move Sandy away from the growling marshal and instead leaned toward him. "Yes, I *chased* them!"

He copied her movement, leaning in until she felt his breath on her face. He held her eyes for several breaths without blinking. In a low dangerous tone, he asked gently, "Why?"

Meri barely heard him over the pulse thudding in her ears. "Because..."

Her brain stuttered to a stop. Why *had* she chased them? At the moment she couldn't remember. His nearness was making it nearly impossible to think. "Because they made me mad?" she finished lamely, feeling as foolish as she no doubt sounded.

He blinked and warmer hazel softened the steeliness. Settling back in his saddle, he looked at her. "You chased them because they made you…mad?" He sounded as if he were choking.

A strangled sound turned Meri's attention to Jonah. The red-faced man coughed out another funny sound before breaking into belly-deep laughs. What in the world was wrong with him? A similar noise from the marshal swiveled Meri's head back to look at him. His lips were clenched, but at the look of perplexed confusion on her face, his own laugh escaped.

Meri's gaze bounced between the two men, a frown creasing her forehead. After half a minute the laughter subsided, leaving grins in its wake. "What is so funny?"

Wyatt shook his head. "I'm not sure, exactly. Just remind me never to make you mad."

"Unless, of course, you *want* her to chase you!" Jonah chuckled.

Meri felt the color flare in her cheeks as the marshal grinned at her. "I might not mind her chasing me, so long as she wasn't shooting at the time."

"If you think for one minute, Marshal, that I'd chase you—"

He interrupted her. "My name is Wyatt, not Marshal, and back to the issue at hand—show us where you found those men and recount what happened from the beginning, please?" Grabbing the offered distraction, Meri led them back in the direction she'd come, explaining what had happened. "When I saw you two, I thought they had circled around and were coming back. I got off the road and under cover." Meri pointed out where she'd first seen the two men.

When they arrived at the spot in the road where the men had stood, Jonah dismounted and studied the ground. "Why don't you take Miss Meri back to town, Captain? I'll follow these tracks and see where they lead."

Meri caught a look that passed between the two men and wondered what it meant. "I'm riding with you two. Three pairs of eyes will see more than one pair."

Jonah swung onto the back of his horse. "I was tracking before you were born, Miss Meri, and although the captain here is pretty good, I've still got him beat. Besides, it's time for you to get back to town. Your pa is gonna be wonderin' where you are. He won't be happy with me if he finds out I let you ride back alone after this little excursion."

"He doesn't need to know about this. He's got enough on his mind right now."

Jonah gave her a stern look. "I'm not keeping this a secret, Miss Meri. The men need to know to keep an eye out for these two."

"I'll take you up on your offer, Jonah, but be careful. Fire a couple of shots if you get into trouble, and I'll come running. Otherwise come see me when you get back to town, and let me know what you find. Coming, Miss McIsaac?"

Meri reluctantly turned her horse toward town, thinking about the unspoken signal that had passed between the two men. "How long have you and Jonah known each other?"

He frowned, thinking. "Almost eleven years, now. He was stationed at the first fort I was transferred to after graduating from West Point." A slight grin quirked his lips. "I was a freshly minted second lieutenant full of book learning and no real knowledge of anything west of the Mississippi. The major over the fort had dealt with know-it-all West Point graduates before. He had a habit of quietly assigning Master Sergeant Jonah Chacksfield the job of keeping an eye on those brash, overeager officers. They outranked him, but Jonah had a way of subtly reining in bad judgment and pointing out a better way without appearing to question an officer's authority, all the while making the idea seem like their own."

"Did he do that to you?"

"More than once. I thought I knew all about Indians after growing up playing with my Cherokee cousins in the wilds of Rocky Gap, Virginia. I could sneak through those woods with the best of them and was more than a fair tracker." A grimace crossed his face. "My first en-counter with a band of Apaches taught me how much I *didn't* know. I came close to getting my men killed that day. It was due to Jonah's guidance and God's mercy we survived that encounter."

They rode in silence for a several minutes. Meri could envision a fresh-faced young army officer decked out in crisp uniform with shiny buttons and a cavalry saber swinging from his hip. She wondered how many female hearts he had conquered. Something he'd said snagged her attention. "You don't look Indian." The words were out before she could catch them.

Narrowed hazel eyes turned toward her. "What is an Indian supposed to look like?"

Meri blushed and shrugged. "I just meant you don't have dark eyes or black hair."

"My grandmother was full-blood Cherokee, but I take after the Scottish side of the family." He grinned at her. "And I can see you have another question. What is it?"

Meri felt relieved that she hadn't upset him with her impulsive question and then wondered why she cared. "You said you grew up with your Cherokee cousins in Virginia. Weren't the Cherokee Indians removed west?"

"Most of them were, but a few escaped into the Ap-palachian Mountains. My family owned their own prop-erty farther north. Indians that actually owned their own land instead of living on communal grounds were by law allowed to stay."

Meri thought about her parents and the boatload of others evicted from their homes in Scotland, and the Indians evicted from their lands and homes in America. Two different nations and cultures, both forever changed because of greed coupled with power.

"You're awfully quiet. Does my being part Cherokee bother you?"

Meri thought she detected a hint of worry. "No." He eyed her for a second, and she looked him square in the eyes. "It doesn't bother me."

The answer seemed to satisfy him, because he smiled slightly. "Good."

Something shifted in the air between them and, growing uncomfortable, Meri turned her focus back to the ride. She was thankful he seemed content to let the silence continue.

They reached the saloon at the edge of town and turned down the street to the livery stable.

"Thank you for coming out to check on me." She didn't understand why a simple thank-you should make her feel so nervous—vulnerable.

He touched the brim of his hat in a snappy salute. "Just doin' my job, ma'am."

Franks greeted them at the door of the livery stable and asked about the gunshots. He listened soberly as the marshal recounted the details while Meri unsaddled Sandy. Turning to her afterward, Franks scolded, "I shore is glad de good Lawd was watchin' out for you, but you might'a stretched his protection a bit far when you chased after dem fellas! Don' you go doin' a fool stunt like da' again, you hear?"

Wyatt turned his horse into a stall beside Sandy. "Don't

go riding alone out of town until we figure out what this was all about and catch those men, either."

The thought of being cooped up in town unable to ride when and where she pleased was smothering. "I shouldn't have chased after those two men, but I'm not going to stop riding just because of them."

"While you're in this town, you'll do what *I* say." His eyes were turning stormy again, she noticed.

Meri opened her mouth to reply and remembered the last time she'd argued with him in this barn. Biting back the words that sprang to her tongue, she spun on her heel and stomped out of the barn. She heard him follow and ignored him hoping he'd go away, but he stayed on her heels all the way to the doctor's house. Reaching the bottom step, she could take it no longer and faced him. "Why are you still following me?"

He took her by the arm, marched her up the steps and opened the door for her. "Since you refuse to abide by my authority in this matter, we're going to take it up with a higher authority."

Meri yanked her arm away from the sparks his touch caused. "What higher authority? God?"

"No. Your father." Leaving her standing at the front door, he stalked toward her father's room.

Wyatt found McIsaac awake and, much to Miss Meri's annoyance, relayed the happenings of the afternoon. He then retreated from the field of battle, more than happy to leave her father to engage her in this particular skirmish. Pulling the bedroom door shut behind him to cut off the glare she aimed in his direction, he shook his head ruefully. One slender female had just caused him to fall back faster than any band of attacking Apache warriors ever had.

His stomach growled, reminding him it was near supper time, and he pointed his steps toward the café. A savory, tantalizing odor greeted him as he entered the dining establishment, and he requested a plate of whatever smelled so good. He chatted with the other diners, feeling the weight of their concern over the missing money, until the hearty stew and hot, buttered bread arrived then he dived into his meal while pondering the events of the past week. Were the bank holdup and today's events random coincidences or did they somehow tie in together?

When he finished his meal, he decided to have a talk with Franks. Meri had described the men's horses, and Wyatt wondered if Franks would know anything about them.

The blacksmith was finishing his own meal in his small living quarters off the back corner of the livery stable, but he warmly invited Wyatt in. Wyatt explained his errand and repeated Meri's description of the men and their horses.

Franks rubbed his head and thought for a minute before replying. "A bay hoss and a gray hoss... Dere's a lot a bay hosses 'roun' here. Dat could describe any a dem. I has sev'ral myself, but I ain't rented any a dem out today. Now de gray...dere's only two a dem in dis area dat I know of—Rufus Bascom's matched carriage hosses and his prize possessions. He's a rancher on past de McIsaac place, and he keeps dem s'clusively to pull his carriage." He paused thoughtfully. "Dey *was* a gray hoss I ain't never seen afore tied in front a de saloon, couple nights ago. It were a big, han'some geldin', but I ain't seen it since."

The only description Meri had given of the men themselves was their clothing and the height difference between the two men. She'd been too far away to distinguish facial features under the brims of their hats. Franks and Wyatt both agreed the clothing description could fit a dozen men in town on any given day.

Wyatt thanked the man for his help and stood to take his leave. Franks followed him to the door. "You be careful wid Miss Meri, she's a han'ful, and she's hurtin', but she's sumpin' special! I don' wanna see her hurt!"

Stepping outside, Wyatt settled his hat on his head. "I'll do my best, but I'm beginning to believe keeping her out of trouble will be the hardest part of my job as marshal!"

Wyatt's next stop was the saloon. The bartender remembered a man who rode a gray horse and gave Wyatt a rough description of the man: tall with shaggy black hair and a mustache, a man who asked too many questions. The bartender said he recognized his type as a troublemaker and was glad to see him leave. Wyatt thanked him and asked him to let him know if he saw the man again or remembered anything else about him.

Leaving the foul-smelling, smoky saloon behind, Wyatt glanced down at the pocket watch his parents had given him upon his graduation from West Point. It was only a little after six in the evening, plenty of time to talk to a couple more people before calling it a day. He walked to the boardinghouse. The bank teller had roomed there before leaving to be closer to his widowed mother, according to Mr. Samuels. At the large two-story house Wyatt asked the proprietress if she knew where the teller had gone.

"Mr. Dunn was such a nice young man, one of my best boarders. I so hated to lose him, and I'm glad he found another job so soon after Mr. Samuels fired him." She offered Wyatt a cup of tea, which he declined.

"He told you Mr. Samuels fired him?"

"Yes. He was naturally upset about it, but I think it almost came as a relief after the way he was treated."

"How was that?"

"In the past few months, he would come in from work with such a sad, tired slump to his shoulders, but I finally got out of him what the trouble was. Mr. Samuels was constantly finding fault with the way he did anything and made the poor boy's life miserable. Then he fired poor Mr. Dunn—said he was just too incompetent. Grouchy old man lost me one of the tidiest boarders I had," she said indignantly.

Wyatt asked her where Mr. Dunn had gone, and she named a town in the next county. He thanked her for her time and left, jotting a note to contact that town's marshal to verify Dunn's whereabouts. Wyatt wondered why Mr. Samuels hadn't mentioned any of this and added it to the growing list of questions he had for the man. However, when he arrived at the banker's house, the housekeeper informed him that as the bank was closed, Mr. Samuels had left town on business and wouldn't return until sometime the following day.

Wyatt turned over the fragmented bits and pieces of information he'd gathered as he walked through the south side of town back toward First Street. When he reached it, he saw Jonah walking toward him in the dim light of evening.

"I just got back in and was coming to find you."

"Let's go to my office and talk."

"You're the marshal, but Mr. McIsaac is my boss, and I think he needs to hear what I found, too."

"I'll take your word for it. Do you want to get something to eat before we head over there?"

"No. Let's get there before it gets any later. I can rustle up some grub afterward."

They hurried to Doc's house and found McIsaac still awake and eager to talk to them. Dr. Kilburn advised them to keep it short.

"I know that look. What's up, Jonah?" McIsaac propped himself higher against the headboard.

"The tracks out on the road, I'd seen 'em before." Jonah's face was grim.

"I figured that's what your look meant earlier," Wyatt replied. "You didn't want Miss McIsaac to know it."

Jonah shook his head. "The tracks of one of those men and his horse matched the ones I found on the ranch after our horse was stolen and returned. The same man I tracked and lost in the cattle drive, and I believe, the same man you were tracking, Cap'n."

"Och! Are ye telling me one of the men me daughter ran into on the road today was that de'il who held up the bank?" McIsaac nearly shouted the question, his brogue thickening noticeably.

"Yes, sir. I believe so. And from the tracks today and some tail hairs I found snagged in the brush, I'd say the gray horse Meri described to us is the one we tracked out on the ranch."

Wyatt quickly recounted what he'd learned from Franks and the bartender about the gray horse.

"The man who came through our ranch was riding a gray horse and had black hair and a mustache." McIsaac's voice was grim.

Wyatt felt his own pulse quicken. "If it is the same man, between the barkeep and yourself, we have a description of our thief. It also means he's been in the area for a while."

"Why would he still be hanging around? Why hasn't he hightailed it out of the area?" Jonah wondered aloud.

"And who was he meeting on the road today?" Wyatt added. "Where did you trail them to?"

"After they left the road, they didn't take time to hide their tracks. They rode as fast as they could to the next town. I lost their tracks once they hit town, but the boy at the livery stable hadn't seen a bay or a gray all day, and the marshal and saloon keeper hadn't, either. I figure they rode on out of there as quick as they rode in, but I couldn't find where."

The three men hashed over this information for several more minutes but were unable to come up with any solid conclusions.

"Did you remember anything else about the bank job?" Wyatt asked McIsaac.

"No, but there's sure something bothering me about it. If I can figure out what it is, I'll let ye know."

"Okay. I'll bring some wanted posters for you to look through, and I'll write up a description of the man you and the barkeep saw and wire it to surrounding towns, see if anyone's seen our thief. I need to talk to Mr. Samuels again and clear a few things up, and I'd like to talk to that bank teller and hear his side of the story." Wyatt eyed both men thoughtfully before he continued. "Mr. McIsaac, I need a deputy, at least 'til we get this trouble solved. The town council gave me authority to hire whomever I wanted. I know Jonah, but more importantly, I trust him. I wonder if you'd be willing to let me hire him away from you, if he's willing."

Mr. McIsaac nodded. "Jonah's his own man. Yer business is with him, not me."

"Jonah?" Wyatt offered his hand.

"I'd be honored to be of service as long as you want me." Jonah grasped the outstretched hand and gave it a firm clasp.

A tap alerted them to a visitor, and they turned to see Meri poke her head around the door. "Oh. I didn't know you had company. I'll be back later to say good-night." She withdrew hurriedly.

"I don't think she's forgiven ye for ordering her not to ride out alone or for tattling to me." McIsaac laughed as they heard her footsteps retreating.

"I was glad to leave that fight in your hands." Jonah and McIsaac laughed at his feigned shudder.

"She's an independent lass, that's for sure. Just like her dear mither was." McIsaac looked at Wyatt thoughtfully. "There are only two men she's ever taken orders from and even then she kicked up occasionally."

"I assume you were one?" Wyatt guessed.

"Aye, and God. Ye just might make the third."

Wyatt felt his pulse jump and a sudden burn in his cheeks. He cleared his throat. "She has spunk, but she's going to give me gray hair if she pulls any more stunts like the one today." Just thinking about the potential consequences of her actions still sent chills down his spine. He'd wanted to shake her earlier for putting herself at such a risk.

McIsaac chuckled, tugging at his own gray locks. "Where do ye think I acquired these? Some things are worth it, though."

Wyatt stood and shook hands with McIsaac, changing the direction of the conversation. He already had Mrs. Van Deusen after him. He didn't need any other potential matchmakers trying to outflank him. "I'd better find my new deputy some food and get him sworn in, or I'll lose him before I've officially hired him."

Bidding their farewells, Wyatt and Jonah departed the house for Wyatt's office.

"Little Creek is a solid little town, recent trouble notwithstanding. It's growing, but there is a lot of good land still available."

Wyatt looked at the ex-sergeant. "Your point?"

"No point. Just got to thinking about your dream to settle down and raise horses. This is as good a place as any."

"Hard to do that when I'm trying to catch a bank robber."

"That won't last forever. Besides, it's high time you started thinking about finding a wife."

"You, too, Jonah? You, too?"

Chapter Nine

Meri stepped outside and felt the warmth of the sunshine bathe her face as she inhaled the heady perfume of fresh spring air. She'd planned to stay with her father instead of attending church, but he'd put his foot down, insisting he didn't need her hovering all day. She smoothed her hands down the glossy purple fabric of her dress. As much as she preferred the freedom of her less cumbersome riding skirts, it was Sunday morning, and according to her upbringing, that meant wearing her best to church.

At least that's what she'd told herself this morning when she'd given in to a fit of vanity and applied her favorite lilac scent, which she'd tucked into her bag on a whim at the ranch. She'd also taken time to twist her hair into a smooth chignon, but a sudden attack of nerves had butterflies fluttering in her stomach as a tiny voice inquired if she were trying to impress anyone in particular.

Ruthlessly squashing the mocking imp, she threw up her head and walked briskly toward the church building. *There's no reason to dither about how you look* or *smell, Meri McIsaac! As long as you're clean and neat, no one will care either way.*

"Mmm…lilacs, I believe."

The masculine voice so unexpectedly close to her ear caused her to trip, but firm hands gently snared her waist, steadying her and sending the butterflies into frenzied acrobatics.

"Steady there. You don't always have to fall at my feet. Besides, I'd hate to see you muss your lovely dress." Mirth danced through the marshal's words.

Meri pulled away from him and walked on, trying to untangle her tongue and ignore the disturbing sensations left by the feel of his hands at her waist. That became impossible, however, when he grasped her hand and folded it around his arm as he fell into step with her. A tingling sensation raced up her arm at the contact, and she jerked her hand back as if she'd been burned.

When the sensation faded somewhat, she found her tongue. "If you would quit sneaking up on me, I wouldn't *be* in danger of falling for you." A huge grin spread over his face, and Meri wished she could bite her unruly tongue off. "That's not what I mean! I meant… Oh, you know what I meant."

"Do I?" His eyes twinkled merrily at her.

Meri tried to concentrate on where she was walking instead of the man beside her. "Don't you have marshal duties to take care of or something?"

"I'm attending one right now."

"What? Pestering innocent law-abiding citizens?" Sparring with him was safer than noticing how sharp he looked in his starched black trousers, white shirt and string tie.

"I'm ensuring that the citizens of Little Creek arrive at church safely," he corrected patiently.

"So you walk everyone to service on Sunday mornings?" Meri couldn't resist a sideways glance at him when he touched her elbow to steady her as they stepped off the boardwalk to cross the street. She could almost imagine her suitor was walking her to church.

"Oh, no, I only accompany the most dangerous. That way everyone else stays safe."

Suitor indeed! Meri corralled the nonsensical thought and searched for a suitable rebuttal.

"Yoo hoo, Marshal." A fog of perfumes enveloped them as three pretty females floated toward them.

Cold reality slapped Meri. Imagining she could compete with such visions of feminine loveliness as these lacy, beribboned, graceful specimens was as foolish as it was dangerous. No man was going to look at a straggly wildflower when such hothouse roses were on display.

She stiffened her shoulders and shored up her sagging defenses. *Who said I was competing against them?*

She quickened her steps to escape, but the marshal stayed with her as did the three young ladies. Their bubbly conversation filled the air, but Meri focused on the little white church building coming ever closer.

When they arrived, she slipped away to speak to Pastor Willis, thanking him for his prayers and asking him to pass along her gratitude to the church family. Squeezing into the end of a pew as the opening hymn was announced, she thought she'd been successful in putting some distance between herself and the marshal, but the rustle of cloth against the wooden pew behind her warned her as someone leaned close and whispered.

"My plan worked. Everyone arrived safely."

The pastor asked the congregation to rise and join in song, and Meri gratefully sprang to her feet, hiding her face behind the hymnbook. As she filled her lungs to join the congregational hymn, the fresh piney scent of shaving lotion filled her nostrils and, distracted, she forgot to sing. Her eyes were on the hymnbook, but her attention focused on the man behind her, his fine baritone voice lifted in joyful praise.

In her perplexity, she nearly missed the pastor thanking the congregation on her behalf, but the smattering of applause when he announced Mr. McIsaac was well on the way to recovery recalled her wandering attention. Other prayer requests were voiced and, after he prayed, Pastor Willis reminded the congregation that the church social was coming up the following Saturday. He then began his message.

Meri opened her Bible to follow along, but her mind drifted over the events of the week until her father's name grabbed her notice.

"We had a pretty big answer to prayer this week in the recovery of Mr. McIsaac. But what about those times when it seems our prayers don't reach any higher than the top of our head?"

Meri looked up expectantly. She'd felt that way many times recently.

He continued, "God hasn't moved, and His grace hasn't failed, but maybe we've let something come between and hinder our relationship with Him. Look at this list in Ephesians 4:31. 'Let all bitterness, and wrath, and anger, and clamour, and evil speaking, be put away from you, with all malice…' Have you allowed one or more of these to fester in your heart and damage your walk with God? The good news is, it doesn't have to be permanent. Put it away from you. He's waiting to forgive and restore sweet fellowship. All you have to do is ask Him. Let's pray."

Meri bowed her head with the rest of the congregation, her thoughts in turmoil. Convicted spirit warred with proud flesh as the pastor's words rattled around her head. A hand touched her shoulder.

"You're coming to lunch with us, dear."

Mrs. Van Deusen's statement startled Meri, and she jerked her head up in surprise. She'd missed the end of service, and her mind scrambled to register what the woman had said.

"Don't worry about your father. Doc announced that anyone who wanted to visit him could come today after lunch, and I've already overheard several people planning to stop in and say hello. He'll have all the company he can stand." She chuckled.

Meri's brow furrowed; she'd missed that particular announcement, too.

Mrs. Van Deusen continued speaking, leaning closer in a conspiratorial manner. "Marshal Cameron is joining us for lunch. It will give you two a chance to get acquainted before the picnic."

Meri surged to her feet, pulse racing. She was not going to get caught in the woman's matchmaking plot. Just the thought of lunch with Wy—that man…made her feel…what? Excited?

"What's wrong, dear?"

Meri hadn't realized she was shaking her head. Reaching for her Bible, she scraped together some much-needed poise. "Thank you for the offer, but I'm…I'm not feeling very well. I'm sorry."

"That's all right. You can rest in the parlor and chat with the marshal while I finish lunch. You just need a good meal and some time to relax." Mrs. Van Deusen patted Meri on the arm.

"No. I'm not hungry. I—I should go lie down. I'm sorry." Meri edged away from the woman as she spoke, heading for the nearby side door.

"Well, okay. Maybe I can have both of you over for lunch later this week before you and your father go home." Stepping closer to Meri, she leaned in and whispered none too quietly, "The marshal is a wonderful man, and all the single girls have been trying to get their hooks in him already. I know you've been busy with your father's injury, but if you don't hurry and fix his attention, some scheming female will lure him away, and you'll lose your chance."

A muffled sound made Meri look over her shoulder straight into the eyes of Marshal Cameron. He stood a couple of pews away, but from the look on his face, he'd overheard every word Mrs. Van Deusen had said. Meri's cheeks heated, but she squared her shoulders and looked back at the matchmaking woman.

Raising her voice slightly and speaking firmly, she spoke to Mrs. Van Deusen but addressed the marshal. "They can have him." Meri left the woman sputtering and escaped out the side door, feeling two pairs of eyes on her back until the door closed behind her.

Midafternoon Wyatt strode toward the livery stable to check on his horse after a cutthroat game of checkers with Mr. Van Deusen. Lunch had been delicious—Mrs. Van Deusen was nothing if not a good cook—but by the time the meal was over, Wyatt's ears were tired from the woman's constant chatter. Most of her conversation had been reserved for singing Miss McIsaac's praises, but he had a sneaking suspicion Miss McIsaac would not appreciate being described as a "poor, motherless lamb." He'd nearly choked on his food at that remark. The last time he'd checked, lambs didn't carry firearms and pursue fleeing gunmen.

Or wear Sunday-go-to-meeting dresses that made their skin luminous.

He'd welcomed the distraction of the three women joining them on their way to church this morning because he had been having trouble remembering his reasons for not pursuing Meri. Unfortunately those overdecorated females had only succeeded in making Miss McIsaac shine like a rare gem amid a pile of imitations.

Wyatt shook his head to dislodge the fanciful thought and entered the barn, pausing to let his eyes adjust to the shadowed dimness.

"Oomph!" His arms instinctively closed around the slight figure that plowed into him, saving them both from hitting the dirt.

A startled squeak reached his ears the same time that it registered he was holding a decidedly feminine form. Firm hands shoved at his chest, and wide eyes blinked up at him from a smudged face.

Meri McIsaac. Except a much-disheveled version of the one he'd escorted to services.

Reluctantly he let his arms fall away, and she stepped back. *Did she have to pull away quite so fast?* He wouldn't think about the empty feeling she left behind. She swiped at a strand of hair that had worked its way loose from her fancy twist, leaving another smudge on her cheek. In the shadowed light of the barn, the wet smear looked like blood.

Wyatt snagged her arm, ignoring her protest. "Where are you hurt?"

She tried to tug away, but he turned her where the light from the open barn door fell across her. He couldn't see the source of any blood, but something smudged her hands, arms and clothing. His heart pounded painfully as he demanded an answer. "Are you hurt?"

"No." She pried her arm out of his grasp and started for the barn door.

Wyatt stepped in front of her. "Then what's wrong?"

Her voice was frantic as she tried to sidestep him. "I

have to get Franks. One of his mares is foaling, but she's having trouble, and I can't get the foal turned."

He grasped her shoulders and peered into her face; she vibrated with worried energy. "Show me. I can help."

"But…" She glanced toward the door as if deciding whether to go for Franks.

"We're wasting time." Wyatt pulled his hands away, unbuttoned his shirt cuffs and began to roll up his sleeves.

His calm actions seemed to refocus her attention, and she nodded abruptly. "Over here."

She led him to a large corner stall in the back of the barn where a chestnut mare lay in a thick bed of straw. Stepping inside the stall, she quietly crooned to the sweating, groaning horse and knelt to stroke its head. "I think the foal is in a breech position, but I couldn't get it turned."

Wyatt knelt beside the horse and stroked it softly before reaching to feel for the foal. "I think you're right." He held still as a contraction tightened around his arm. When the contraction eased, the mare struggled to rise to her feet. "Hold her still. I'll try to work with her contractions and turn the baby."

Meri murmured soothing words and stroked the distressed mare, preventing her from rising.

Wyatt worked as quickly as possible and finally maneuvered the foal into a better position. Wiping his arm on the straw, he sat back on his heels to let the mare finish her job. "Where is Franks?"

"He went to play checkers with Faither. I said I would keep an eye on her, but we didn't think the foal would come this early. They usually wait 'til late at night to foal." She moved away from the mare to watch. "I was outside with the other horses, so I don't know how long she's been pushing, but when I checked on her, I knew she was in trouble." She drew in a quick breath. "Oh. Here it comes."

Wyatt and Meri watched as a tiny horse quietly entered the world. The tired mare didn't immediately notice her newly arrived offspring, so Wyatt cleared the sac away from the foal's face and head. "Come on, momma. This is your job."

The foal began to struggle, and one little hoof kicked the mare, bringing her head up and around. Meri sank down in the straw with her back against the stall and watched as the mare began to lick her baby.

Wyatt sat down beside her. "It never gets old, does it?"

She shook her head, wonder and excitement filling her face as she brushed back the loose strand of hair again.

Wyatt turned slightly, resting his shoulder against the stall, and studied her. She'd changed from this morning's pretty dress into a simpler skirt and blouse. She had smudges on her face, arms and clothes; her hair was falling out of its fancy twist and bits of straw clung to her, but she didn't notice them. She'd seen a problem and dived in to fix it, heedless of the damage to her clothes and the rather unpleasant task.

Her attention focused squarely on the foal struggling to get to its feet. "Is it a colt or a filly?"

"A good-looking colt." Wyatt's attention never wavered from her. He didn't have to look, he'd checked earlier.

A pleased smile stretched across her face. "Franks will be happy." She rested her head against the stall and let it roll to one side until she was looking at him.

Wyatt grinned back at her, but he was finding it a bit hard to think straight. Or breathe for that matter. She was a tousled mess, and she'd never looked more beautiful. When she smiled at him the way she was doing now, her eyes warm and shiny, it was downright dangerous. A man could get addicted to seeing it. He leaned in closer, not stopping to second-guess himself.

Her eyes flickered, and her breath hitched. She straightened away from the wall and looked down at her hands. "Thank you."

Would he have kissed her if she hadn't pulled away? He settled back against the boards of the stall and took a much-needed lungful of air. "For what?"

"For helping her." She motioned to the mare now on her feet grooming her baby. "I was scared we would lose them both." Her voice dropped to a whisper. "And I'm tired of things dying on me."

The despair in her voice made Wyatt's heart ache. He gently reached over and tucked the wayward strand of hair behind her ear as he spoke softly. "I'm glad I could help."

Raw, open vulnerability filled the brown eyes that turned to look at him, and Wyatt forcibly restrained his hand from touching her face. If her smile was dangerous, this look was downright deadly.

To his plans.

He forced a grin onto his face. "The would-be horse thief and the marshal. We make a pretty good team of nurses."

She blinked, and that fast, the look was gone. Replaced with a shielded wariness that made Wyatt regret the teasing comment.

"Miss Meri, where is you at?" Franks's deep voice rattled the silence.

Meri sprang to her feet. "In here." Her voice broke, and she cleared her throat. "You have a new colt."

The moment was gone. Wyatt had the cold comfort that his plan to remain unattached until he had a safer profession and a place of his own was still intact. Which was exactly what he wanted.

Wasn't it?

Chapter Ten

Monday morning after her father again ordered her to quit hovering about him, Meri wandered over to the mercantile. Bored and feeling a little guilty about missing lunch with the Van Deusen's the previous day, she volunteered to help around the store for a spell. Mr. Van Deusen took her up on her offer since his wife was at her weekly quilting circle, and Meri worked off some energy wielding a dust rag over the many items in the store. But the quiet morning and even quieter storekeeper left her mind free to brood over Pastor Willis's nagging sermon.

The message and scriptures resonated in her spirit even as her mind argued against the conviction that had settled in since yesterday. Bitterness wasn't her problem. Yes, she had lost her mother, but she'd had her far longer than some people had their mothers. She'd had a relatively easy life: wonderful parents, wonderful place to grow up, a life she loved. The knot in her chest was grief not bitterness, she reasoned, but her spirit wouldn't accept that answer, and the argument continued.

She was carefully dusting some delicate china dishes displayed in the front window when a tap on the glass pulled her out of her thoughts. Marshal Cameron smiled as he tipped his Stetson, and Meri's heart skipped a beat before hastily correcting its lapse and inserting a few extra. He resettled his hat, and Meri forced her eyes back to her task as she replaced the dusted dishes. It was time to get back to the ranch. Being in town this long was affecting her thinking! She was *not* going to become one of those silly females who got all flustered and—and *silly* whenever a good-looking man happened to glance their way.

And a good look at herself in the mirror upon returning to her room yesterday showed she was nothing a man, good-looking or otherwise, would do more than glance at. What a scruffy mess she'd been. Dirt and dried blood all over her face and clothes, hair in a tangle with straw in it.

There had been a camaraderie between them as they'd helped deliver the foal. She'd actually been comfortable with him, but then she'd made a fool of herself when he'd tucked her hair behind her ear. For a moment she'd thought he was going to kiss her.

She shook her head and rubbed fiercely at a smudge on the shelf. How wrong she'd been. He was simply being kind when he could have laughed at her grimy, disheveled condition. He'd certainly retreated fast enough when she'd looked at him like…like a moon-eyed calf.

Meri felt her cheeks heat. She'd obviously forgotten to stick in her good sense when she'd packed her bag at the ranch. The man drove her crazy with his know-it-all grin and bossy attitude!

Didn't he?

Spinning on her heel, she stepped away from the window and her chaotic thoughts. She slammed into a solid immovable object. "Oomph!"

Warm hands steadied her. Meri closed her eyes and breathed in his scent. The feel of powerful hands gently encasing her shoulders and the fresh cleanness of his aftershave swirling around her were…

Pulling away, she frowned, irritated at her illogical reaction. "Do you enjoy sneaking up on everyone, or is it just me?"

His eyes twinkled at her from a straight face. "It must be you since I don't get this reaction from anyone else. I thought you saw me coming this time."

"You were outside. I didn't realize you were going to be right behind me." Meri pointed toward the front window, the forgotten dust rag waving from her outstretched hand like a flag. Jerking her hand down, she gripped the offending rag in both hands. His eyes were laughing at her, but her own eyes didn't seem to care. The traitors kept straying upward to catch another peek.

"So I noticed."

"Noticed what?" Meri's eyes entangled in the hazel trap.

"I noticed you didn't realize I was behind you." He tucked his hands into his back pockets as the laughter moved south and quirked the corner of his mouth.

"Oh." She really did need to pay more attention to this conversation, but she was a little busy avoiding those all-seeing eyes. She focused on the rag in her hands.

"Then again, maybe you ran into me intentionally."

"What!" Meri's eyes widened; her gaze slammed into his.

"I thought that'd get your attention." The satisfied smirk was back. "Now, the reason I came in was to see if you wanted to walk with me. I'm headed to see your father."

"No! I mean…" She glanced around hastily before remembering the dust cloth in her clenched fists. She lifted it triumphantly. "I'm not finished here. You go on." Meri stepped around the well-built form blocking her path and industriously attacked a shelf she'd dusted earlier.

"I'm in no rush. Take your time. I'll be outside taking advantage of that new bench."

Meri watched him walk away out of the corner of her eye and heard the bell chime over the door as he exited. How had she missed that when he'd entered? Peering over her shoulder, she was in time to see him glance at her on his way to the bench located just past the big window. He smiled again, and she whipped back around to scrub at an invisible spot. She was not walking back to Doc's with that man. She'd lose what little sense she still possessed at this rate. She'd already proved she had the conversational ability of a goose today. She needed some space to get her head, and her heart, working intelligently and normal again.

Mr. Van Deusen came out of the storeroom from straightening stock. "You've got things looking spick-and-span. Run along and enjoy the rest of the morning."

"I think I will. I'll wash up before I head out."

Meri tossed a quick glance toward the window. No one was visible. Heading into the storeroom, she rinsed out the dust rag, washed her hands, hung up her apron and slipped out the back door.

Wyatt chuckled under his breath, stretching out his long legs and leaning back against the bench. He had smiled and laughed more since meeting Miss America McIsaac than he had since his parents had died and maybe even longer.

He had excelled in army life, but losing friends in battle and taking the life of another human being tended to sober a man very quickly. Killing was occasionally a necessary part of protecting people's lives and property, but only a callous, heartless individual was unaffected by it. Wyatt was neither callous nor heartless, but his naturally sunny, cheerful disposition had grown graver, and he laughed much less easily. The deaths of his parents had further dampened his ability to smile or laugh easily.

Until a shapely spitfire of a lass had landed at his feet.

Wyatt didn't try to contain a grin. Had she been just a tad reluctant to pull away after she'd run into him? And that poor dust cloth. It had been wrung within an inch of its life before she'd remembered its presence. Her spitfire attitude reminded him of a scared, hissing kitten, yet the confused shyness blanketing her brown eyes had belied the indignant tone.

Winning her trust and...friendship would outweigh the risk of a few scratches along the way. Her relationship with her father and Franks showed a character that was deeply loyal and loving. Her spunky independence might clash with Wyatt's desire to protect her, but beneath the pretty exterior and prickly attitude, there was a heart worth winning.

Wyatt snapped his reckless thoughts back to attention. He should have continued on his way after catching a glimpse of Meri fetchingly framed in the mercantile window instead of stopping to see if she wanted to accompany him back to Doc's. He wasn't in a position to win *anyone's* heart. Asking someone else to bear the burden and hardship of his job wasn't fair. He couldn't even come close to providing the kind of place and life Miss McIsaac was used to, so it was no use daydreaming about it. She deserved someone who could give her a safe, comfortable life.

Wyatt surged to his feet. The thought of another man winning her heart was as abhorrent as facing an angry skunk.

"Somethin' I can help you with, Marshal?" Thomas Van Deusen interrupted Wyatt's thoughts.

"No, just stopped to see if Miss McIsaac was ready to head back to Doc's."

The storekeeper leaned against the door frame. Sly amusement on his face. "Might be a while."

Wyatt's brow furrowed. "Oh? I thought she was close to finishing. Hasn't she been here awhile?"

"Yep."

The man certainly was the opposite of his voluble wife. If two words were needed, Thomas made do with one. Suspicion bloomed in Wyatt's mind. "She went out the back door, didn't she?"

"Yep."

"How long ago?"

"Couple minutes, maybe."

A little more information would have been helpful, Wyatt thought ruefully. "Did you happen to see which way she went?"

"Nope."

The man's eyes twinkled in a bland face, and he slowly, deliberately looked up the street. Wyatt followed his gaze in time to see a familiar yellow blouse and tan skirt step nimbly around a passing wagon and disappear between the buildings on the other side of the street a couple of blocks away.

"Thanks!" Wyatt tossed the word over his shoulder, his feet already moving in her direction.

"If you ever catch that girl, you'll have your hands full." A chortle punctuated the storekeeper's words.

Wyatt's eyes narrowed. Oh, he fully intended to catch this particular handful! She'd find it wasn't so easy to escape from a soldier-turned-marshal.

Concerned citizens stopping to inquire about his progress in catching the thief impeded his chase, however. Swallowing his frustration, Wyatt kindly put them off, saying he was waiting for reports to come back from area towns, which he was. He didn't tell them that at the moment he was on the trail of more important quarry!

He was passing the small community park, thinking she might have succeeded in eluding him after all, when he heard a shout that sounded like the woman he was pursuing. Taking off at a run, he raced toward the sounds of a fight issuing from behind a house at the edge of the park.

Rounding the corner, he skidded to a halt. A relieved puff of air left his lips. Meri was unhurt.

Two half-grown boys rolled around the ground, throwing punches and kicks that were mostly ineffectual. Meri was unsuccessfully trying to grab the closest combatant, and Wyatt threw up a prayer thanking the Lord she wasn't injured.

As the prayer crossed his heart, a booted foot found a target in the shape of Meri's shin, and she stumbled. Her gasp moved Wyatt forward to put a stop to the fight, but the sound of a fierce growl brought him to standstill after only two steps.

"That's it!" Meri grumbled as she limped toward the well and hauled up a dripping bucket. "If you want to play dirty, then you're going to get a bath!"

Wyatt leaned against the side of the house curious to see what would happen. Neither Meri nor the continuing-to-tussle boys had caught sight of him, as yet.

Meri emptied the bucket of water into a washtub that had been propped up against the well. Dropping the bucket back down to the water with a splash, she refilled it and poured a second bucketful of water into the tub. She repeated the procedure a third time then leaned down, hefted the full washtub to her hip and limped slowly toward the boys who were still rolling around the ground. Wyatt was impressed. That tub of water had to be as heavy as it was bulky, but she toted it with seeming ease. She neared the boys and paused, waiting.

A grin cocked the corner of his mouth; this was going to be downright entertaining.

The boys rolled toward Meri, fists and feet still flying. Calmly upending the tub of water on the unsuspecting victims when they came within range, Meri drowned the boys in the resulting waterfall.

The fight came to an abrupt end when the boys found they were unable to fight or breathe underwater. Gasping coughs replaced furious grunts, and they struggled to untangle themselves. Wyatt smothered a groaning laugh at the boys' howls when Meri reached down, grabbed each waterlogged boy by an ear and dragged them over to a low woodpile.

"Sit!"

They wilted onto the stacked wood, staring wide-eyed at the woman towering over them, muddy rivulets running down their faces.

"I would like to know why two boys, who claim to be best friends, are suddenly trying to kill each other?" The disarmingly quiet question was met with silence as the two boys glanced nervously toward one another before dropping their gazes to the ground. The silence stretched thin as Meri waited, arms crossed.

Wyatt wondered who would break first and saw the toe of Meri's shoe begin to tap the ground. Both boys glanced nervously at it. Wyatt almost felt sorry for them.

The shorter of the two boys broke the silence with a rush. "Sue Ann said Danny told her he was taking her to the picnic Saturday, and that I couldn't go with them!"

The second boy shot to his feet. "That's a lie! I never did no such thing!"

The first boy shot up, too, and faced him. "Quit calling me a liar!"

"Danny! Billy! Sit down!" The snapped order cowed the boys back to sitting positions.

"Danny, did you ask Sue Ann to the picnic?"

Danny's "No!" was vehement.

Billy scowled at his friend. "Then why would Sue Ann say you did?"

Meri interrupted before Danny could reply. "Hmm... sounds like a Proverbs problem."

"Huh?" Both boys glanced at her curiously. Wyatt was just as curious to hear her explanation.

"Proverbs says, 'A forward man,' or in this case girl, 'soweth strife: and a whisperer separateth chief friends.'"

"What do you mean?" Billy frowned.

"It sounds like someone is trying to break up your friendship by 'whispering' things that aren't quite true, and you fell into the trap of suspecting your best friend instead of her."

"Why would she do that?" asked Danny.

"Proverbs says, 'a lying tongue hateth those that are afflicted by it...'"

"Sue Ann hates us?" Billy asked.

"Well, I think she might be jealous of your friendship and saw this as a way to break it up."

"Why?" This came from Danny.

"Maybe because she likes you and wanted to get your attention."

"But lying is wrong!"

"Yes, and you should pray for her, but I'm more concerned with your friendship at the moment. Proverbs also says, 'Thine own friend...forsake not...' and 'It is an honor…to cease from strife.' Do you want to be honorable friends?"

Both boys nodded, squaring their shoulders.

"Then there's one more piece of advice from Proverbs. Shake hands and apologize."

"Where does it say that in Proverbs?" Danny's brow furrowed skeptically.

"Proverbs 6:3. 'Make sure thy friend.' I want to make sure you're friends again, so shake hands."

A bubble of laughter swelled Wyatt's throat at the sight of the bedraggled, dripping boys solemnly shaking hands and giving shamefaced apologies. Both were developing shiners, but their sheepish grins showed the incident was well on its way to being forgiven and forgotten.

"I know another way to make sure you're friends," Meri added.

"What?"

"I hear there's a three-legged race at the church picnic. Since you're both already dirty, this would be a good time to find a piece of rope and practice working with each other. By the end of the week, you should be able to beat all the competition." Wyatt could hear the grin in Meri's voice and wished he could see her face.

Excitedly discussing where a suitable length of rope could be found, the boys wrapped their arms around each other's shoulders and began to practice, hopping away from Meri.

When they disappeared from view, Meri turned and caught sight of Wyatt, a grin lingering on her face.

Wyatt shook his head and shivered theatrically. "I'm glad you're not my mother."

Her grin faded. "Why?"

"I've never heard so many Proverbs thrown into a tongue-lashing in all my life!"

Reluctant amusement crept back over her face. "My mother used Proverbs on me all the time. She said they were more effective than anything she could come up with since God promised *His* word wouldn't return void, but He never promised the same thing about her words!" A short laugh punctuated her statement.

"You were pretty thorough, but I think you missed a couple that apply."

"Oh?" It was amazing how quickly her suspicion returned.

"Proverbs 27:6 and 17." He waited.

Her eyes narrowed as she sifted through her memory. Shaking her head, she said ruefully, "I don't recall what those verses say."

"'Faithful are the *wounds* of a friend…' and 'Iron sharpeneth iron; so a man sharpeneth the countenance of his friend.' Danny and Billy certainly had the wounds to show for their sharpening session today!"

Meri snickered, and Wyatt grinned, pleased with himself.

"You are terrible, Marshal!" Laughter wove itself through her voice.

He grinned, pleased with the sound. "Just following your example, Mac."

Lingering humor ruined the effect of her scowl. "My name is not Mac."

"And mine's not Marshal. It's Wyatt, or Cameron, if you prefer."

Meri edged around him. "On that note, I think I'll say good day."

"Not so fast." Wyatt touched her arm to stop her, unsuccessfully ignoring the spark that jumped between them. "I've not forgotten that you snuck out on me."

The way she looked at her arm made him wonder if

she had felt that spark, too. "I never said I was going with you."

Was there a hint, just a hint, of coyness in her reply?

He assumed a serious expression. "I've always tried to be an 'honorable' man, so I'm going to 'cease from strife' and not argue the point—"

Meri rolled her eyes.

"—but since my job is protecting the citizens of Little Creek and danger seems to be just around the corner lately, I wouldn't be doing my job if I allowed you to walk the streets alone and unarmed." Reaching for her hand, he tucked it around his arm and guided her steps toward Dr. Kilburn's house.

Meri was remarkably quiet, and surprisingly, she left her hand on his arm. After several moments she spoke. "I'm not exactly unarmed, you know."

Wyatt heard a trace of amusement. "Are you carrying a hideout gun?"

"I'm talking about a different kind of weapon," she hedged. He noticed she didn't say no. "It's called the '...sword of the Spirit, which is the word of God...'"

"Ah. In that case, I'll escort you to protect the town from *you!*"

A snicker escaped her, and Wyatt laughed. She cast furtive glances in his direction as they continued to walk along in silence until they reached the doctor's house. Stopping, he nudged her around until she was facing him. "If the town council hears about this, I may lose my job."

There was a slightly dazed look in Meri's eyes as she wrinkled her brow in confusion. "What do you mean?"

"If they hear how you keep charging in and facing down danger on your own, they'll decide they don't need me and hire you because you're cheaper."

She waited, eyes narrowed expectantly.

"The town has to buy the ammunition for my gun, but the last time I checked, swords don't need bullets!"

Warm brown eyes rolled again, and he saw her bite the inside of her lip to hide a smile. "Don't worry, Marshal. Your job is safe from me. I do *not* want to deal with the nuisances of town life."

Wyatt nodded sadly in agreement. "There *are* some nuisances, like people who don't listen to the marshal—" he looked pointedly at her before continuing "—but I must admit that there is some compensation."

"Like what?"

"Some nuisances are prettier than others...Mac."

Her eyes sparked, and he removed his hat with a flourish, sweeping her a low, courtly bow. Then he turned and walked swiftly back toward his office, whistling retreat as he went.

Chapter Eleven

The initial replies to the telegrams Wyatt sent out had been disappointing; there were no reports of anyone matching the description of the suspect. Tuesday morning, however, Wyatt received some much-needed information. A marshal in an adjoining county wired that the bank teller was living and working there, and a man matching the thief's description had been seen.

Leaving his new deputy in charge, Wyatt saddled his stallion, Charger, and rode out to gather further information on the identity or whereabouts of the bank bandit. He spent part of the long ride in prayer over the case, asking the Lord to guide his steps and open his eyes to the truth about the theft. When he wasn't praying, his thoughts ranged between mulling over the case and picturing Meri's smile the previous day.

It felt good to be astride his own horse again. Charger had developed a troublesome limp on the last of their journey from Texas to Little Creek, and Wyatt had given him ample time to recover. Now fresh and raring to go, Charger eagerly covered the long distance as fast as Wyatt would allow him and listened willingly whenever Wyatt shared his thoughts aloud.

Midafternoon, they arrived at the office of the marshal who'd sent him the telegram. After a discussion of all the particulars of the bank robbery, the two men walked over to the saloon. However, upon talking with the bartender and several of the regulars, Wyatt learned little he didn't already know.

The man in question had come in for a meal and a drink, but hadn't spoken beyond giving his order. His clothing matched what the thief had worn, but the description of his physical appearance was vague enough to have been anybody. And the horse he'd ridden was sorrel, not gray. A quick stop at the livery stable confirmed there was a gray horse in town, but as she had just presented her proud owner with a lovely filly a couple of days previous, she couldn't have been the horse Meri had seen Saturday. The livery stable owner didn't know of any other gray horses in the area.

At this dead end Wyatt turned his attention to the bank teller Mr. Dunn. Like Wyatt, the marshal was newly hired and knew little about Mr. Dunn. He did know Dunn was the newest employee of the bank and resided at a local boardinghouse. He pointed toward the bank and said although it was near closing time, Wyatt might be able to catch Mr. Dunn there.

Mr. Dunn had already gone for the day, but the manager invited Wyatt into his office, curious about the holdup. Wyatt filled him in on a few details and asked what he knew or thought about Mr. Dunn. The man informed Wyatt that in the time Mr. Dunn had worked for him, he had found him a hardworking, conscientious employee. In addition Mr. Dunn's family lived in the area, and the bank manager had known them for years. They were well respected in the community, and he was glad to have been able to hire their son. He also confirmed that Mr. Dunn had been at work the day of the holdup in Little Creek. Wyatt thanked him for his time and upon receiving directions to Mr. Dunn's lodgings, departed.

At the boardinghouse he was informed Mr. Dunn had a room there but ate his meals at his folks' place and was probably still there. Wyatt was feeling hungry himself when he finally located the Dunns' residence. An older gentleman answered his knock, and after introducing himself and explaining his errand, Wyatt accepted the offer of a meal while they talked and was ushered into the kitchen of the small home.

The older man introduced himself as Mr. Dunn, the local schoolteacher. He then presented his wife, his youngest daughter and his son George. Requesting everyone to be seated, he spoke the blessing over the food. "Enjoy the meal while it's hot. We'll discuss your business after we've eaten."

With a minimum of conversation, everyone dug into the simple but tasty fare. When Mrs. Dunn served a delicious dried-apple pie, Mr. Dunn turned to Wyatt. "We heard about the robbery, but how can we be of help?"

"I've been unsuccessful in tracking down the culprit, and since your son was employed at the bank, I'm hoping he can shed some light on a few inconsistencies I've run across in my investigation." Turning to George, he continued, "I've heard a couple of different reasons why you left Little Creek. Would you tell me your side of the story?"

George, a bookish-looking young man wearing wire-rimmed spectacles, set down his fork and wiped his mouth before responding succinctly. "Because I was fired."

"Your former landlady said as much. The banker had a slightly different story."

The young man scowled. "I can only guess what that old skinflint told you."

"George!" Mrs. Dunn's shocked reply softened her son's face, and he shot her a look of apology.

"I'm sorry, Ma, but he was a hard man to work for."

"Would you elaborate, please?" Wyatt asked.

"I went to Little Creek to work in the bank because I wanted to try and make it on my own. I knew I could get a job in this town because everyone respects my father, but I wanted to make it on my own name. Mr. Samuels was okay to work for the first couple of years, but after his wife died, I couldn't seem to do anything to please him. It was as if he no longer trusted me."

"What do you mean?"

"I had more responsibilities when I started working for him. The longer I was there, the less he let me do. He wouldn't let me near the safe, and the only money I handled was what he placed in the teller's drawer. He got so suspicious that if he needed to leave the bank, he'd send me home early and lock up 'til he got back. He frequently accused me of accounting mistakes and finally outright accused me of stealing before he fired me. He didn't even give me a chance to defend myself. By that time I was so tired of it all, I just let it go and moved back home."

"Why didn't you quit sooner?"

"He didn't used to be that bad. I was going to tough it out 'til he got better, but then he fired me. I thought I could make it on my own. Guess I was wrong."

"Maybe the grief over his wife's death was more than he could handle." Mrs. Dunn patted her son's arm soothingly.

"Maybe—" his voice was doubtful "—although he sure was more attentive to her after her death then he ever was before."

"What a thing to say!" Mrs. Dunn chastised again.

"I'm sorry, Ma, but he was. When he did talk about

his wife, which wasn't often before she died, he wasn't very complimentary, and he spent all hours at the bank. After she died, he was constantly talking about how he missed her, and he'd send me home so he could lock up and visit her grave. I think he spent more time with her after she died than before." Addressing Wyatt, he asked, "How much did the bank robber get?"

"Mr. Samuels said the man cleaned out the safe, but he won't divulge the amount taken until the culprit is apprehended. I was hoping you could tell me how much was normally kept in the safe."

"Like I said, Mr. Samuels wouldn't allow me near the safe, and he certainly didn't tell me that information. The only money I ever saw was what was in my drawer for the day. Mr. Samuels put it in the drawer each morning and took it out each afternoon. For all I know, that was the only money in the bank!" George Dunn said sarcastically.

Wyatt changed the subject and gave the description of the thief. "Did you ever see anyone that matched that description or acted suspiciously?"

George thought for a minute before replying. "No. I rarely dealt with anyone I didn't already know. Mr. Samuels made me send any newcomer directly to him."

"Were there any 'newcomers' recently?"

"No. Wait. Somebody came in one day when I was coming back inside from dumping the wastebasket. Mr. Samuels hustled him into his office and sent me home. I heard him lock the door behind me when I left."

"Did you get a good look at him?"

"I didn't see anything but his back before he entered Mr. Samuels's office. Anyway, he hurried me out of there and didn't say anything about who it was. I didn't ask, either, as he didn't take kindly to questions. About a week later, I was out of a job."

Wyatt had been scratching notes as George talked and now returned the little book and pencil to his pocket. Thanking the family for the meal, he asked George to send word if he remembered anything else that might be of use and stood to take his leave. "One more question. I know you were here at work the day of the holdup, but did you have anything to do with the robbery? Revenge on Mr. Samuels perhaps?" He watched George closely.

"No! I don't like the man, but I'm not a thief!"

The man's shock seemed genuine, and Wyatt didn't press him further, taking his leave of the family.

Deciding against riding back home in the dark, he stabled his horse at the livery and bedded down in an empty stall at the invitation of the stable owner. Crossing his hands behind his head as he lay on his bedroll, he sifted through the information he'd learned.

There were so many odds and ends that didn't seem to fit anywhere. Was George Dunn telling the truth or was it a case of sour grapes over losing his job? Then again, the banker had said George left to be near his widowed mother, and there was clearly no widowed mother. Why would the banker lie? Or had George lied to the banker and about the banker?

Wyatt had seen the empty safe in the minutes after the holdup; he'd seen the bandit riding away; he'd seen the wound on the banker's head from his fall; he'd seen Mr. McIsaac bleeding on the floor. A robbery had occurred, but every clue led to dead ends and conflicting testimony. If only he could get some solid answers.

He fell into a fitful sleep, dreaming he was in pursuit of the bank robber. Every time he neared the elusive thief and reached to grab him, the man melted away leaving only questions in Wyatt's hands. Before daylight he rolled his bedroll, saddled Charger and hit the trail for

Little Creek. A little before noon he reached town, his first stop, the bank to speak to Mr. Samuels.

But its doors were locked, and his knock brought no response. At the man's house the housekeeper informed him Mr. Samuels was out of town visiting investors in the hopes of replacing the bank's capital, since the marshal couldn't seem to find the stolen money. Ignoring the not-so-subtle dig, Wyatt politely inquired about the banker's return, but was informed condescendingly that Mr. Samuels would come home when he'd finished his business and not before.

Again Wyatt was left with unanswered questions as he rode Charger to the livery where he was met by the blacksmith and Jonah.

"I saw you ride up to the bank and figured I might catch you here," Jonah said.

Recounting what he'd learned, Wyatt unsaddled and rubbed Charger down before turning the animal out with Franks's geldings to graze. Franks and Jonah confirmed that the banker had frequently complained in public about his "worthless bank help" although the young man had been unfailingly polite to customers.

No new pieces of the puzzle appeared as the three men discussed the findings but agreed Wyatt needed to pin down the banker when he returned. "The town's been real quiet since you and Miss Meri left," Jonah said dryly.

"Meri left? Where? When? She wasn't supposed to ride out on her own," Wyatt snapped.

Franks chuckled, his hammer clanging a horseshoe into shape as Jonah replied to the question. "McIsaac talked Doc into letting him go home. Between Miss Meri and Mrs. Van Deusen, they filled a wagon bed full of quilts and bullied McIsaac into lying down in the back for the ride. They headed home yesterday afternoon."

Wyatt resumed breathing. "Anything else I need to know about?"

"Nope, like I said. It's been quiet without you two to stir up trouble."

"Then let's go get some food. After that I need to catch up on some reports. See ya later, Franks."

Meri straightened and stretched her aching back. The sun was warm, but the breeze cooled her sweat-dampened skin as she leaned on her hoe and checked her progress. The garden was coming along well and looked as if it would deliver an abundant harvest this year. It was also weed free, thanks to her hard work.

It was good to be home and back in the thick of ranch life. Faither was anxious to be back out on the range he loved, and Meri didn't know how long she could keep him off a horse, but at least for now he'd agreed to work in his office for a few days. She'd worried the trip home would tax his strength and set his recovery back, but he appeared invigorated by the fact that he was home, and she was pleased with how well he seemed to be doing. He tired quicker than normal, but that was fading a little more each day. Before long, he'd be back to full strength.

Meri, on the other hand, had about worn herself out making sure he took it easy while trying to outwork her own disordered thoughts. Coming home was supposed to restore life to normal, but normal had packed its bags and departed for parts unknown. Pastor Willis's sermon continued to nag her heart, and Wyatt Cameron seemed to have taken up permanent residence in her thoughts. When ignoring them didn't work, Meri tried to keep herself too busy to think, and evidence of her frenzy lay all around her.

They had arrived home Tuesday afternoon; it was now

Friday. In that time she'd cleaned the chicken coop and horse stalls before progressing to every corner of the barn. She'd cleaned and oiled every saddle and bridle she could lay her hands on, and Barnaby good-humoredly accused her of trying to put his men out of a job. She would have tackled the inside of the house if Ms. Maggie and her father hadn't shooed her out from under their feet, so she tackled cobwebs on porches and weeds in flower beds instead.

Looking over her latest endeavor, Meri viewed the weed-free garden with satisfaction.

Now what? a little voice asked mockingly. *You can't run forever.*

Hoofbeats caught her ear, and welcoming the interruption, she turned, shading her eyes to see the oncoming rider. Meri's heart gave an odd little skip as she recognized the figure on the beautiful bay. She groaned. Just when she'd managed to stop thinking about the man, he had to show up!

Sure you stopped thinking about him...for all of five minutes!

Wyatt lifted his hand in greeting.

Meri glanced down at herself. She was a mess! Sweat dripping, dirt smudges everywhere and her hair probably a wild tangle from the wind teasing it all morning. She couldn't meet him looking like this! Dropping the hoe along with any attempt at dignity, Meri raced for the back door.

The kitchen door slammed in her wake, and Ms. Maggie jumped away from her bread dough, slapping her hand to her chest. "Good grief, girl. What's wrong?"

Meri slid to a halt and attempted to retrieve the composure she'd left in the garden dirt. "Um, the marshal. He's here. I'm going to my room."

The housekeeper shook her head in exasperation, and Meri ran up the back stairs as a knock rattled the front door. Reaching the sanctuary of her room, she frantically washed up, donned a clean pink blouse and fresh skirt and with trembling fingers rebraided her windblown hair. Finally she plopped down in her rocking chair, hands shaking and nerves fluttering.

Why was she so worried about her appearance? She wasn't vain about her looks, at least not much. They'd had visitors to the ranch when she wore the stains of hard work, but never before had she raced away to clean up, then remained hidden in her room.

Meri rocked the chair vigorously. *I am not hiding! Besides, he didn't come to see me. He came to check on Faither.*

"Meri? Are ye coming down, lass? Ye have a visitor." Meri jumped as her father's voice echoed up the stairs.

Taking a deep breath and checking her appearance in the mirror once more, she noticed she was visibly shaking. Meri uttered a quick, desperate plea.

"Lord, help!"

The prayer had been instinctive, and a sudden thought froze her in her tracks. Maybe it wasn't that the Lord wasn't hearing her prayers, maybe it was that she'd actually stopped praying except for an occasional desperate yelp. Had she prayed at all since she'd gotten home?

"Meri?"

Shelving the thought, she called, "Coming, Faither."

Feigning courage, she opened the door and hurried to the stairs. She'd fully expected to see both men waiting at the bottom and breathed a sigh of relief when they weren't. Descending the stairs slowly, she heard voices coming from her father's study and headed that direction.

"Ah. There she is." Both men stood from overstuffed

chairs as she entered the book-lined room where her father's desk stood. Most of the books had been collected by her mother and lived undisturbed until long winter evenings. "I've invited Cameron to stay to lunch. Ms. Maggie said it would be ready shortly."

"It's ready now. Come and get it." The housekeeper spoke behind her.

Meri followed the woman back to the kitchen. "I'll help you put it on the table."

"It's already on the table." The woman waved Meri toward the door.

"Where?" Meri looked at the bare kitchen table.

"We have company. It's time that big dining table was used again, and this is as good a time as any. Now shoo, you have a guest."

Entering the little-used dining room, Meri was surprised to see the housekeeper had set the table with a linen cloth, napkins and Catriona McIsaac's good china. When had she had time to do it all? Surely Meri hadn't spent that much time in her room?

Marshal Cameron held a chair for her to the right of her father, and she slid into it while avoiding his eyes. His hand brushed her shoulder, and Meri nearly jumped out of her skin at the reaction the simple touch caused. Glancing at him as he took his seat across the table from her, she intercepted a penetrating look and dropped her eyes to her plate, wondering why he was here.

After McIsaac asked the blessing and their plates were filled, Wyatt and her father continued a discussion that must have started in the study before she'd come down. It seemed that once again there were more dead ends concerning the bank robbery.

Meri chewed and swallowed automatically, losing track of the conversation. He wasn't here to see her. He was only here to keep her father informed. So why did her heart pound just a little faster every time she caught his eyes on her?

Because you've allowed yourself to imagine something that isn't there. The man is simply doing his job. Once it's done, he'll move on. Meri fought to keep her wandering gaze on her plate and off their handsome guest.

The interminable meal ended, and McIsaac leaned back in his chair, propping his elbows atop the armrests and crossing his hands over his stomach. "I believe ye had something ye wanted to ask me daughter, Cameron."

Meri stiffened, waiting, but neither man spoke. She darted a look at her father, but he merely pointed toward Wyatt. She steeled herself to brave the hazel-green eyes watching her.

"Ah. There you are. You've been very quiet." His smile was gentle instead of teasing.

Meri felt her cheeks color. When had he gone from the most annoying man she'd ever met, to the most handsome? Taking a deep breath, she forced a composure into her voice that she was nowhere close to feeling. "What is your question?"

His gaze shifted to the table, and Meri felt like she'd lost something—which was nonsense. How could you lose something you didn't have in the first place?

He looked back, determination gleaming in his gaze. "May I escort you to the church picnic tomorrow?"

Chapter Twelve

Meri's breath froze in her throat. Had he really come to ask her to accompany him to the picnic? Her—Meri McIsaac? The old maid of Little Creek?

Hope sparked then an appalling question doused it. After those two men had shot at her, Marshal Cameron had said she wasn't to go riding outside of town alone. Had he simply decided it was part of his job to escort her to the picnic—a way to keep an eye on the troublemaker? Had her father asked him to take her since he was staying home?

Her father cleared his throat, reminding her Marshal Cameron was still waiting for an answer. She swallowed the lump of mortification that stuck in her throat, and it hit her stomach like a cannonball. "Thank you, but I'm not going to the picnic. I don't want to leave Faither alone." At least her voice didn't sound as embarrassed as she felt.

"Ach. I don't need a babysitter, lassie. Frankly, I could use a break from yer frantic cleaning, and so could ye. Ye've worked yerself to a frazzle this week. Now it's time for a little fun." He looked at Wyatt. "When will ye be here to pick her up?"

"But..." Her feeble protest was lost in the continuing conversation.

"I'll be here about ten o'clock in the morning. That should give us plenty of time to get there before the meal at noon. When do you want your daughter home, sir?"

"Have the lass home before dark."

"Yes, sir."

They stood and shook hands as if they'd completed a business transaction. Apparently, her suspicions weren't far from the mark. Dazed, she watched them walk out of the room toward the front door. "Wait! Don't I have some say in this?" she demanded, scurrying to catch up.

Both men replied in unison, "No."

"Why do I get the feeling I've been ambushed?" She sounded peeved, but it was better than melting into a puddle of humiliation.

Wyatt laughed as he stepped outside and off the porch. "See you in the morning."

As he loped his horse away, Meri turned to her father and took a deep breath. "Why—"

He held up his hand. "Ye need a break, and ye wouldn't have gone on yer own. Don't forget, ye'll need to make something for the dessert auction." McIsaac turned to go in the house.

She stopped him. "Did you ask him to take me?"

The surprise in his eyes was genuine. "Wheesht, lass. Why would I need to ask the man to escort me beautiful daughter to the picnic? He's smart enough to have the idea for himself. Now, if ye'll excuse me, I'm wee bit tired. I think I need to lie down." The twinkle in his eye belied his plea of fatigue as he left her standing on the porch.

Meri threw the third dress across her bed in frustration. She was working herself into a dither over what to wear to the picnic.

You're being ridiculous, Meri!

Running downstairs, she found Barnaby exiting her father's study.

"Can I do something for you, miss?"

"Would you have someone saddle Sandy and bring him around, please?"

Faither followed him out of the room. "Lass, a gentleman brings a buggy when he's taking his girl to a picnic. Ye don't need yer horse."

"I am *not* his girl. I'm riding Sandy in." She smiled winningly at the foreman. "Will you do it, Barnaby? Please?"

Looking at McIsaac, who only shrugged in exasperation, he sighed. "Yes, if that's what you want."

"Thank you." Planting a quick kiss on the cheek of each man, she turned and ran back up the stairs to her room.

"This is gonna be interesting," Barnaby muttered.

Determination filled her as she headed back to her wardrobe and grabbed an outfit. It wasn't what most females would wear to a picnic, especially when they were escorted by a handsome gentleman, but then again, she wasn't most females. When Wyatt Cameron arrived at her doorstep with a buggy, she would meet him on horseback. As Meri McIsaac, the content-to-be-single cowgirl. Not a delicately dressed husband-hunting female.

Donning the outfit, Meri scoffed at herself. Obviously her rebellion only stretched so far. She'd pulled out her newest, fanciest riding habit. The long and full divided skirt was a buttery-soft fawn-colored leather, paired with a crisp white blouse and belted at the waist with a black leather belt. A black velvet ribbon circled the collar of the blouse in a feminine bow. A matching fawn-colored leather vest with shiny black jet buttons topped the blouse, and a tan flat-brimmed hat and black boots completed the ensemble.

Meri studied herself in the mirror. She'd smoothed her hair into a neat braid, coiled and pinned at the base of her neck and neatly tucked beneath the brim of her hat. A flush warmed her cheeks, and the color of the skirt and vest mimicked the color of her hair and the light tan on her skin. She'd always thought the outfit was pretty and polished, but all at once, she saw the contrast she'd make against the backdrop of dressed-up females.

"Well, if your aim was to stand out like a sore thumb, America McIsaac, you're going to accomplish it in rare form." Looking at the little clock on her nightstand, she muttered, "And it's too late to change your mind now. He'll be here soon."

Giving in to a last-minute impulse, she opened her jewelry box, pulled out a pair of jet earbobs and fastened them to her ears. Tucking a handkerchief in her pocket, Meri avoided the mirror again and left the room.

The clock was chiming ten as she stepped onto the porch. Sandy was standing patiently at the hitching rail, groomed and saddled, and a distant horse and rider were approaching the house.

Meri blinked, surprised. He wasn't driving a buggy?

Swallowing past a bundle of nerves, she focused on the horse he was riding. It was the tall bay with the white star she'd seen in Franks's pasture the day she'd first met the marshal. The same horse he'd ridden yesterday, come to think of it, but in her haste to get to the house and change, she'd not spared the animal any attention.

Wyatt rode up beside Sandy and leaned his arm against the saddle horn, tilting his hat brim up with one finger. He wore his holster and star, but a black string tie adorned the collar of the spotless gray cavalry-style bib shirt that stretched across firm shoulders. Dark blue pressed trousers and polished boots covered the muscular legs that draped around the horse. "Great minds think alike."

"They do?" Meri asked guardedly.

Wyatt pointed to Sandy. "I didn't figure you'd want to ride in a buggy on this pretty day, so I took a chance you'd be ready to ride."

This man seemed able to read her like a book. It was a bit disconcerting to say the least.

Wyatt swung his leg over the front of the saddle and slid lightly to his feet. Sweeping off his hat and holding it against his chest, he bowed deeply. Meri had originally thought the gesture was his way of mocking her, but today it felt…courtly.

"You look fetching." His eyes swept over her, frankly admiring as he straightened to his full height.

Meri dropped her own eyes in confusion. This didn't feel like an escort simply to keep her safe. "Thank you." Stepping off the porch, she walked over to the magnificently tall bay and held out the back of her hand for him to smell. "Who is this handsome fellow?"

She felt Wyatt move up behind her, and his arm reached around to stroke the horse's neck. "Meet Charger. He came with me all the way from my folks' place in Virginia. I haven't been able to ride him until this week because he developed a limp on our way up from Texas. It's good to be back on him."

Meri withdrew from the disturbing awareness the man was causing and walked around the sleek animal, stroking him as she circled. "Is he a thoroughbred?"

"Yep, from old Virginia bloodlines. I hope to have a place someday where I can run a few head of good horse-flesh. He's my start. He's also a good friend. We've been through a few scrapes together, and unlike some people, he's never let me down."

"He looks like he could cover some ground." Meri swung up on Sandy.

"He can, and he's raring to go today." Wyatt stayed on the ground.

"Then let's not keep him waiting, Marshal."

He glanced at the house. "Do we need to take anything with us for the picnic?"

"No. The housekeeper and some of the hands are bringing food in the wagon. They'll leave here shortly." Meri's nerves were beginning to make Sandy antsy, but the marshal didn't seem in any hurry to leave.

"Who's staying with your father?"

"The bunkhouse cook. He and Faither are having a chess rematch. They're evenly matched right now, and each one swears he's going to be the winner of the tie-breaker."

The man finally swung up on his horse. "Well, then, Miss Mac. Let's go, shall we?"

Meri's father stepped out the front door. "Have a nice time. I trust ye'll take care of me daughter?"

"Yes, sir! I won't take my eyes off of her."

Meri caught her breath sharply. His eyes were dangerous when they sparkled like that.

"What's that, Meri-lass?"

She cleared her throat with a cough ignoring Wyatt's grin. "We're going to be late."

"Well, who's stoppin' ye? Get goin'."

Meri and Wyatt turned their horses and rode out of the ranch yard. Silence stretched between them for several minutes before Meri broke it. "You know, I never knew our town was so compassionate."

"How so?" Wyatt's tone indicated he knew something was coming.

"They took pity and hired such a forgetful person for so important a position."

"Meaning me, I suppose."

Meri nodded, looking appropriately sad but hiding a grin.

Wyatt made a show of looking all around and down at himself. "What did I forget?"

Meri shook her head gloomily. "See? You can't even remember to remember that my name is *not* Mac!"

Wyatt's hangdog, mournful demeanor was comical, but she smothered the impulse to laugh. The man didn't need any further encouragement. "Yes. Unfortunately it's a highly contagious condition. I contracted it from a certain young lady who can't seem to remember that *my* name is not *Marshal!*"

She was regretting her choice of subjects. *Hoist on your own petard, Meri.*

"There is a cure, however." Wyatt paused, catching her eye before continuing quietly, "When you can remember to call me Wyatt or even Cameron, I believe my memory will improve, and I'll be able to remember *your* name." Earnestness peered through the teasing expression.

Meri searched for a reply that would rescue her from the hole she'd entrapped herself in. "But you *are* the marshal. It's…it's a term of respect," she finally managed weakly.

A laugh burst from Wyatt's lips. "If the way you obey orders is any indication of the level of your respect, I'd much rather you just call me by my name!"

Meri didn't know whether to laugh or search for a witty rebuttal, so she did neither. She ran.

Touching Sandy with her heels, the horse sprang into

a full gallop, taking advantage of the long open stretch of road and leaving the marshal behind in two jumps.

Charger strained to follow Sandy, but Wyatt held him in check, taking a few moments to admire the slim figure that moved as one with her horse. The color of Meri's apparel matched the coloring of the flashy palomino, and highlighted the golden glints in her hair. Horse and rider presented a striking image as they flew down the road. He had wrestled with himself about asking her to the picnic and in the end had decided to do it, trying not to examine his motives too closely. It was a day to enjoy the burgeoning spring, not worry about the future.

The distance between them widened, and Wyatt stroked Charger's sleek neck. "Okay, fella, let's show those two what Virginia boys can do." Charger leaped into action, long legs stretching easily to eat up the distance.

Meri glanced over her shoulder, and her eyes widened when she realized they were gaining. Turning back, she leaned low over Sandy's neck and urged him to greater speed. The sturdy palomino surged forward with renewed effort, but Charger's longer legs relentlessly narrowed the gap between them. In minutes they were alongside Meri and Sandy.

While Wyatt was momentarily checking Charger's speed to match Sandy's, Meri's eyes flashed at him, gleaming with competitive excitement. He tapped the brim of his hat in a salute. Charger tossed his head impatiently at the delay, and Wyatt let him go. Surging forward in a renewed burst of speed, they quickly left Meri and Sandy behind.

Wyatt allowed him to run several more strides before guiding him down to a smooth lope. Flashing a look over his shoulder, he saw Meri racing to close the distance

Charger had put between them. As they came alongside, Wyatt slowed Charger's pace again, but Meri ignored the gesture, tapping her own hat as she and Sandy raced past.

Wyatt growled, half amused, half irritated. The stubborn woman didn't know when she was beaten because she refused to quit! He allowed Charger to leap after the palomino immediately this time, and they were alongside the pair almost instantly. Nudging Charger in close to Sandy, Wyatt snaked an arm around Meri's waist and pulled her off her horse and across the front of his saddle in one fluid movement.

Shock widened her eyes and one hand convulsively clenched Sandy's reins as Wyatt slowed Charger to a walk. Sandy quietly followed alongside, eyeing his unseated mistress curiously.

Wyatt looked down into her surprised face and grinned at the traces of dirt Charger had kicked up on her when they'd passed. Right arm cradling her back, right hand holding Charger's reins, he used his left to pull out his handkerchief and gently wipe her face. "You've got a little dirt here…and here…" Wyatt heard her sharp intake of breath as he wiped the dust off.

She was a frozen bundle of tension for half a second longer before she snapped into frantic motion. "Put me down…" she squeaked as she struggled to slide off his lap.

Wyatt tightened his arm around her, pinning her into place. "Nope. You haven't asked me nicely, yet." Her stubbornness was no hardship; he could hold her all day. He refused to lose this battle of wills.

"Would you put me down…please?" Meri tried again to pull away and slide down.

"Uh-uh. You still haven't asked correctly." He could feel her trembling. The horses had continued traveling at a brisk walk, and they would soon be in view of town.

Wyatt wondered how long the stubborn woman would hold out before realizing she was in danger of being seen…sitting on the marshal's lap!

They were at the final turn toward town before she gave in. The ramrod-straight spine was as stiff as a poker, but her voice was wobbly as she spoke. "Please put me down, *Mr. Cameron.*"

Wyatt looked into nervous brown eyes before she cast a quick look down the road toward town. Wyatt brought Charger to a stop. Sandy kept his nose even with Meri's feet.

"That's not exactly what I had in mind, but I guess it'll do. For now." He tugged the reins out of her hand and moved Sandy into position before smoothly, regretfully, swinging Meri back into her saddle. His arms immediately missed the feel of her.

She fastidiously straightened her skirt and vest and adjusted her hat, before reaching to take the reins from his hand.

He moved them out of range and cocked an eyebrow at her.

She exhaled noisily. "*Thank you.* Now would you *please* give my reins back, Mar…?" She bit off the last word but not quickly enough.

She was persistent, but she had met her match. Wyatt grinned and reached to pick her off her horse again. "Ah, ah, ah, Miss Mac. That's not my name."

Meri nudged Sandy with her heel, and he swung his hindquarters away, placing the horses in a T position and putting Meri temporarily out of reach. She lifted her chin regally and focused somewhere over his shoulder. "As I was saying, Mr. Cameron, thank you. Now I suggest we get a move on if we plan on attending the picnic."

Wyatt wondered what she'd do if he hauled her off her horse again and kissed her senseless.

Probably slap your fool head off!

Wyatt chuckled before handing over the reins. It might just be worth it, but he'd back off and accept the unspoken truce for now. He waved toward town. "After you, Miss *Mac*…Isaac."

Chapter Thirteen

Meri stood outside the marshal's office and contemplated the abnormally quiet street. The townsfolk must already be at the picnic grounds. She would have been there, too, but for the fact she had wanted to leave Sandy in Franks's pasture for the afternoon. That detour had given her a few extra moments to recover her composure after being held by…Mr. Cameron, as well as giving her a chance to duck into Franks's living quarters and wash the remaining dirt off her face.

Walking back toward the picnic grounds, Wyatt had stopped at his office to check in with Jonah who would be keeping an eye on the nearly deserted town while everyone was at the picnic. Meri had waved hello through the open door and now waited on the porch while the two men talked.

Letting her idle gaze linger on the bank, she relived the terrifying moment when she'd seen her father lying bleeding on the floor. A shudder rippled through her at how close death had come to robbing her again.

Something flashed inside the bank.

That was odd. She had assumed the bank would still

be closed and the banker at the picnic with the rest of the town.

She walked down the boardwalk toward the bank, staying on the opposite side of the street. She'd just take a quick look-see and make sure everything was okay, although from what she'd heard, there was nothing left to steal. Meri stopped across from the bank, in the shadow of the dressmaker's shop. The bank's large front window shed light into the dim recesses of the building, and a figure stood just on the edge of the pool of sunlight.

Meri let out a breath she didn't know she'd been holding. It was only the banker. After being shot at, she was imagining trouble behind every bush.

Another silhouette moved into view. Whoever was in there was certainly having an animated conversation with the banker. Their body language shouted irritation. Someone unhappy with the bank's closure, maybe?

The two figures moved out of sight, and Meri walked back to the office, arriving as Wyatt stepped out with Jonah.

"Best not keep the lady waitin' any longer, Cap'n. I know where to find you if I need you."

"I'll send someone with food so you won't miss out on the good cookin'." Wyatt tucked Meri's hand under his arm, covering it with his free hand, and stepped off briskly toward the church grounds.

Meri allowed her fingers to curl lightly around Wyatt's arm. She should pull away, but it felt good, hand nestled in the crook of his arm, hidden under his own. She had a sudden wish that her entire person could hide. The whole town was about to see her walk in on the marshal's arm.

Her. Meri McIsaac. The I'd-rather-be-riding-the-range-than-going-to-a-party spinster was being escorted to the spring picnic by the most eligible bachelor in town. She could hear the catty tongues now. They'd say he felt sorry for her or something along those lines.

Maybe he did feel sorry for her, or maybe he still wasn't sure she and Faither were merely victims of the bank robbery. Maybe he was trying to get close enough to find out if they were somehow more deeply involved.

He definitely had you close enough when you were on his lap!

Heat flooded her face as she remembered the feel of his arms around her. She hadn't wanted to leave them, and that realization had made her desperate to get out of them. Besides, why would she want to be held by someone she wasn't even sure liked her; someone who only did it to prove a point? She had to get her unruly emotions under control. When she'd let them peek out after they'd helped the foaling mare, he'd backed off as if she'd stuck a gun in his face.

"I've heard one of the highlights of the picnic is the dessert auction. What's it all about?"

Meri grabbed the distraction from her disconcerting thoughts. "The women bake special desserts, and the highest bidder gets to enjoy it with the lady who made it. The proceeds go to something the church or school needs. Originally the women were supposed to keep their dessert a secret, and the buyer found out only after he'd purchased the dessert. But we've been doing it so long that everyone pretty much knows who made what before the meal is even served."

"Did you make a dessert for the auction?"

There was no way she was answering that question truthfully. "I didn't even know I was coming until yesterday, and I rode in on horseback, in case you forgot, not a good way to carry a dessert."

"That was an evasive answer. A simple yes or no would have sufficed."

"You have a very suspicious nature, Mars…sir."

"Hazards of the profession, Mac…ma'am."

The man was as dogged as she was. She bit back an unexpected grin as she looked up at him. Her gaze tangled with his, and she caught her breath as his laughing hazel-green eyes sobered and darkened. Meri ducked her head and concentrated on something safer. Like breathing.

Reaching the picnic grounds behind the church building, they paused to survey the scene before them. Women in brightly colored frocks mingled around tables covered in various sizes of dishes, and the sounds of cheery chatter filled the air as they assembled the upcoming meal. Deeper voices and more muted clothing identified the male portion of the gathering, and happy shrieks marked children busily at play.

"There's Marshal Cameron, now," a high-pitched voice squealed.

Meri jerked her hand away from Wyatt's arm as a group of young women headed toward them, maneuvering for Wyatt's attention. She gave ground as the women talked over each other, giving broad hints regarding the choicest dessert on which to bid. The fluttering eyelashes and simpering voices were enough to give her a headache. Retreating from the field without firing a shot, she left the victors to their spoil.

She spent the next hour helping with setup and food preparation as families continued to arrive and contribute their food dishes, but Meri unconsciously kept track of Wyatt as he moved around the picnic grounds. Sometimes he was talking with a group of men; sometimes a young lady and her mother would be smiling and chatting with him. Finally the women called Pastor Willis over to ask the blessing on the food, and afterward, Meri busily dished up food for little ones or those with full hands.

Ms. Maggie tried to shoo her away several times, but she stubbornly continued serving. When the last straggler headed for a place to sit, she filled her own plate and planted herself next to Ms. Maggie. She took a long-awaited drink of cool, tart lemonade.

"Mind if I share your blanket?"

Her head snapped up to see Wyatt holding a plate full of food. She'd thought he would have finished eating already. There had certainly been plenty of invitations for him to join certain picnic blankets. Not that she'd counted.

"Go right ahead, young man." Ms. Maggie grinned.

The blanket had seemed roomy until he sprawled his large frame across one side. Now it felt entirely too small. Meri watched him attack his food while she picked at her own, appetite lost in a stomach full of busy butterflies.

"The ladies of Little Creek have certainly outdone themselves today." Wyatt wiped his mouth in satisfaction.

Meri noted he had the manners to use one of the cloth napkins Ms. Maggie had provided instead of his sleeve, unlike some of the other men on nearby blankets.

"So you came west from Virginia?" Ms. Maggie asked.

"That's where I grew up, yes. My parents are gone now, but my brother and three sisters still live there. They're all married, and my brother lives on the home place."

"You don't plan on going back?" Meri asked, mangling a piece of chicken with her fork.

"Not to live. I've been out West too long. It's my home now."

"What was it like growing up in Virginia?" Ms. Maggie set her empty plate aside.

Meri nibbled on her food and watched Wyatt's face light up as he answered Ms. Maggie's question and regaled them with stories of growing up in the wilds of Virginia with his Cherokee cousins.

"I learned to read the woods before I learned to read. In fact, I didn't want to learn to read at all, told Ma I'd never need it." He chuckled ruefully. "She sure reminded me of that when I was taking the exams to enter West Point, but she'd made sure I had a sound education, and it stood me in good stead. After graduating West Point, I was shipped west as a shavetail second lieutenant."

Meri voiced a question she'd been wondering about. "Why did you leave the army?"

For a second she wondered if he was going to answer, but then he took a deep breath and began, "I got word about two years ago that my father was gravely ill, and I obtained a leave of absence to go home. He rallied for a few weeks after I arrived, and we had a wonderful visit, but it didn't last long enough. He started failing again, and within a month of my arrival, he slipped away in the night." His voice grew rough. "Mother took it so hard." He paused to clear his throat. "I resigned my commission so I could stay with her. I thought if I was home for good and she had all her children back around her she'd eventually come through the grief."

He slowly shook his head. "We didn't realize how deeply she felt the loss of her other half. Cy and Hanna Cameron were two sides of one coin, and she just lost the will to go on without him. Within a year of Father's death, we buried Mother beside him. My oldest brother had the family farm well in hand, and after all these years of working it and staying by the stuff, he deserves it. My sisters are all married and live nearby, but I just didn't feel like it was home after Ma passed. I started itching to be back out West but didn't have a desire to return to the army, so I said my goodbyes and started drifting. I was down in Texas working as a deputy when I heard about Little Creek looking for a marshal. The sheriff down there was kind enough to send a recommendation, and here I am."

Meri was stunned. He'd recounted his tale so calmly, it had taken a moment for her to grasp the fact he'd recently lost *both* of his parents. He knew better than she the pain of loss.

She was on the verge of apologizing for bringing up sad memories when Mr. Hubert's voice rang out across the picnic grounds. "Graaaab your partners, and let the games begin." The town barber loved being the master of ceremonies and brought a certain flair to the festivities.

Wyatt sprang to his feet, pulling her up with him. "Let's go. I signed us up as partners in the three-legged race."

"Uh-uh." She shook her head and dug in her heels, but she was no match against his gentle, persuasive strength. "We're going to fall flat on our faces."

Ms. Maggie made a shooing motion with her hand. "Oh, go on. Have some fun."

Wyatt tugged her, protesting, toward the gathering competitors. "I think you'll be surprised what we can do if you'll work with me instead of against me."

"I'd rather not," she blurted, heart racing.

"Scared?" he challenged.

Meri glared at him. She was, but she'd never admit it. "Okay, fine. But don't say I didn't warn you."

Reaching the starting line, Wyatt took one of the long strips of cloth the barber handed out to contestants. "Tell you what. If we win this race, I won't call you Mac any more—"

"Deal!"

"—today." The impish smirk reappeared on his face.

"You can't change the rules just like that."

"I didn't change the rules, you interrupted before I finished." Wyatt knelt beside her and tied their booted ankles together, her right to his left, leaving the holstered pistol on his right hip free of obstruction.

She was immediately grateful for the shorter riding skirt instead of a frilly dress as he looped the cloth around her ankle. "Has anyone ever told you how vexing you are?" She shouldn't be able to feel his touch tingle through her leather boot.

Wyatt looked up at her. "I think you just did."

Standing, he wrapped his arm around her waist, and Meri tried to hide the shiver that ran down her spine. Why did a simple touch from him cause her to react like a wild horse, flinching and shying at the slightest thing?

"Are you cold?"

Apparently she hadn't been successful. "No."

"Have you ever done this before?"

"It's a little late to be askin' that." Her insides might be a quivering mass, but her tongue apparently still worked.

The children's portion of the race ended, and Billy and Danny ran up to Meri, blue ribbons fluttering from their hands. "Thanks for tellin' us to practice, Miss Meri. We won!"

"Good for you." The boys ran on almost before Meri got the words out.

"All right, ladies and gents. Line up. Let's see if you can do as good as those youngsters."

It took a second to figure out which foot should move first, and she stumbled, but Wyatt's arm around her waist kept her upright.

"If you'll wrap your arm around my waist, I think you'll find it a tad easier," Wyatt instructed casually. As if his arm around her waist was the most natural thing in the world.

Meri tentatively complied, trying to ignore the feeling of his broad back against her arm. Other young ladies seemed to have no qualms about wrapping their arms about their partners, and apparently it wasn't a big deal to anyone except her. Well, if those giggling females could do it, then Meri McIsaac should certainly be able to do it. She concentrated on her feet as they stumble-hopped toward the starting line.

"Con…tes…tants! At the sound of the bell, make your way to the big oak down by the creek, circle the tree and head back to the finish line. If you fall, you're disqualified. First team across the line wins the blue ribbon. On your mark…"

"This is gonna hurt," Meri muttered under her breath.

"Get set…"

"Have a little faith, and remember, start with your right foot."

The bell rang, and all the teams shuffled, hopped and tripped their way toward the oak tree as fast as three legs could carry them. The field of contestants was swiftly whittled down as couples lost their balance and fell, laughing good-naturedly. Meri nearly followed their example several times, but Wyatt's strong arm kept her safe.

"Work *with* me," he whispered near her ear each time she stumbled.

She was having more than a little trouble concentrating on anything but the distracting sensations caused by his arm around her waist, but eventually they were circling the oak tree and heading back the way they'd come. Meri looked up to see there were only two teams ahead of them.

"Stay with me, Mac, we're almost home free."

As he spoke, a young man and his pretty partner fell

and landed in front of them. Meri braced herself for the inevitable tumble, but Wyatt pulled her up short, and they sidestepped the fallen, laughing couple. Reaching clear ground again, Meri caught the exhilaration of the competition and the rhythm of the race, and a giggle bubbled up.

"You ready to make a run for it? I think we can catch them."

"Let's do it!" She tightened her arm around his trim, muscled waist.

She regretted the words as soon as they left her mouth, for Wyatt surged headlong, and Meri realized how much longer his legs were. He'd been holding back, and now she struggled to match his longer stride and faster pace.

The onlookers were cheering on their favorites, yelling out encouragements as Meri and Wyatt gained on the last team. She felt his arm tighten, and he lifted her slightly. Her feet were barely touching the ground. She might look like she was helping, but he was doing all the work himself.

She wasn't going to complain because his move paid off. They swept across the finish line, mere inches ahead of the other team, to the cheers and applause of the picnickers.

Meri untangled her arm, leaning over to catch her breath from the last mad dash. "You did it," she panted happily, reaching to untie the scrap of cloth that bound their ankles.

"*We* did it."

"Congratulations on a race well run." Mr. Hubert thrust a scrap of blue silk at them before hurrying to announce the next contest.

Wyatt handed the ribbon to Meri. "I told you we could do it if you worked with me."

"And since we won, you have a deal to keep." She cocked her head and grinned triumphantly.

"I'm a man of my word. I won't call you Mac again. Today." He placed his hand over his heart.

"Laaaadies and gentlemen! The potato-sack race!" Mr. Hubert's voice boomed again.

"Come on." Wyatt grabbed her hand. "I signed us up for this."

Meri noticed a few females shooting daggers at her, and others that had their heads together whispering as they watched. She was the subject of gossip once more. "You go ahead, I'll watch from the sidelines." And fade back into the woodwork.

"But I was the 'Champeen' potato-sack racer of my county," Wyatt pleaded boyishly.

"Then by all means, go. Have fun." Why did her mouth say one thing when she really wanted something else?

"I see." He shook his head morosely. "You're afraid to be beaten by a Virginia boy."

"We'll see about that," Meri growled. Let the biddies talk. They always did, anyway. No matter what she did or didn't do.

She stalked over to the pile of potato sacks, grabbed one and marched to the starting line, Wyatt beside her all the way. She stepped into the sack and pulled it up around her waist. "It's time to put up or shut up, Marshal." Meri watched him start to speak and cut him off, grinning. "And you can't call me Mac, remember?"

The starting bell sounded, and Meri gripped the top of the rough burlap, hopping frantically in the direction of the finish line.

Don't fall. Don't fall. Don't fall! The words accompanied the beat of her frenzied jumps.

Wyatt's long legs carried him past her, but Meri kept

hopping, trying to avoid those that fell and took others down with them.

The finish line grew closer. Wyatt was hot on the heels of the young man in the lead, and Meri was behind Wyatt. She would have laughed at the sight of the marshal leaping like a gigantic jackrabbit, but she needed all her breath to catch up.

Suddenly the young man slipped and went down right across Wyatt's path. This time Wyatt was unable to avoid the fallen contestant and toppled to the ground over the poor fellow. Meri hopped as swiftly as she could, crossing the finish line a mere breath ahead of the remaining contestants.

A familiar arm snaked around her shoulders as she accepted her ribbon, and Wyatt pulled her into quick side hug. "I knew you could do it." Wyatt's flushed face beamed at her as he released her.

"Champeen potato-sack racer, huh?" Meri felt another giggle bubble up. Good grief. She sounded like those silly females earlier.

He shrugged, unperturbed. "Did I mention I was only ten at the time?"

"Laaaadies and gentlemen! The egg race!"

Wyatt grabbed Meri's hand and led her to a table holding spoons and eggs.

"Don't tell me. You signed us up for that one, too," Meri groaned dramatically.

"Yep."

"I don't want egg on me." A protesting laugh accompanied the words.

"O ye of little faith. They're hard-boiled."

Mr. Hubert explained the rules and handed each team a spoon and an egg. "This is a relay race. The team that crosses the finish line first without dropping their egg will win the blue ribbon. There are several flags between the starting line and the finish line. One team member will go to the first flag. When the bell sounds the team member at the starting line will place the spoon in their mouth and their egg on the spoon. They will then carry the egg to their partner at the first flag and pass the egg to them, without dropping it and without using their hands. The new egg holder will head to the next flag, where their partner will meet them to pass the egg off again. And so on and so forth until they reach the finish line. First team across with an undamaged egg still on the spoon wins. Drop the egg, and you're disqualified. Touch the egg with your hands, and you're disqualified. Take your places!"

Wyatt thrust the egg at Meri and jogged to the first flag. Accepting the inevitable, Meri put the spoon between her teeth and laid the egg in the bowl of it. When the bell sounded she carefully made her way toward Wyatt. She reached him with little trouble, and by concentrating on the spoons instead of the nearness of his face, she was able to exchange the egg smoothly. Racing to the next flag, she watched as Wyatt carried the egg toward her on the next leg of the relay. He moved quickly, but the journey and the exchange again went smoothly.

This was easier than she'd thought it would be! She set off for the next flag, balancing the egg easily and moving quicker. Just as she reached Wyatt, her toe connected painfully with a rock hidden in the grass. She pitched forward.

"Mmph!" Her teeth clamped hard around the spoon handle as her hands flew out. She closed her eyes tight, bracing for the impact.

Solid hands caught her shoulders and stopped her descent toward the ground.

The egg wasn't so fortunate.

She heard a dull smack, and the sulfurous odor of rotten egg filled the air. Wyatt looked down, nose wrinkling at the smell emanating from the slimy mess dripping off his shirtfront. He gingerly pulled the fabric away from his body, leaning over to swipe the worst of it off into the grass.

Meri was helpless to stop the laughter that erupted at the look of disgust on his face. He pulled out his handkerchief to wipe his hands free of the odiferous slime. "I appreciate your concern."

"I thought you said they were hard-boiled." She gasped breathlessly.

"Apparently I was wrong," Wyatt replied dryly.

A fresh round of giggles choked her. "Looks like the yolk's on you."

Wyatt rolled his eyes and groaned. "I think now would be a good time to take Jonah some food and change into a fresh shirt."

"If I'd known all it took was a little egg to get out of all these games, I'd have tossed it a little sooner."

"You little imp. I think you did this on purpose."

Meri escaped the yolk-soaked handkerchief that threatened retaliation, and hurriedly retrieved the basket of food Ms. Maggie had put together for Jonah.

"Hurry back, Marshal," Mrs. Van Deusen called out. "The dessert auction starts as soon as the horseshoe tournament ends."

"I wouldn't miss it. I can almost taste those desserts I've been hearing about all day."

Wyatt took the basket of food from Meri. "I'll return shortly."

"Watch out for bad eggs, Marshal," she warned, tongue in cheek. It was absolutely ridiculous that a man covered in rotten egg should look so attractive.

"Next time, warn me a little sooner." With a wink, he spun on his heel and jogged away.

Wyatt whistled as he changed into a fresh shirt. He was dangerously close to becoming attached to Miss Mc-Isaac, but he didn't care when he remembered her slender arm around his ribs, her delight when she'd won and her spontaneous laughter at the egg mishap.

He tucked his shirt in and swung his holster back around his hips. He might have let his guard down around Meri—that only had the potential to damage his heart— but he refused to let his guard down when it came to protecting the town. He was keeping his eyes open and his gun handy to ensure everyone had a memorable, safe picnic.

"Someone sounds awfully chipper today. Might it be due to a certain young lady?" Jonah looked up from his plate of food as Wyatt came out of the back room.

"Evidently you weren't as hungry as you professed, if you have time to talk instead of enjoying that pile of food the ladies sent you."

Jonah grinned and changed the subject. "I took a turn around town a while ago. Looks like ever livin' soul is at the picnic. I didn't find a thing stirrin'."

Wyatt opened the front door and settled his hat on his head. "Thanks. I think I'll take a quick look around myself before I head back."

"Glad to do it. Don't take too long. Miss McIsaac'll get tired of waitin' around and find some other good-lookin' fella to share dessert with."

"Go back to your food, you old coot, before I regret making you my deputy." He grinned, removing any sting from the words.

Jonah's laugh followed him down the boardwalk.

Wyatt strolled around the different businesses lining the main thoroughfare through town before heading back to the picnic grounds. Jonah was right. Little Creek was as quiet as a graveyard.

The games were over and picnic goers were slowly gathering around the table that held the decorated dessert baskets, but Wyatt didn't see Meri. He glanced around, searching for her. Had she left?

A waving figure caught his eye. Naoma Van Deusen grinned widely and pointed to the tree-lined stream bordering the picnic grounds. Maybe he should have made her the town deputy, the way she managed to keep track of everyone's movements. Tipping his hat toward her, he followed the sounds of voices and splashing coming from the creek. Quietly slipping through trees, he paused to watch, unnoticed.

A barefoot Meri was wading in the creek alongside Danny and Billy. He grinned, appreciating the glimpse of slim ankles as she held her skirts above the water. The woman wasn't afraid to get dirty, and when she relaxed, she wasn't afraid to have fun. She'd make a good mother.

The thought startled him. Thoughts like that were dangerous territory for a man who had nothing but dreams on which to build a future. A family needed more than dreams to survive. A family needed a home, security.

Then maybe it's time you take that money you've been squirreling away and stop planning and start doing.

He shoved aside the frighteningly intriguing thought. He was simply enjoying a picnic with a pretty girl while keeping an eye out for trouble.

He stepped onto the creek bank toward the slender woman who was bent over intently watching something in the water flowing around her ankles. She sure made a fetching picture.

Stop it, he commanded himself. Even if she *was* the first woman that made him want to, he wasn't ready to plan a future around her.

So why was it impossible to walk away from her?

Chapter Fourteen

The day wasn't overly warm, but the exertion of the games made the cool shade and running water of Little Creek look especially inviting. Plopping down on the bank, Meri watched Danny and Billy try to capture a school of minnows with their pails while her thoughts wandered to the dessert auction.

She'd evaded Wyatt's question earlier because she *had* prepared a dessert last night but was now regretting it. She only had herself to blame. In trying not to compete with the town girls, she'd gone totally in the opposite direction. Take her outfit today, for example. It was neat and functional, but painfully plain compared to the bows, ruffles and frills on the bright colorful dresses the other young women wore.

Her dessert was another attempt at self-sabotage. Not that her dessert would taste bad, she'd made it plenty of times and father and Franks liked it, she'd just never prepared a dessert for the auction before. The desserts on display today would be fancy pies, luscious cakes and other dressed-up treats designed to make an impression, but what did she bring? A pan of plain-and-simple boring old gingerbread.

Oh, it would make an impression all right. She could hear the snickers and see the looks of pity now. She dropped her head into her hands. *Ugh!* She'd never particularly cared before what people thought of her. Why was she so worried about it now?

Because you're not worried about what people *think. You're worried about what* Wyatt Cameron *will think.*

"I am not!" Meri's head flew up as she uttered the words aloud.

"Aren't what, Miss Meri?" Danny asked from the edge of the creek.

"Nothing, Danny. Just arguing with myself, I guess."

"Miss Meri, you told *us* it was an honor to cease from strife. Isn't arguing with yourself strife?" Billy spoke up, a rascally look on his face.

Meri grimaced as her words returned to haunt her. Mother had always said to season your words with a little salt because you might have to eat them someday.

"Yes, it is. So I'm going to cease right now." Discreetly removing her boots and socks, she stepped into the icy stream, holding the hem of her riding skirt clear of the running water as she waded.

So she was different from most of the young women in town. They weren't enjoying the cold water flowing around their ankles or seeing silvery flashes of tiny fish dart over their feet. She was glad she'd given in to the urge to join the children in the water. It was relaxing and relatively peaceful as Billy and Danny moved upstream to investigate the tadpoles the other children had found.

Standing motionless in the ankle-deep water, Meri bent over to watch little creatures swim out of hiding. A variety of aquatic life, that had found it advantageous to hide from inquisitive little boys, now returned to their various underwater tasks around Meri's bare feet.

"I was beginning to think you'd run off and left me again."

Meri straightened and spun around, but the slick stones under her feet shifted at her sudden commotion, and she lost her balance. With a startled cry she sat down hard— chilly ankle-deep creek water splashing upward as she landed.

Drops were still falling from the splash when she surged to her feet, streams of water pouring off the soft leather skirt. A hand reached to assist her to the creek bank, but Meri's hands were busy shaking the water out of her clothing as she waded out of the streambed. A quick glance showed Wyatt biting his lip and struggling not to laugh. "For the luv' a— Is this gonna' be a habit?"

"What, you falling for me?" He cocked his head innocently.

"No!" Embarrassment scorched its way across her face.

"Me sweeping a beautiful woman off her feet?"

Meri couldn't have looked at the man if her life depended on it, and she retreated into silence. She was digging herself deeper every time she spoke. She dripped her way over to her boots and stockings. Sitting down with her back to Wyatt, she quickly pulled on the dry footwear. A hand cradled her elbow as she stood, and Meri pulled away from the disconcertingly welcome contact, heading downstream away from the picnic.

"Where are you going? The dessert auction is just starting."

"I'm going to get Sandy and go home. I'm all wet, in case you forgot." Falling into the creek might not be such a bad thing after all. It gave her an excuse to leave before her dessert came up for auction.

Hands halted her escape and turned her back toward the picnic. "You'll dry quickly in this warm sun, and everyone will be too busy with the auction to notice a little damp clothing."

"I want to go home." Meri hated the whine she heard in her voice.

"Come on. I've got my mouth all set for dessert," he coaxed as he inexorably drew her along with him up the creek bank into the sunshine to a blanket just on the edge of the picnic area.

It was the blanket they'd sat on for lunch, but it had been moved to a new location farther away from the other scattered picnic blankets. Meri sat reluctantly. At least no one seemed to have noticed her dripping emergence from the trees. Everyone was already gathered around the dessert table where Mr. Hubert was explaining the rules of the auction.

Wyatt dropped down alongside her, leaning back on his elbows, legs outstretched.

"Aren't you going to go bid?" And leave her to her embarrassed misery, free to slip away when he purchased a fancy dessert and the baker claimed her good-looking prize?

"Since I'm new to this, I'm going to study how this all works for a minute."

Bidding started on a plump canned-peach pie with Mr. Hubert reminding bidders that the money raised would go toward a new church piano. The pie sold for fifty cents to the husband of the proud baker. The next items up were a cherry pie, an apple pie and a dried-berry cobbler. Wyatt commented on each item but didn't bid, laughing when a bidding war started over the cobbler.

"Mrs. Van Deusen makes the best cobbler in town. Sometimes Mr. Van Deusen wins it, sometimes he doesn't," Meri informed him.

The bidding went to two dollars before Mr. Van Deusen triumphantly carried away the cobbler, magnani-mously offering to share with the loser but only after he'd had the first piece. An angel food cake, another pie and delicate cookies were the following items, but still Wyatt sat and watched.

Nerves were nearly strangling her. Why hadn't she escaped when Wyatt had gone to change his shirt or per-sisted in leaving after her fall in the creek? Then she wouldn't be sitting here agonizing over which girl would claim Wyatt with her dessert. At least she'd found another reason to be glad she'd chosen this particular outfit. The leather skirt hadn't absorbed the creek water, and she was drying faster than a regular dress would have allowed.

"I thought you wanted dessert."

"I do, but my mouth's all set for something specific, and I haven't seen it yet."

Meri looked at the girls standing close to the dessert table. She'd seen a couple of them talking to Wyatt ear-lier; maybe he was waiting on one of their confections.

Another cobbler passed without a bid from Wyatt.

"You're going to run out of choices." Maybe biting her tongue would silence it.

"Nope, they're just saving the best for last." He smiled, unconcerned.

They were down to the last three desserts, and Meri's heart thudded painfully as tension built inside her. She smothered a groan as a thought occurred to her.

You could have at least brought some cream to gar-nish the top of your gingerbread, but you can't even get that right! You are your own worst enemy!

Wyatt stood abruptly and walked toward the dessert table. This was it. This must have been what he was wait-ing on. Which girl would walk away on his arm?

"Dig deep, fellas. This one will make your mouth

water." Mr. Hubert carefully reached into a ribbon-frilled hamper and pulled out a tall, beautifully frosted chocolate cake.

A murmur of excitement rippled across the assembled crowd. Mr. Hubert started the bidding at fifty cents, and bids flew fast and loud. A pretty blonde stood by the dessert table beaming proudly. Finally Mr. Hubert closed the bidding at four dollars.

Meri strained upward to see who'd won.

It...*wasn't* Wyatt.

She sat back with a squishy thud. One of her father's ranch hands smugly accepted the basket of cake and escorted the attractive girl to a picnic blanket.

"Next up, folks..." Mr. Hubert reached into a basket and pulled out a small square pan.

Meri's heart stopped. It looked even plainer than she'd remembered.

He sniffed the pan. "Gingerbread, and it smells wonderful. I don't know who the baker is, but if it tastes as good as it smells, it'll be a real treat. Who'll start the bidding?" The words had hardly left Mr. Hubert's mouth before a firm, ringing voice spoke.

"Five dollars."

Meri's heart started again with a painful bound.

"Did you say...*five...dollars?*" Mr. Hubert stuttered.

She strained to hear the answer through the roaring silence.

"Yes. I bid five dollars."

Meri's heart and lungs had functioned automatically for nearly thirty years, but they seemed to have forgotten how to perform their most basic functions. Her eyes and ears, on the other hand, were capturing every detail in agonizing clarity.

"Our new marshal must like gingerbread, folks. Anyone want to give him a run for his money?" The crowd laughed, but no one bid. "Come on, folks, who'll give the marshal some competition?"

"Five twenty-five." Franks walked toward Wyatt, a big grin showcasing pearly teeth.

"Five fifty," Wyatt countered.

"Five seventy-five," Franks shouted.

The bidding war continued, and Mr. Hubert's gaze bounced between the two men. When the bidding neared eight dollars, Wyatt leaned over to Franks and whispered something. Turning back to Mr. Hubert, he bid again. "Eight dollars!"

Mr. Hubert looked at Franks, but that gentleman only shook his head, grinning.

Mr. Hubert slammed his hand down on the table. "Sold!"

Wyatt walked to the table and handed some bills to the auctioneer.

"Now that the marshal's won his dessert, will the baker step forward to claim her dessert partner?"

Meri was frozen to the blanket. She couldn't even stand up, much less walk up there.

Mr. Hubert called again for the lady to come claim her dessert partner, and the assembled picnickers glanced around curiously. Wyatt leaned over the table and said something. Mr. Hubert smiled, nodded, then carefully picked up the next dessert and called for bids, recalling everyone's attention to the last item of the auction.

Meri's eyes were glued to Wyatt as he returned and carefully set down his burden before seating himself.

"Ahh, good things come to those who wait." He winked at her and reached into the basket, pulling out the pan of gingerbread and inhaling deeply. "Smells delicious."

Meri watched in a daze as he carefully cut two large

pieces of thick, dark gingerbread and slid them onto plates. Opening a small crock that he'd pulled out of the basket along with the plates, he spooned something over the top of the fragrant cake.

Whipped cream!

"Just the thing to top it off," Wyatt said satisfactorily, handing her one of the plates

Thank you, Ms. Maggie. She must have brought it along with the rest of the food the ranch had supplied today and tucked it in the basket when Meri wasn't watching.

He forked a generous piece into his mouth and chewed. "Umm…good." A second bite quickly followed the first.

Meri found a voice that sounded nothing like her own. "This is what you had your mouth set for?"

"Yep!"

His smirk wasn't nearly so intimidating or irritating when surrounded by smudges of frothy whipped cream.

"You *knew* there'd be gingerbread?' He nodded, his mouth full. "How?"

He stuck another piece into his mouth and pointed at her untouched plate with his fork. "I have my sources, and you're not eating your gingerbread."

Meri took a small bite, too distracted to enjoy it. "What did you say to the auctioneer?"

"I just told him I knew who the lady was and to go on with the auction." His eyes twinkled merrily.

"How did you know there would be gingerbread here?"

He slowly chewed and swallowed before speaking. "I have to protect the identity of my sources, or I'd have people afraid to bring me information."

Meri's eyes narrowed. "You knew I brought gingerbread—" she pointed to her plate "—all this time?"

Wyatt popped another forkful into his mouth and nodded, grinning roguishly. "It was kind of fun watching you squirm."

"Why would you wait around for my gingerbread when you could have had your pick of much fancier desserts…"

…and fancier girls?

Wyatt cut another serving for himself and slathered it with cream. "First off, I haven't had gingerbread since my mom made it for me as a boy, and I really like it." Wyatt carefully forked a cream-covered piece into his mouth, chewed slowly and swallowed before continuing. "Second, I really didn't want to sit with any of those man-eating females!" He shivered theatrically.

Meri looked down at her forgotten piece of expensive dessert. Putting a piece into her own mouth, she chewed without tasting. He didn't scc her as a threat? Was that good or bad? Finally she could resist no longer. "You're not afraid *I'm* a 'man-eating female'?"

Hazel eyes twinkled. "Nope."

Meri took another bite to give her mouth something to do besides ask foolish questions. The last one had left her confused as to whether she was relieved or offended. If she kept opening her mouth, she was going to drown in these dangerous waters.

She hurriedly finished her dessert as Wyatt set his plate down and leaned back with a full groan. "That was delicious. My compliments to the cook."

She gathered up the used plates and utensils and restored them to the basket.

"What's your hurry?"

"I'm uncomfortably damp, and it's time I headed home." She reached to set the pan of gingerbread in the basket.

"You're not taking all that gingerbread, are you?"

Meri had to smile at the pitiful puppy-dog expression Wyatt assumed. "No. I'll send it home with you."

Wyatt immediately resumed a cheerful smile. "Good. I told Franks I'd share it with him if he'd stop driving up the price. I wouldn't want him to come after me when I don't bring him any of it. He said it'd be delicious, and he was right." Wyatt rubbed his stomach in appreciation.

"Did everyone know what you were up to?" she whispered in a mortified tone.

Wyatt chuckled ruefully. "No. Franks knew the gingerbread was yours and wanted to make me work for it."

Meri ducked her head in bewilderment and shooed Wyatt off the blanket so she could pick it up, avoiding his eyes as he helped her fold it neatly. Taking the blanket and basket from her, he walked her toward the ranch wagon.

Nearing the accumulated variety of wheeled vehicles, she saw the banker climbing into his buggy. "Hello, Mr. Samuels."

He nodded shortly. "Miss McIsaac. Marshal."

"I'm glad you were able to make it to the picnic. I saw you were busy with someone at the bank earlier."

Mr. Samuels picked up the reins and slapped the back of the horse, and the buggy moved away at a quick clip.

Meri turned to watch him go. "That was abrupt. I wonder what his problem is."

"I was just about to ask you the same thing," Wyatt said.

"What do you mean?"

"You didn't try to run off with *his* horse or something, did you?" There was a teasing glint in his eye.

"Very funny. No, I didn't take his horse or something. I haven't done anything to him except be polite."

Wyatt chuckled at her sarcasm. "Then why worry about it?"

"I don't know. He's never been overly friendly, but he's never been outright rude, either. First he ignores me at the cemetery, and today he acts like he can't get away from me fast enough."

"He's probably just distracted by the bank robbery."

"I guess." Meri shrugged her shoulders, dismissing the subject.

Setting the basket and blanket in the bed of the wagon, Meri transferred the dirty plates and utensils to another container and handed the basket containing the gingerbread to Wyatt.

"We can pick up the basket and pan next time someone comes into town." She ducked her head. What did one say at the close of an occasion like this? "Thank you for bringing me and for buying my dessert." Spinning away from him, she set off in a brisk walk for the livery stable. She hadn't taken two steps when she felt him beside her.

"You're not getting rid of me that easy. This day's not over until I've escorted you home."

Meri sighed resignedly as she continued walking, but didn't argue. At least she told herself it was a resigned sigh. She ignored the fact it had sounded happy.

The ride back to the ranch was slower and less competitive than the ride in, and Meri was very quiet, responding to Wyatt's attempts at conversation with monosyllabic replies. When he failed to get a rise out of her by teasing her about her dip in the creek, he allowed silence to accompany them the rest of the journey, contenting himself with stolen glances at his fellow traveler.

After they reached the ranch house, Mr. McIsaac invited Wyatt into his study, and Meri disappeared after shyly thanking him again. Mr. McIsaac quizzed him about the picnic, laughing heartily at the account of the games and creek incidents. "Did ye snag her gingerbread?"

"I did. It was as good as you said it'd be." He nodded his appreciation to the older man.

McIsaac rocked back in his chair with a satisfied grin. "Most folks think the fancier the package, the better the dessert will be, but there's a wealth of flavor waiting to be discovered in that unassuming little cake. And like that gingerbread, the boys in town never looked past the fancier-dressed females to see the treasure underneath her intimidating independence. Until now I thought that was unfortunate, but ye might hold a different opinion."

Wyatt did. But he wasn't ready to admit it out loud. "Did you ever figure out what was bothering you about the bank robbery?"

Ian McIsaac's eyes measured him for a moment before nodding. "I finally remembered this afternoon, but I don't think it means anything."

Wyatt sat down, pulling the little notebook from his pocket. "Tell me anyway."

"After I hit the floor, something was said before I passed out. That brigand shouted, 'Where's the rest of it?'"

Wyatt looked up from his notes when McIsaac didn't continue. "Anything else?"

"No, that's it. 'Where's the rest of it?' I was hoping I'd heard something important. Maybe that's why it took this long to remember. It wasn't anything big." Ian McIsaac's voice was regretful.

"I'm beginning to think the pieces that don't look relevant to the case are the ones that are going to solve it," Wyatt said thoughtfully as he tucked away the little notebook. "I need to get back to town and give Jonah a break. Tell your daughter I enjoyed her company today."

McIsaac followed him to the front door, bidding him good afternoon.

Wyatt shelved thoughts of Meri and her reaction to the dessert auction and pulled out his little notebook as he rode toward town. Splitting his attention between his surroundings and his notes, he mulled over the pieces of the frustrating case. The only conclusion he'd come to by the time he reached town was that he needed to talk to the banker.

He pointed his horse toward the man's house. It was time he pinned Mr. Samuels down on a few unanswered questions.

Chapter Fifteen

This time when he knocked on the banker's door, the housekeeper admitted him into a dark stuffy parlor.

"Can I help you, Marshal?" The banker's tone belied his offer of helpfulness.

"I have one or two more questions."

"That seems to be all you have."

Wyatt ignored the verbal jab. "I talked to your former employee. He has a slightly different account of why he left." He watched the man's face closely, but the lack of light in the room made it difficult to read his expression.

"I can only imagine what George Dunn told you." He sniffed.

"He said you fired him. Did you?"

"Yes."

"Why didn't you tell me that in the first place?"

"Because it had nothing to do with the robbery, and I dislike casting aspersions on a man who isn't around to defend himself." The little man puffed out his chest pompously.

"Why did you fire him?"

"He was unreliable, and I could handle the business until I found someone more competent."

"He said you accused him of stealing."

"I told him his incompetence was as bad as stealing. As usual, he misunderstood."

"The townsfolk seemed to think highly of him."

"They didn't have to work with the young jackanapes. I fail to see how this has anything to do with the holdup, Marshal," Samuels said impatiently.

"Why did you shout at McIsaac when he was trying to stop the thief?" Wyatt changed course abruptly.

"What?" The man startled as if struck.

"McIsaac said you yelled something when you saw him start to pull the gun and that's what caused him to be shot."

"No. I was trying to *keep* him from being shot."

"And yet you neglected to tell me this when I first questioned you."

"I fail to see how yelling at someone during the confusion of a robbery has any bearing on catching the culprit." Mr. Samuels stood to walk out of the room.

"I have one more question before you leave." The man was pricklier than a cactus and sourer then a barrel of pickles.

"What, pray tell, can it be this time?" The banker sighed sarcastically.

"What happened to Mr. McIsaac's gun?"

"His gun?"

"Yes. Mr. McIsaac would like it back, but I didn't see it at the bank that day, and no one else seems to know what happened to it."

"I assume it was taken along with the bank's money. Are we done here?"

"You didn't see if the bank robber picked it up?"

"I was dealing with my own injury at the time!"

"You've been out of town a lot lately. Have you made any progress toward getting the bank reopened?"

"It's been difficult, but I think I've talked a few investors into lending capital to reopen the bank. I should hear word in the next week or so. I'm sure they would be much more amenable should they hear that the perpetrator has been caught. And that was *three* questions, Marshal. Are you quite finished?"

"For now. Thank you for your time."

The housekeeper ushered him out the door, and he was glad to exit and feel the evening sun on his face. That gloomy house would make anybody cranky. He unwrapped Charger's reins from the hitching post and led him down the street.

Who was telling the truth? An employee who'd been fired, one everyone else seemed to like, including his new boss, or the banker everyone seemed to find difficult?

One of the more blunt citizens he'd questioned had commented, "He runs a mortuary, not a bank. When he undertakes your money, you never see it again!" Another had said, "He doesn't run a bank, he runs a natural history museum. Naturally, when he loans you money, you're history!"

He'd been tempted to laugh at the tongue in cheek answers. Mr. Samuels might not be popular, but didn't most people fear bankers to some extent, especially if they held the mortgage on your land?

"Howdy, Marshal."

"Hello, Billy. Danny. Aren't you tired from the picnic?" The two boys ran up to Wyatt as he led Charger down the rutted street.

"Nah. We're workin'. We're private eyes, like Mr. Pinkerton. You need any help with anything?" Billy asked hopefully.

Wyatt had an impulsive idea. "As a matter of fact, I could use your help. Danny, don't you live near here?"

"Yep. Right over there." Danny pointed proudly to a two-story home a short distance away.

"I need some information, but it has to be kept strictly between us or it will be useless. I'll pay for this information." Wyatt jingled a few coins in his pocket for emphasis.

"We know how to keep secrets," Billy said defensively. "We didn't tell anyone you made Miss Meri fall in the creek. Besides, private eyes don't go around spilling the beans about their cases."

Wyatt eyed them thoughtfully. They were such a familiar sight around town people paid them little attention unless they wanted an errand run or some small task done. The boys might prove valuable eyes and ears at times when sight of the marshal would put people on their guard.

"Good. Here's what I want you to do." Wyatt leaned close to the boys and spoke quietly. "I want you to watch Mr. Samuels's house. Let me know if you see anyone visit him or if you see him leave with a bag like he's going out of town. Can you handle that?"

"Sure."

"Don't try to follow him or sneak up on him. Go about as you normally do, and just keep your eyes peeled for anything out of the ordinary. Can you follow that to the letter?"

Billy and Danny nodded, taking his instructions very seriously. Wyatt pulled out two half-dollar coins and handed one to each boy.

"Our first paying case." Billy clutched the coin proudly, awe filling his voice.

"We won't let you down, Marshal." Danny solemnly

shook Wyatt's hand, and Billy followed suit. Both boys hurried off, talking to each other in low guarded voices, and Wyatt returned to his office to relieve Jonah, wondering if he would regret his impulsive decision.

It stormed hard that night, and the McIsaacs didn't show up at church the following day, but Pastor Willis reminded the congregation to pray for them: the anniversary of Mrs. McIsaac's death was coming up later in the week.

As the week progressed, Wyatt missed seeing Meri every day but resisted riding out to the ranch to see her. Instead he kept his hands busy with his duties and his mind and heart busy in prayer. He prayed that God would help him bring the bank robber to justice, and that He would heal Meri from her mother's loss.

When Billy and Danny breathlessly showed up on his doorstep early one morning, Wyatt began to believe the first prayer was close to an answer. Little did he guess both prayers were about to be answered almost simultaneously.

Meri was grooming the fourth horse of the morning when her father stalked into the barn. She could tell by the way he walked he had something on his mind but ducked her head and pretended not to see him, continuing to comb snarls out of the horse's tail. But the comb was plucked from her hand.

Her father calmly untethered the horse and turned him into the paddock.

"I wasn't done with him," she protested.

"Yes, ye are." McIsaac led her over to a wooden bench. "Sit."

Since his order was reinforced with a gentle, irresistible push, Meri sat.

He turned, folded his hands behind his back and

paced a few steps before coming back to stand in front of her, planting his feet determinedly. "It's high time ye dealt with whatever's bothering ye." He spoke kindly but firmly.

"Nothing's bothering me." She tried to speak convincingly, but her father's eyes bored into hers, and she glanced away uneasily.

"Do not lie to me, lass. Ye've nearly driven everyone crazy this week. If ye're not bossing the hands around on some new project ye've thought up, ye're hovering 'til I trip over ye, or ye're pacing back and forth sighing up a windstorm."

"I am not."

"The fences on this ranch have never been in as good a shape as they are now, thanks to the men trying to get away from the next crazy scheme ye've cooked up. Ms. Maggie is upset because ye've rearranged every cupboard on the place, and even though Dr. Kilburn cleared me to return to riding, ye nearly panic every time I even think about going farther then the front porch."

McIsaac sat down beside her, wrapped an arm around her shoulders and pulled her stiff body into a hug as he continued talking. "I don't know why we lost Catriona so soon, and there will always be a hole left by her passing, but, lassie, it is okay to move on. It's okay to be happy again. Mither would be the first to tell ye she's happier and healthier with her Savior than she could ever be down here. I'm not saying the grief over her loss will ever be completely gone, and that's okay. But yer anger is not okay. It's an infection that keeps eating away at yer insides, and until it's dealt with, ye won't get better." McIsaac stood and gave a short whistle.

Barnaby entered the barn leading a saddled Sandy. How had they managed that without her noticing?

"Ye always seem to think better on the back of a horse, and I think part of yer problem is that ye haven't had a good ride in a week or more. Sandy's ready, and yer hat, canteen and rifle are on the saddle. Go, take Sandy for a run, and don't come back 'til ye've had a heart-to-heart talk with yer Heavenly Father."

McIsaac pulled Meri up from the bench and laid the reins in her hands, looking into her eyes for a couple of heartbeats. "Be careful, and pay attention to yer surroundings—"

The familiar warning was one she'd heard since childhood.

"—but it's time to face whatever ye're running from." He kissed her on the forehead, turned and walked out of the barn.

Meri looked at Sandy who shook his head up and down as if to say "Hurry up, let's go."

"All right," she muttered grudgingly. She swung into the saddle and guided the horse outside.

Sandy hit their favorite trail at a smooth lope, but the familiar thrill of the horse's smooth rhythm and the sense of freedom were missing.

The anniversary of Mither's death was only two days ago. How can Faither tell me to get over it? How can he be okay when I feel so stuck, so rotten?

Her father had been sad on the anniversary of her mother's death, but it was not the despairing anger she felt. Anger?

Yes. She'd been angry. A lot. She'd tried to tell herself it was grief, but if she were completely honest with herself, it looked and acted a lot more like bitter resentful anger.

She turned Sandy off the trail, and the horse snorted his surprised displeasure at the sudden change of plans.

"Sorry, boy." Meri patted his shiny blond neck. "I think it's time I faced something."

A half hour later Meri dismounted, flipping the palo-mino's reins around a decorative spike atop the cemetery fence. The wrought-iron railing didn't enclose the entire grounds; it extended partway up the slope, ending just past the ornate marble crypt near the tree line. Taking a deep breath, she pushed open the gate, cringing as it protested with a metal-on-metal squeak, and entered the burial ground. She slowly walked past each gravestone, reading the names as she passed, delaying the inevitable. All too soon she reached her mother's headstone.

Catriona McIsaac
1825-1882
Beloved Wife
Beloved Mother
Beloved Child of God

The cold gray stone could never communicate the true meaning of the life it represented.

Meri felt a tear run down her cheek, and wiped it away in surprise. She hadn't shed tears since the funeral. Even when her burning eyes and aching throat had begged for the cathartic release, her eyes had remained stubbornly dry. She sank to her knees in the soft grass.

"Oh, Mither. I miss you so much it hurts." Another tear slid down, and all the grief and anger of the past year boiled up with it, refusing to be contained any longer. "God, why did you take her? You could so easily have healed her! Why did You let her die?"

The sound of the vicious words rocked her back on her heels. She'd never spoken the questions aloud, but they had festered just below the surface slowly infecting her whole being.

Meri finally accepted the truth that had been gnawing at her spirit since Pastor Willis's sermon. "I have been so angry with You, Lord. You could have healed Mither of pnuemonia, but You didn't and I couldn't accept that. I've blamed You for her death. I've been angry and bitter that You allowed that to happen to us, to me, and that anger has become a barrier pushing me away from You."

As confession cleared the windows of Meri's soul, the tears began to flow in earnest. "Father, You say that all things work together for good to them that love You. I don't understand how Mither's death is good, but she was Your child, and I know You love her more than I ever could. Forgive me for being angry at You, for acting like a spoiled child who gets mad when things don't go my way. I'm tired of fighting You. I'm tired of being angry and hurting all the time. Please forgive me."

Sobs shook her shoulders and tears poured, but as she cried out to a loving Heavenly Father, long-lost peace began to seep through the cracks in her heart, softening the hardness and restoring what bitterness had choked out. Long minutes passed before her tears began to dry, and snatches of Scripture watered peace deep into her soul.

A few more tears leaked out as she pictured her mother in Heaven at Jesus's feet. She had focused entirely on what she had lost when she should have been focusing on what her mother had gained. Her father was right. Mither was happier with her Savior than she could ever have been here on earth.

Meri shifted to pull a handkerchief from her pocket and realized she'd sat on her legs so long she'd lost feeling in them. Gingerly stretching them out, she leaned against the headstone, wiping her face and wincing as sleeping limbs awakened with a rush of fiery prickles. But in spite of aching legs and tear-soaked eyes, Meri felt better than she had in months. The oppressive weight was gone, and her heart felt light and clean. She would always miss her mother, her friend and confidante, but sweet peace had replaced aching sadness, and Meri basked in the calm that followed the long storm.

Fatigue washed over her, and she leaned her head back against the cool stone, letting her eyes drift shut. She had almost dozed off when a soft nicker made her jump. Sitting up, she saw Sandy was not looking at her. He was watching the high end of the graveyard, ears pricked intently.

Meri rose to her knees to follow his gaze. What had caught his attention? The only thing up there was that silly marble tomb, imposing in its haughty grandeur and looking down on lowly rank-and-file headstones.

She froze, heart pounding. Had the door on the crypt… *moved?*

Shivers raced up her spine, and she jumped to her feet and sprinted to Sandy's side, unsheathing her carbine and spinning back to scan the area in one quick move. Nothing stirred. She would have doubted she'd seen anything except Sandy was still cautiously looking toward the top of the cemetery between quick bites of grass.

A thought caused Meri to take a deep breath and laugh at herself as her racing heart slowed. Boys had probably found a way into the crypt and thought to scare her.

Let's see who scares whom!

Meri reentered the burial ground, thankful she'd thought to leave the gate open thus avoiding its noisy squeak, and walked toward the two imposing lions flanking the door of the marble monstrosity.

"I know you're in there. You can come out now," Meri called out sternly.

Silence fell and she heard nothing but the swish of her own footsteps through the grass as she reached the last row of gravestones and stopped. Darting a glance around, she saw nothing but her own horse calmly grazing.

"I said, come out," she ordered again, but nothing moved.

She thought she'd only *started* to doze off, but maybe she'd actually been asleep and dreamed this whole thing up.

No. Sandy saw something, too.

Another shiver raced up her spine as she squinted at the latch on the door. It was undone and the door stood slightly ajar. It had never been used, but who would want to hide in there? That seemed terribly unnerving, even for a bunch of mischievous boys.

"I have a Winchester carbine aimed straight at this door. Come out with your hands up. Now!" The words sounded braver in Meri's mind then they did when they hit the air.

She held her breath as she waited, but still nothing happened. She argued with herself before slowly stepping within reach of the cold marble edifice and touching the toe of her boot to the metal door. She swallowed hard as the door moved smoothly and silently inward.

You're crazy! You could have gotten on Sandy and ridden home, but no, you have to go investigate!

Meri stepped back hastily, bringing the rifle up as sunshine illuminated the shadowed crypt. It was too late to turn and run now. Something—no, someone was in there. Meri backed farther away, voice squeaking when she ordered, "Hands up! Come out where I can see you."

Her heart beat furiously in her ears as the shadows in the crypt shifted toward her.

Chapter Sixteen

Daylight washed over the shadows, and they melted, leaving behind two men. One wore an amused expression on his face and a star on his shirt; the other wore a similar star but a sheepish expression. Both men raised their hands placatingly as they exited the marble structure, Jonah pulling the door shut behind him with one hand.

"You!" Meri's knees suddenly threatened to buckle, and the barrel of her carbine drooped toward the ground.

"May we put our hands down, or are you going to use that on us?" Wyatt grinned and motioned toward her gun.

She kept the barrel pointed toward the ground but shifted it toward Wyatt. "That depends on how you answer my question. What were you and Jonah doing in there?" It took some effort, but she kept the tremor out of her voice.

But then dismayed realization dawned. "How long have you been up here?" She cringed, thinking how she'd blubbered over her mother's grave.

"Long enough to realize you wouldn't appreciate an audience," Wyatt said softly.

She almost dropped the carbine. Of all the people to witness her tears… She didn't know whether to melt in mortification or… She tightened her grip on the gun and took a step toward Wyatt and Jonah. Jonah stepped back.

Wyatt stood his ground with a crooked grin. "You just figure out if you shoot us there won't be any witnesses?"

How does he always *know what I'm thinking?* "Would you quit changing the subject?" she huffed. "How did you two get up here? Where are your horses?" She moved another half step closer, but Wyatt still didn't budge. It was hard to intimidate a man who didn't scare.

"Which question would you like answered first?" Wyatt scratched his forehead with a knuckle, nudging his hat up.

The man was impossible. He had no right to look so devastatingly attractive when she was upset with him. "How 'bout all of them?"

"Well, let's see…" In one swift move Wyatt's hand came away from the brim of his hat and swiped the barrel of the carbine to one side. Stepping in close, he pulled the gun from her abruptly nerveless hands.

Meri stiffened as he leaned down, hat brim nearly touching hers, forcing her to look up at him. He held her gaze for several breathless heartbeats. "You were saying?"

Meri blinked and scuttled backward trying to collect her scattered wits. What had she been saying? Glinting green-gold eyes had short-circuited her brain.

Crack! Crack! Ping!

She jerked, feeling the sounds like a physical blow.

"Get *down!*" Wyatt roared, and lunged at her, wrapping her in his arms. The ground rose up to meet them with a thump, and he used their momentum to roll down to a row of headstones for cover. Pain radiated through her as they slammed to an abrupt halt against a wide stone marker. She groaned. Her arms were pinioned to her sides by Wyatt's arms, and she couldn't breathe against his weight pinning her to the ground. "Stay down! You okay, Jonah?" Wyatt shifted Meri out of his arms, tucking her tightly against the base of the marker.

Jonah hollered he was unhurt, and Meri decided to argue with the bossy marshal when she'd recovered enough breath to speak more forcibly. Her back loudly protested the sudden contact with the ground, and her lungs ached with the effort to refill them.

"Can you see anything?" Wyatt removed his hat before peering cautiously around the bottom edge of the headstone.

"No, but those shots sounded like they came from farther down the slope. Maybe those cedars left of the road," Jonah barked.

"We're pinned down pretty bad," Wyatt gritted out. "Let's see if we can shake something out of those trees." He levered Meri's carbine open—he'd managed to hold on to it in their tumble for cover—and jacked a shell into the empty chamber. He left his own pistol securely in its holster and aimed for the clump of trees about a hundred and fifty yards down the slope. Firing two quick shots, he paused and repeated the action. "See anything move, Jonah?"

"No. Wait! You hear that?"

"Yeah, sounds like a horse leaving fast—with or without the rider I can't tell. He's using his cover too well." He sounded disgusted.

"There haven't been any more shots fired at us since those first two. Maybe he's hightailing it out of there."

"Let's see if we get any bites." Wyatt grabbed his hat, slowly raised it above the top of the headstone and held it there a second. The deafening silence was broken only by the return of tentative birdsong.

"Try your hat, Jonah, maybe he's playin' 'possum."

Jonah repeated Wyatt's actions, but no further gun-shots sounded. "You think he's gone?"

"If he's not, he soon will be." Wyatt peered around the base of the stone. "Look at that dust coming. Someone must have heard the shots and decided to come investi-gate. All we have to do is lay low 'til they get here." He turned and sat, tucking his back against the stone. He swiped his arm over his damp forehead and looked at Meri. "You shock me, Miss McIsaac. I figured you'd be trying to take that gunman down all by yourself. Instead you followed my order to stay down. I'm surprised and proud of you!" He grinned.

"You had my rifle. What was I supposed to use?" Meri had to force the words through her tight throat. She was feeling completely useless and nearly cross-eyed with diz-ziness. "I think you broke my shoulder when you threw me down and landed on me, you big ox." It hurt to breathe.

"Now, now, Mac, don't call names. It isn't ladylike. And I didn't land on you, I cushioned your fall."

"If that's what you call cushioning a fall…"

"Drop your weapons and come out with your hands where we can see them!" The command rang out below them.

"Where have I heard this before?" groaned Jonah.

"Take it easy, fellas. It's just us," Wyatt shouted before he and Jonah got cautiously to their feet.

"Marshal? What's all the shootin' about?" The man sounded closer, but Meri was having trouble recogniz-ing the voice through the pulse hammering in her ears.

"Some polecat started throwin' lead at us. You can see where one of 'em hit the top of that tombstone over there." Jonah motioned toward a marker near where they'd been standing when the shots had been fired.

"Where's Miss McIsaac? Her horse is down here," another voice asked.

"She's right here." Wyatt looked down at Meri as he spoke. "You're taking the order to stay down a bit too seriously, Mac."

"Don't call me Mac. I'm still trying to catch my breath." Meri struggled to push herself up, but a bolt of pain streaked through her, and the bright afternoon spun wildly, colors dimming and blurring together. She slumped back as Wyatt whispered her name, and the world went black.

Wyatt fell to his knees beside Meri, yelling her name. She didn't respond. He reached under her motionless body to lift her into his arms and something warmly wet and sticky met his touch. Heartsick, he withdrew a hand covered in thick red blood.

He should have known something was wrong. She just didn't lie around taking orders. "Somebody go get Doc! Now!"

Pastor Willis ran to his horse, leaving Mr. Van Deusen and Mr. Hubert standing by helplessly. Wyatt gently shifted Meri. Torn blood-soaked fabric met his eyes.

Mr. Hubert hissed sharply as he peered over Wyatt's shoulder. "That looks pretty bad."

Wyatt grunted acknowledgment as he finished turning her over carefully. "There wasn't blood on the front of her shoulder. Did it go in or just cut her up?" He reached for his knife, and slit the torn edges of the fabric, pulling it away from the wound to look.

"Looks like she caught a ricochet." Mr. Van Deusen knelt beside Wyatt. "They make wounds like that."

A jagged furrow plowed up her back, ending in a ragged hole just below the top of the shoulder. Wyatt yanked off his neckerchief and pressed it onto the wound. "Hold that in place, and put some pressure on it!" he barked.

Mr. Van Deusen complied, and Wyatt lifted the hem of Meri's riding skirt and ripped a wide strip off her cotton petticoat. Tearing the strip lengthwise, he knotted the two ends together to make a longer strip and wrapped it around her shoulder, holding the improvised bandage in place. With infinite care he rolled her onto her back and into his arms. Standing, cradling her limp form, he saw Jonah leading his own horse and Charger down from the trees where they'd been hidden.

"Figured you'd want to get her into town quick—looks like she's still losing quite a bit of blood. I'll go after the shooter and leave a trail for you to follow after you get her to Doc's." Jonah's tone was brusque, but his hands were gentle as he took Wyatt's fragile armful.

Wyatt leaped into the saddle and wrapped the reins around the saddle horn. Reaching down, he tenderly retrieved his precious burden and cradled her once more. He looked toward Mr. Van Deusen and Mr. Hubert. "You men stay here and make sure no one enters that crypt. If anyone tries, you hold them prisoner 'til I get back."

"What? Why?" Matching looks of confusion covered their faces as they glanced from the mausoleum back to him.

"I'll explain later. Until then, make sure no one goes anywhere near it. Your word on it?"

"Our word, Marshal." Both men nodded solemnly, still bewildered.

With a nod of thanks, Wyatt used his legs to guide Charger out of the gate and toward town. The big horse stepped carefully but quickly as if he understood the gravity of the situation.

Wyatt struggled to pray beyond one-word syllables, and his heart ached at the pale face cradled against his chest. "Lord, help her. Help me. Hang in there, Mac. Stay with me."

Meri groaned and mumbled something.

"What is it?" He lowered his head to catch her words.

"…not…Mac," she breathed.

Wyatt's chest rose and sank on a relieved sigh. "You just keep fighting, sweetheart, and I'll call you any name you want." But she was beyond hearing.

He shifted a hand until he could feel the pulse at her wrist. Weak, but steady. He hugged her a little closer and resumed praying. "Father, please, stop the bleeding and heal her body."

The ride was interminable. He prayed and wondered why the doctor hadn't already met him. He was at the edge of town before he saw Franks riding toward him. "Where's Doc?"

"Deliverin' a baby. Brotha' Willis rode ta git 'im. Doc's wife is waitin'." Franks turned to ride alongside Wyatt, glancing worriedly at Wyatt's limp bundle.

When they arrived at the Doc's, Franks dismounted and reached for Meri. Wyatt reluctantly relinquished her so he could dismount but quickly reclaimed her as soon as his feet touched the ground.

"Bring her in." Mrs. Kilburn waved them through to the examination room. "Lay her there." She pointed to the exam table, and Wyatt tenderly lowered Meri onto her uninjured side.

Mrs. Kilburn immediately set about removing the bandage he had hastily fashioned and examined the wound critically. "You two step out of the room, but don't go far."

Wyatt and Franks retreated to the office. Wyatt slumped into a chair, suddenly aware of his weak knees.

"How bad…?" Franks's deep bass trembled a little.

"She caught a ricochet that tore up her shoulder. Looks like one of the first shots glanced upward off a headstone, slicing up her back before angling into her shoulder. She's lost some blood. She woke up on the ride in, but almost immediately lost consciousness again." Wyatt sketched the details of the ambush then dragged in a deep breath before continuing. "Can you round up someone to go get her father?"

Franks didn't waste time answering. He just turned on his heel and ran out the door.

"Marshal, can I have your assistance?" Wyatt reentered the exam room at Mrs. Kilburn's call.

"Pastor Willis went after my husband, but he's all the way out past the Bascom place, and if he's in the middle of delivering that baby, it'll be a while before he can get here. The bullet stopped just under the skin on the top of her shoulder. I can get it out. I've assisted my husband enough to be able to handle it, but an extra pair of hands will make the job easier. Once it's out, I can get the wound cleaned and bandaged until Doc gets back."

Wyatt looked at the fragile creature lying facedown on the table, a heavy sheet pulled discreetly over her. All her spunk and fire extinguished, she looked tiny and helpless.

"Have you ever done anything like this before?" Mrs. Kilburn questioned gently.

Wyatt gritted his teeth and nodded. "Yes. Many times after a skirmish with the Indians I'd assist the army surgeon, even dug out a few bullets on my own when he wasn't around."

"Good. Wash up," the efficient nurse directed. She carefully folded back a corner of the sheet and bared Meri's bloody shoulder.

Wyatt ached all the way to his soul at the sight of the ugly, seeping wound marring pearly skin.

Mrs. Kilburn pointed out a small bluish lump that bulged the skin along the top of her shoulder. "There's the bullet, just under the skin. This shouldn't take long. Hold that lamp for me and be ready to apply pressure after I cut it out." She handed him a bright reflecting lamp and thick cloth then leaned over Meri with a sharp scalpel.

In seconds she had removed a small deformed piece of lead and dropped it with a clatter into the bowl beside her. Wyatt pressed the cloth firmly over the oozing hole, while the woman briskly rewashed her hands. Then she returned and thoroughly cleansed the wound before applying a thick layer of ointment.

"Doc will check this over when he returns. Now, you wait in the office while I bandage her up. If my husband still hasn't returned, I'll have you carry her to a bed where she'll be more comfortable."

Wyatt collapsed onto the chair outside the door and dropped his face into his hands. He was a trembling bundle of limp bones. All he'd done was hold a lamp and press a bandage over the wound, and he was a mess. What had happened to the coolheaded lieutenant who calmly cut arrows and bullets out of the flesh of his comrades?

Dragging his head out of his hands, he stared at the quivering members. He'd more than likely cut off his own hand if he had to do anything like that right now.

Time dragged until Mrs. Kilburn summoned him again. "Help me move her to the room her father was in."

Wyatt cradled the delicate woman in his arms. The torn bloodstained blouse and riding skirt had been replaced with a long loose gown. He could feel the bulky bandages swathing her shoulder as he followed the doctor's wife down the short hallway. Laying Meri on her side, he stepped back, and Mrs. Kilburn tucked pillows behind her back and gently laid a quilt over her.

"I'll stay right here with her 'til Doc gets back. You go get the coyote who did this to her."

The woman's fierce expression would have made Wyatt smile on any other day but this one. He nodded grimly and exited the house. Leaping onto Charger, he raced back to pick up Jonah's trail.

If it took the rest of his life, he would not rest until he had caught the man who'd shot Meri.

Chapter Seventeen

Wyatt was halfway between town and the cemetery when he recognized Jonah and Barnaby riding toward him, their rifles trained on a man astride a gray horse riding slightly in front of them, hands bound securely behind his back.

"How's Miss Meri?" Barnaby asked anxiously, keeping the barrel of his rifle aimed unswervingly at the battered-looking man as their horses came to a halt.

"Doc's out of town on another call, but Mrs. Kilburn got the bullet out of her shoulder. She was still unconscious when I left." He gestured toward their prisoner. "Looks like you caught him."

"Yep." Grim satisfaction surrounded the single word.

"He looks a little worse for the wear." Wyatt eyed the man's bloody, bruised face and dirt-smeared torn clothing.

"He got off easy." Barnaby's eyes glinted dangerously. "I came real close to shootin' him off his horse and leavin' him for the buzzards."

"Where did you come from, by the way?" Wyatt asked the foreman.

"I was shadowing Miss Meri on her ride today. I knew you two were somewhere around 'cause I found your horses, and then I spotted you in the doorway of the crypt about the same time Miss Meri's horse did. When I heard the shots and saw you take her down and get her behind cover, I started working my way closer to him." Barnaby jerked his thumb toward the bound prisoner. "When this skunk lit out, I rode cross-country to cut him off."

"I caught up to them about the time Barnaby was ex- plainin' the finer points of the consequences of shootin' a woman." Jonah's chuckle held no humor. "From the tracks his pretty gray horse is leavin', this is the same rat that stole McIsaac's horse and shot at Meri the first time."

"I don't know what they're talking about, Marshal," the man broke in belligerently. "I was just drifting through and suddenly this crazy fool jumps out of nowhere and knocks me off my horse."

Barnaby patted the stock of a second rifle resting in the saddle scabbard. "His rifle's been fired recently."

"I shot at a rabbit."

"His tracks lead straight back to those cedars he shot at us from. I found these before I trailed him to where Barn- aby had him cornered." Jonah pulled two brass cartridges from his pocket. "I'll also wager he's our bank robber."

"Why did you shoot at us?" The man turned his head away and refused to answer Wyatt's query. "Do you know anything about the bank robbery?" Again he vouchsafed no answer. "All right then, before we take him to jail, I need to make a quick stop at the cemetery."

"You want us to take him on in and lock him up?" Jonah stuffed the cartridges back into his pocket.

"No. I want him to see what we found this morning."

The four men rode toward the cemetery, Jonah and Barnaby vigilantly keeping their guns on the prisoner. Mr. Van Deusen and Mr. Hubert heard them coming and walked out from the tree line where they'd been keeping watch. They lowered their guns when they recognized the riders.

"You gonna explain why we've been keeping guard over a bunch of dead people and an empty tomb, Marshal?" Mr. Hubert peered at Wyatt quizzically, chuckling ruefully as he added, "I'm beginning to feel like those Roman soldiers in the Bible."

"This tomb isn't as empty as it appears." Wyatt dismounted, walked between the two marble lions and swung open the metal door.

He disappeared inside and scraping sounds were heard before he reappeared carrying several canvas bags. Dropping them on the ground, he untied the top of one and displayed its contents, keeping his eyes on the face of the suspected robber.

There were gasps from everyone except Jonah and bitterness spewed from the lips of the bound man. "That scheming double-crossing little weasel! I knew there was more money than what I…" He clamped his lips tight.

"I assume this is what you've been roaming the countryside looking for?" Wyatt retied the bag of money.

Mr. Hubert stared wide-eyed at the loot. "What is all that?"

"I believe that's the money from the bank," Jonah replied sardonically.

"How did it get here?" queried Mr. Van Deusen.

"I think our prisoner has a pretty good idea." Wyatt motioned toward the man on the gray horse. All eyes turned toward him, but he only glared sullenly.

"Maybe a little time cooling your heels in jail will loosen your tongue." Wyatt removed the rolled slicker from the back of his saddle and tied the three moneybags in its place. Flipping open the slicker, he draped it over the bags, concealing them from view.

"You gonna' drop that off at the bank on our way to the jail?" Mr. Van Deusen asked.

"No. It's going into the safe in my office. It's evidence. And I need all of you to keep quiet about it." Wyatt swung atop Charger.

"Why? Looks like we got the man who took it." Mr. Hubert waved his hand toward the sullen prisoner.

"He may have been the one to hold up the bank, but he didn't take this money." Wyatt cut off further questions by riding out of the cemetery toward town.

The next few hours flew swiftly. Wyatt locked the money in the office safe and secured the prisoner behind bars. He provided the man with a bucket of cool water and some rags to clean up with, but the man refused to talk.

Jonah returned from the banker's house with news that the man had packed a bag and departed an hour or so previous. The housekeeper had no idea when he would return.

Barnaby rode to the doctor's house for word on Meri and returned to inform Wyatt that Doc and Ian McIsaac had arrived. Although Meri was still unconscious, Doc said she was simply weak from loss of blood and the shock to her system and should make a full recovery barring infection.

Leaving Franks in charge of the jail and the prisoner, Wyatt and Jonah snuck away from town in opposite directions. Slowly and silently they worked their way into the woods behind the graveyard, hiding themselves and their horses. Then they sat down to wait.

The last light faded from the sky. Wyatt strained his ears for any sound, his senses on full alert. Was he trying to close the trap on an already-escaped prey? The squeak of the gate at the lower end of the cemetery broke the heavy stillness.

Motionless, he and Jonah watched a shadowy figure sneak up the slope through the silent gravestones. When it disappeared into the crypt, they glided soundlessly from their hiding places. A muffled oath echoed from the interior of the pale mausoleum, and the sinister shape hurtled out the door.

"Put your hands up. You're under arrest," Wyatt ordered, gun held ready.

Crack! Crack!

Flame stabbed the darkness, and Wyatt felt a tug on his sleeve as the bullet tore past. His own gun fired simultaneously with Jonah's, and the indistinguishable figure slumped to the ground. They cautiously neared the man, and Jonah kicked the gun away from his hand. Wyatt knelt and rolled the groaning man over. Mr. Samuels's pasty face shone in the dim moonlight.

"You were right, Cap'n."

"Regrettably." Wyatt hauled the man none-too-gently to his feet. "Let's get him into town, see what shape he's in and hear what he has to say for himself."

Bright sunlight streamed in the window when Meri forced her eyes open. Why was she in Doc's house? Had she only dreamed her father was back home? No. It couldn't have been a dream. She was in the same room her father had occupied all those terrible days.

She sat up, gasped and fell back against the pillows as a wall of pain collided with her shoulder. Blackness threatened to swamp her, and her breath hissed between clenched teeth. What was wrong with her?

The sharp teeth of agony gnawed interminably, but when it began to ease, the events of the previous day flooded back. In spite of the physical pain, the weight of sadness and anger she'd carried so long was gone. Her spirit was light, and the world looked brighter in spite of the torment in her shoulder.

Thank You, Lord, for not giving up on me.

As the prayer filled her heart, a little smile turned up the corners of her mouth. She felt better and hurt worse than at any other time in her life. *Why* am *I hurting so badly?*

Meri gingerly fingered her shoulder, feeling the bandages under the fabric of the gown. The image of Wyatt taking her to the ground replayed in her memory, and a sudden blush heated her face. She'd made an idiot of herself in front of him. *Again.*

She groaned. Why was she so quick to lose her composure with him? So much for getting things right between herself and the Lord. It lasted mere seconds before she promptly flared up at the marshal, forgetting all about her newfound peace.

Footsteps warned her of someone's approach, and she looked toward the open door. Dr. Kilburn walked in followed by her very-worried-looking father.

"And how is our patient?" Doc moved to her side, lifting her wrist and looking at his pocket watch.

"Why am I here?"

"You were shot yesterday. Don't you remember?" Her father looked concerned

"I remember hearing gunshots and Wy…Marshal Cameron throwing me to the ground. My shoulder hurt, but I thought it was because he landed on me."

"No. One of those bullets ricocheted off the top of a headstone and ripped upward along your back to your left shoulder. You lost quite a bit of blood before Wyatt got you here and helped get the bullet out."

At Meri's questioning frown, Doc explained, "I was at the Adams place delivering a baby boy. Mother and baby are doing fine, incidentally. Anyway, that ricochet spent the last of its energy cutting up your back before burying itself in your shoulder just below the skin. My wife cut the bullet out. Marshal Cameron was her extra pair of hands before leaving to round up the gunman."

Doc stirred something into a glass of water and gently raised her head to allow her to sip it. Meri grimaced at the taste of the liquid and the ensuing pain when her shoulder protested even that slight movement.

"What is that stuff?" she gasped.

"Laudanum. I'll need to change those bandages soon, and this will take the edge off the worst of the pain."

"They caught him, in case ye were wonderin'," McIsaac announced, grimly pleased. He seated himself by the bed.

"Who was it?"

"The same eejit who shot me." The burr in McIsaac's voice intensified.

"The bank robber?"

"Aye, and he better be thankful he's surrounded by iron bars, or..." McIsaac's jaw clenched; his hands knotted into fists.

"Why would he shoot at us? I thought he was long gone." Meri blinked slowly, heavy drowsiness creeping in.

"It's a long story. I'll let Marshal Cameron tell it. He's the one who figured it out."

Her father's voice faded as she struggled to stay awake, but her eyelids had grown too heavy.

A piercing cry filled her ears when someone rolled her over, and the burn ravaging her shoulder blazed into an inferno. Hands were a million teeth gnawing her flesh, and another cry stabbed her ears. She dimly recognized her own voice before gratefully surrendering to unconsciousness.

Time ceased to exist. Meri was vaguely aware of a damp cloth on her face or a cool trickle of water down her throat, but these blurred and floated together in a crazy pain-racked dream.

It was dark when her eyes opened, and the memory of intense pain kept her motionless. The burning ache in her shoulder was still very much present, but Meri marveled at the restored peace warming her soul. She thanked the Lord for his gracious love, and asked forgiveness as she recalled again the events at the graveyard. *Lord, why do I lose my cool around Marshal Cameron? I really have been quite unpleasant, and I'm sorry. Why can't I just ignore him and go on?*

A quiet little voice whispered in her heart, stopping her thoughts in their tracks.

Maybe you can't ignore him because he's dangerous to your heart.

No! she argued silently.

Maybe you're in love with him. Maybe that's what you're fighting.

I am not in love with him!

But in spite of her denial the words dug into her heart, and Meri was wide-awake as slow realization dawned.

How can I be in love with him? He drives me crazy. He's bossy. He laughs at me. He... He... His horse is faster than mine. The thought was petty, and she knew it. Laughing hazel eyes peered through her memories coaxing her to join in their merriment. They are rather pretty eyes, she admitted with a sigh.

Another memory lit up the dark room. A handsome man placing an outrageous bid and sitting across from her to indulge in his hard-won gingerbread. More images paraded past. An arm supporting her during the three-legged race; his chagrin at losing the sack race, but his delight in her win; the look on his face when rotten egg dripped down his shirtfront.

Meri grinned. Since when did a man look good in rotten egg? She sighed again. At the very least the man fascinated her. She was beginning to believe it went much deeper than simple fascination.

"Are ye awake, lass?" McIsaac's whisper broke the silence, and she jerked at the sound. Biting back a moan, she breathed past the pain. "Yes."

The strike of a match warned her, and she closed her eyes as the lamp flamed to life. Squinting against the sudden brightness, she watched her father pour a glass of water. Bringing it to her, he carefully raised her head to allow her a drink. The cool liquid tasted wonderful, and Meri drank the entire glass before resting her head back on the pillow. "Thank you. That tasted so good."

"How do ye feel?" He placed a hand on her forehead.

"Sore."

"I heartily sympathize."

"Now I know why you were unconscious so long. You didn't want to deal with the pain." Meri grinned at him.

"Me secret comes to light at last." He shook his head in mock shame.

Silence fell for a moment, and Meri swallowed hard before she spoke. "Faither?"

"Aye, lass?"

"Will you forgive me for my terrible attitude the past few months? I know I've been a pain to be around, but the Lord finally got my attention. I was angry and blaming Him for Mither's death, thinking He wasn't hearing my prayers. I kept telling myself I was sad, but I was taking out my hurt and anger on those around me." Meri choked on the sudden rush of tears.

Arms surrounded her in a gentle hug. "Wheesht, lass. I

knew ye were hurting, and I prayed ye'd let the Lord heal ye as He has me. Of course I forgive ye. I love ye more than me own life. I'm so grateful the Lord spared ye."

He pulled away, tears glistening on his cheeks. Pulling a handkerchief from his pocket, he dried her tears before wiping away his own. "Yer mither would be laughing at the both of us. She always said she was the only stoic Scot in the family."

Meri grinned at him. For the first time since her mother's death, the mention of her didn't send a shaft of pain through her heart. Instead the memory of her mother's teasing statement whenever father got emotional was heartwarmingly pleasant. They softly reminisced until Meri's eyelids drooped again, and her father turned the lamp down low.

Leaning over, he softly kissed her forehead, his Scottish brogue rumbling softly against her ears. "Sleep well, lass. Yer Faither will be watching over ye. And so will I."

The day passed in a confusing blur, laudanum keeping the worst of the pain at bay, but making Meri's brain so foggy, wakefulness and sleep swirled together in a surreal tangle. She wasn't sure if she dreamed Wyatt's voice, but the word *sweetheart* spoken in a rich baritone brought a drowsy smile to her lips.

The sun was high in the sky the following day when she finally woke with a clear head and ravenous hunger. Her father was busily scanning the newspaper, but at the sound of her growling stomach, he lowered the paper to his lap. "Ye're awake. And hungry from the sound of it." A relieved smile lit his face.

"I'm starving."

The door swung open, admitting Dr. Kilburn. "How's our patient feeling today?" Meri's stomach rumbled in answer. "Sounds like your appetite is in good working order." Doc laughed as he felt her head and reached for her wrist. "We'll get it quieted down in a few minutes. Until then, how are you feeling?"

"Still trying to figure out which end is up." Meri shifted slightly, regretting it instantly as the pain reminded her why she was flat on her back, or rather, propped up on pillows.

Dr. Kilburn smiled. "Your wound is looking good, no sign of infection, and you haven't had any laudanum for several hours. How's the pain?"

"Bearable, as long as I don't move."

"Then don't move. It's going to take some time to heal, and you'll be sore even after that. Now, how about some food?"

"Yes, please."

He left the room, and soon Mrs. Kilburn breezed in with a fragrant-smelling tray. Setting it down on the bedside table, she turned to Meri. "Do you want to try sitting up?"

"Yes, I'm tired of lying down."

Meri thought better of the idea when Mrs. Kilburn helped ease her into an upright position, but she gritted her teeth and refused to let a whimper escape. Mrs. Kilburn artfully arranged the pillows to support her while keeping pressure off the damaged shoulder, and Meri gratefully sank against their softness. Pain had effectively quieted the noisy rumbling of her stomach, leaving her nauseous instead.

"I don't think I'm hungry anymore." A bead of sweat trickled down her back.

"I brought some nice broth to start with. Why don't you try a few sips and see if it doesn't calm your stomach?"

Meri felt very weak and helpless as the woman spooned

broth into her mouth, but after a few swallows, Mrs. Kilburn proved she knew what she was talking about.

Meri's appetite returned with a vengeance. The broth disappeared quickly, and she gratefully accepted the soft, buttered bread. "Thank you. That tasted wonderful."

"We'll give you something a little more substantial for supper, but Doc wanted to make sure you handled this okay before trying anything heavier." She gathered up the dishes. "I'll be back in a few minutes to help you freshen up. You'll have guests before long. You're quite our most popular patient." Mrs. Kilburn grinned and winked before bustling out of the room.

"What did she mean?"

McIsaac lowered the paper he'd been quietly reading. "I'm not sure who's left to run the ranch since most of the hands rode in at various times yesterday to 'check on you' and carry news back there. Half the town has stopped by to check on 'Miss Meri.' Franks is more worried than I've ever seen him."

She was humbled so many people cared about her, but had Wyatt not stopped in? Was that why her father hadn't mentioned him? Maybe she *had* only dreamed the sweetheart endearment.

Mrs. Kilburn returned, interrupting her musings. Hustling McIsaac out of the room and closing the door behind him, she helped Meri with a personal urgent need. When she was settled back in bed, exhausted, Mrs. Kilburn brushed Meri's hair smooth and tamed it into a neat braid. Then she bathed Meri's hands and face in refreshing warm water before arranging a pretty little crocheted bed jacket about her shoulders and straightening the colorful quilt around her waist.

"There," she said, stepping back to admire her work. "Don't you make a lovely picture?"

"If you happen to like looking at what the cat dragged in."

"Absolutely not!" the woman argued stoutly. "You look fashionably pale, and I know a certain lawman who won't be able to take his eyes off you." A distant knock sounded, and Mrs. Kilburn smiled knowingly. "I suspect that's him now." She eyed Meri's blooming cheeks. "Ah, you're not quite so pale now. Feel up to a little company?"

Meri's heart was in her throat, so she could only nod. First she was disappointed when she thought he hadn't dropped by, and now she feared seeing him again.

Fickle female! You don't know your own mind.

"I'll show him in then." Mrs. Kilburn pulled the door closed behind her.

Meri barely breathed, straining to hear identifiable voices. When she heard steps approaching, her heart shuddered to a stop.

You don't even know if it's him.

But she did. She recognized his steps on the wood flooring. Her stomach lurched as they came to a stop outside the door, and a light tap caused her heart to explode back into action.

"Come in." It was more croak than voice, but it did the job because the door swung inward.

Chapter Eighteen

Wyatt stepped into the room and stood looking at her for a long moment, his eyes seeming to absorb every inch of her. His powerful presence shrank the space until it felt too small to hold two people comfortably, and Meri felt he could see all the way through her. She wanted to lower her gaze, but it tangled irretrievably in his.

He exhaled a noisy sigh. "You look so much better today. You had me worried, Mac."

Meri opened her mouth to protest the name then shut it abruptly. She might actually be starting to like it.

"Uh-oh. I thought you were doing better, but maybe I ought to call Doc."

"Why?"

"You're not arguing with me. You must be feeling worse than I thought." The sparkle in his eyes belied the concern in his voice, and Meri felt an answering grin struggle for freedom.

She sobered quickly, however, and dropped her eyes to the quilt. "I need to apologize for that."

"Apologize for what?"

"Apologize for always arguing with you."

"You don't *always* argue with me. I seem to recall we worked pretty good together at the picnic."

Meri ignored the heat in her cheeks and forced herself to continue. "I've been fighting the Lord on some things, and I allowed it to affect my attitude and how I treated those around me, you especially. I've been rude to you, lost my temper…" Meri felt tears sting her eyes but refused to release them. "I've asked the Lord to forgive me, now I'm asking you to forgive me." The apology was hard enough without blubbering all over the man.

"Forgiveness granted, and I have a confession of my own."

Her eyes flew to his.

"You're not completely at fault here."

"I'm not?"

"No." He chuckled. "I did my fair share of provoking you."

"Why?"

"Unlike most females of my acquaintance, instead of fussing about a ruined dress, a mussed hairdo or even acting helpless when you landed at my feet that day at Franks's, you came up fighting. I liked your spunk and wanted to see it again. You mind if I sit down?"

The question caught Meri off guard. "Of course."

"You want me to leave?"

"No! I mean… Yes, you can sit down."

"You had me worried for a minute there. I was afraid you were going to throw me out on my ear," Wyatt said good-naturedly, seating himself in the chair by the bedside.

If the room had shrunk when he'd walked in, it now felt positively minuscule. Meri looked down at her fingers mindlessly twirling a bed jacket ribbon. She folded her hands, forcing her gaze back toward Wyatt. He was watching her with a look she couldn't decipher, but it made her stomach quiver. She rallied her retreating courage; just because she was more accustomed to arguing with him didn't mean she was incapable of carrying on a normal, civil conversation, despite evidence to the contrary.

Lifting her chin slightly, she broke the silence. "Thank you."

Those intense eyes never left hers. "For?"

"For saving my life."

A breathtaking smile curved his lips. "The Lord saved your life, but it was absolutely my pleasure to be of some assistance. You scared a few years off my life when I realized you were bleeding. I'd rather not experience that again, if you don't mind."

"I'd rather not repeat it myself. It's painful. Would you tell me what happened after I was shot? Faither said the bank robber and the man who shot at us were the same person and you had him in jail. And you never did tell me why you and Jonah were out there in the first place."

Wyatt leaned back in the chair and crossed one ankle over his knee. "There were a lot of pieces that didn't add up about all that, and I couldn't figure out why the bank robber was still hanging around."

"Why did you think he was still around?"

"Jonah matched the tracks where he stole your ranch horse to the ones on the road where you…"

Meri interrupted. "The two men I saw on the road—I knew you and Jonah were acting funny. One of those men was the bank robber?"

"Yes. His name is Ernie Mullins."

"Who was the other man?"

"Mr. Phineas Samuels."

Meri's eyes grew large, and her mouth dropped opened in surprise. "Mr. Samuels?"

Wyatt nodded grimly.

"But—I don't understand."

Wyatt related what he'd learned from the bank clerk. "I'd already figured out someone else was involved in the bank job, and when every inconsistency kept leading back to Mr. Samuels, I began to have my suspicions. I could never pin him down on any explanations, and then you mentioned seeing him at the cemetery and his strange behavior. It just added to all the things pointing his direction. I put a couple pairs of eyes to watching him and sure enough it led back to the cemetery."

"I still don't understand why you were there."

"Mullins was hanging around because he didn't find a safe full of money like he was expecting. The majority of the money was gone long before he arrived. Mr. Samuels had been embezzling a little at a time and engineered the robbery to cover his tracks. He didn't expect Mullins to realize there had to be more money somewhere and want more than his share of what he cleaned out of the safe. Mullins was trying to scare Mr. Samuels into giving him a bigger cut. That's what you saw on the road that day and what you saw through the bank window the day of the picnic." He shook his head. "There is absolutely no honor between thieves."

"I can hardly believe it." Meri was stunned.

"You were the other wrinkle in Mr. Samuels's plot."

"Me? What did I do?"

"You'd seen too much. Or so Mr. Samuels thought."

"I didn't see anything. I wasn't anywhere around when the bank robbery occurred."

"You saw Mr. Samuels in the cemetery, you saw him out on the road with Mullins and you saw the two of them in the bank. When you mentioned that at the picnic, he thought you were putting it all together and panicked. He told Mullins if he got rid of you, he'd give him a larger cut. You were too hard to get to at the ranch, but Mullins got his chance when you rode into the graveyard. He wasn't shooting randomly that day. He was aiming for you."

Meri shivered at how close he'd come to being successful. She decided not to dwell on that thought. "What were you doing there?"

Wyatt shifted in the chair and leaned forward, elbows on his knees. "Jonah and I were following a hunch—one that played out. Mr. Samuels had been 'depositing' money in that ridiculous crypt. He buried it under a loose stone in the floor, believing no one would ever think to look in there. We'd just uncovered it when we saw you. We didn't want you asking questions and were waiting 'til you left, but Sandy caught us peeking out."

Wyatt threw his head back suddenly and laughed. "I wish you could have seen your face when we walked out. You looked like you were expecting a ghost, but you got me instead."

"I came close to shooting you just for scaring me." Meri couldn't hide an embarrassed grin.

"I thought for a moment you *were* upset enough to pull that trigger." He grinned back at her to show there were no hard feelings and continued his story. "Word got to Samuels that you were shot, and he went to retrieve the money before hightailing it out of the country. He got quite a surprise when he found an empty hole in the ground instead of his money. We were waiting when he burst back out the door."

"You got him."

"And found your father's missing gun, too. Samuels had it and used it. Ruined a good shirt, too." He scowled.

"He shot you?" Meri jerked forward and yelped as the injured shoulder objected to the sudden move.

Wyatt was gently easing her back against the pillows before she realized he'd moved from his chair. "Easy does it. Give it a minute, the pain will pass." He gently rubbed her arm. "Breathe, sweetheart. Want me to get Doc?"

"No," Meri bit out, eyes closed and teeth clenched against the searing burn. Maybe she hadn't dreamed up the sweetheart endearment in her drugged stupor after all.

A cool cloth touched her skin. She opened her eyes, surprised to see Wyatt tenderly dabbing her forehead. Concern radiated from him. "Is it easing up any?"

"Yes." It wasn't great, but it was bearable, given the distraction of his fingers against her forehead. "Go on with your story."

He studied her closely before folding the cloth. Laying it over the edge of the basin, he reseated himself. "Okay, but no more sudden movements," he cautioned anxiously.

"I think I'll take you up on that advice." She breathed shallowly as the pain began to ebb.

"Following orders? That would be a first for you, wouldn't it?" Wyatt asked seriously.

"Funny. I can understand why you're a lawman. Your career as a jester was so short-lived." Meri grinned dryly.

Wyatt swiped his hand across his brow. "Pshew! Now that's the Miss McIsaac I know and…I was beginning to worry that I didn't have the right room."

She rolled her eyes with a grin. "You didn't say if Mr. Samuels hit you or Jonah."

"He missed on both counts and only tore up the sleeve on my shirt. We didn't miss."

"Is he dead?"

"No. Jonah and I winged him, one on each side. He's

sitting in jail with two very sore arms awaiting the U.S. Marshal to transport him to the county seat for trial."

"Sounds like you both nearly missed."

His eyes narrowed playfully. "No, Miss Doubting Thomas, we hit exactly what we were aiming at. We didn't want to kill him. We wanted him to stand trial."

"What will happen to him?"

"That'll be up to a judge, but he'll be tried for the attempted murder of you and your father as well as the theft of the bank's money."

Meri shook her head in unbelief. It was bewildering that the man who'd attended church with them year after year had tried to have her killed! "But he was hurt in the holdup, too."

"I've not been able to get out of either of them whether Mullins hit him or if Samuels did it to himself, but either way, it was done to make the holdup look real."

"Why would he do it—rob the bank?"

Wyatt shook his head, thoughtfully quiet for a moment before answering. "I asked him that myself, and a lot of pent-up anger spewed out. Says he deserved to have the money because God never did anything for him. He's raved about his poor childhood, the loss of a baby son, a wife that withdrew after the baby's death, every little slight anyone's ever done to him and on and on. Bitterness poured out of him like a festered sore. He doesn't even sound rational half the time. I guess he let all his disappointments weigh on him until he snapped."

"So the money's all back?"

"Every penny according to the records we found at Samuels's house. We even got back most of what Mullins took. He'll stand trial for attempted murder, as well."

"What will happen to the bank?"

"That's up to the bank's investors. Apparently, they

were part of Samuels's problem. Several of them wanted him replaced as bank president and had been working toward that end. Samuels knew about it and decided to get revenge along with what he thought he deserved."

She leaned her head back against the pillow. Just hearing the whole sordid story tired her out. "What a mess."

"I can't help but think about Pastor Willis's message a couple weeks ago. Samuels is a prime example of letting anger and bitterness fester until it ruined him. I suppose he's had a hard life, but so has everyone to some extent, and he'd made something out of himself. But instead of letting the Lord help him through his difficulties, he allowed every little problem to grow out of proportion until he was willing to kill to get what he wanted."

Meri blushed to think how close she'd been to starting down the same path. She didn't realize her eyes had drifted closed until they flew open when she heard Wyatt stand up from his chair.

"I can see I've bored you to sleep," he teased gently. "I'll let you get some rest before Doc comes in and runs me out." He pulled out his watch. "He gave me a time limit, and it's almost up."

"Thank you for explaining what happened." She swallowed the yawn that threatened.

"You are most welcome." Wyatt bowed. "May I drop in to see you again?"

"Could I keep you away, Marshal?" she teased.

"If you really don't want to see me, Mac, I won't come, but I'm hoping that's not the case." Wyatt was completely serious.

"I…" She cleared her throat in nervous confusion. "I don't mind if you come by."

Wyatt grinned hugely. "Good." In the blink of an eye he picked her hand up from the quilt and, leaning over, kissed it gallantly. Straightening, he squeezed her fingers before releasing them, gave her a jaunty grin and headed out the door.

Meri was speechless. Her eyes followed the broad shoulders until they disappeared. She was still staring, pondering his actions, when Dr. Kilburn stepped into the room and after a quick look at her, ordered her to get some rest. She had no desire to sleep; her mind was too busy ordering her heart not to indulge in foolish dreams, but the kiss on her hand accompanied her into dreamland where chivalrous knights wore shiny badges instead of rusty armor and rode beautiful bay stallions instead of washed-out white horses.

When Wyatt arrived back at his office Friday afternoon, a U.S. Marshal was waiting to escort the prisoners to the county seat. He also requested Wyatt's assistance in delivering the two men. Wyatt thought the trip would be a quick there-and-back, but he had to stay long enough to testify in a preliminary hearing Monday morning.

The time away gave him plenty of time to think. Almost losing Meri to a gunman's bullet brought a new perspective to his belief that he needed to wait until life was safe before thinking about a wife and family. Seeing the hardship military life placed on wives and families, he'd erected a barrier to keep himself from being hurt or hurting someone else. The loss of his parents had shown him he couldn't control circumstances around him, only his response, but still, he'd tried to protect himself with a wall around his heart.

Then Miss McIsaac had sailed a rangy black horse over his carefully fortified barriers as if they were no more substantial than a cobweb fence.

Although she had struggled for a while, she'd proved

she was resilient enough to deal with the loss of her mother. Was her self-sufficient independence strong enough to deal with the uncertainty of his job and an unknown future? He hoped so, because the thought of not having her in his life was as scary as almost losing her to that bullet.

Whether he was an officer of the law or a simple horse breeder, it was impossible to guard completely himself or those around him from loss. He could, however, stop waiting for life to be perfect and go after the woman who made him laugh and his heart beat faster. After years of trying to control his future, it was time to trust the One who held the future in His hands.

Equal parts excitement and fear accompanied him on his return to Little Creek. Her reaction to him, whether it was a fiery retort, an all-out retreat or the shy softness she'd worn the last time he'd seen her, suggested she wasn't completely indifferent to him. He clung to that hope as he let Charger pick his own pace—fast— toward home.

Chapter Nineteen

Meri caught herself glancing up nervously every time the door rattled, but the longed-for sight of a particular star-toting individual did not appear. The pain in her shoulder was less severe, but she was achy and chafed at the unaccustomed inactivity of the past several days. She had slept a great deal due to the laudanum, and when she was awake, she'd had a steady stream of visitors. It felt like she'd seen everyone in town. Everyone except the one person who she most wanted to see.

Not too many days ago you were convinced you couldn't abide the man, yet here you are working yourself into a dither wondering why he hasn't come by to see you again. Just because you've decided you lo—like him after all, doesn't mean he's of the same opinion.

But he called you sweetheart and kissed your hand, the little voice argued.

He was merely being a gentleman.

She couldn't bring herself to ask his whereabouts, but when Jonah casually mentioned Wyatt had escorted the prisoners to the county seat, her internal argument ceased.

For all of ten minutes.

In spite of her unsettled emotions, however, her soul

rested in the peace of restored fellowship with her Heavenly Father.

Meri had been injured Thursday, and by Tuesday morning, she had developed a case of cabin fever. By keeping her arm quiet in the sling Dr. Kilburn had fashioned, pain was kept to a dull ache, and he allowed her to be up and about as she had energy. He also gave her the welcome news she could return home the next morning if she promised to curtail any riding or lifting for another week.

Mrs. Kilburn assisted her into real clothes, a pale yellow blouse and simple blue skirt, and pulled her hair up and away from her face in a soft twist. Meri then celebrated her impending release by escaping the enclosing walls of the house for Mrs. Kilburn's shady garden.

After exploring every nook and cranny of the verdant bower, Meri made her way to the pretty bench tucked under the rose arbor. A few buds were just beginning to peek open, subtly perfuming the air, and some thoughtful soul had padded the bench with a thick quilt and several soft pillows. She gratefully tucked her uninjured side into the pillowed corner and lifted her legs to rest on the seat, more drained than she would have admitted. It was good to be outside in the fresh breeze, but getting shot definitely took the starch out of a person.

Leaning her head against the high-backed seat, she allowed her mind to wander as she listened to a chipper little sparrow singing his heart out as he hopped to and fro on his bird duties.

She was drifting on a drowsy daydream somewhere between sleep and wakefulness and didn't immediately notice when floral-scented air changed to spicy bay rum. She enjoyed the new aroma for several breaths before the contrast dawned on her. Her eyes flew open, and her gaze riveted to the shadow lying across her lap. A wave of shyness washed over her, and she hesitantly turned lowered eyes toward her visitor.

Shiny black boots, firmly anchored to the ground and tucked beneath spotless black trousers, stood inches outside the rose arbor. Her eyes slowly traveled up the sleek, solid form. A holster circled narrow hips, and a crisp red shirt with silver buttons was belted into the pants. One hand dangled a black Stetson by the brim; the other hand was tucked into a back pocket.

The spick-and-span, too-handsome-for-his-own-good marshal appeared as if he'd just stepped out of a bandbox. He didn't move nor speak during Meri's scrutiny and, swallowing past the lump in her throat, she forced her eyes to his face. There was no smirking grin or teasing eyes as there had been the first time she'd met this man. There was only a soft gaze and a hint of upturned lips.

Intense hazel eyes snagged hesitant brown eyes as the thick silence continued. Meri felt his piercing gaze read her every thought. She tried to read him, but unfamiliar with this new language, she remained unsure of what she saw in his eyes and on his face. Her gaze dropped, breaking the connection, and a sense of loss registered.

"Excuse me, ma'am."

The husky sound drew Meri's eyes back to the tall shadow-casting figure who bowed slightly, still keeping one hand tucked behind him.

"I don't think we've been properly introduced. Allow me to present myself. I am Wyatt Cameron from Virginia by way of Texas."

A smile dawned in Meri's heart in delight of the pretentious tone he assumed and the haughty tilt of his head.

"Some might know me better by my job description here in Little Creek—Marshal Cameron."

She resisted the laugh that bubbled at his continued air of superiority but a little burble escaped her.

Wyatt lifted an eyebrow at the outburst. "Please do not interrupt my introduction, ma'am."

She pulled her face into some semblance of matching dignity while the impish twinkle in his eyes made her heart do an undignified jig.

"Now where was I?" He pretended to ponder a second. "Ah, yes. I was raised in the fine state of Virginia by my parents, Recyrus, better known as Cy, and Hanna Cameron. I graduated from West Point a second lieutenant in the United States Army. I served for over ten years and attained the rank of captain but resigned my commission after the death of my father."

Wyatt's voice had taken on a serious note as he mentioned his parents, and he paused a moment before continuing. "Might I ask whom I have the honor of addressing?" The condescending tone had returned.

She held out her hand in feigned hauteur. "*Miss* America McIsaac, sir."

He stepped toward her. Setting his hat on a nearby table, he cradled the offered hand in his own and saluted it with a kiss.

Delightful tingles raced up her arm, and she admired the lustrous head of hair bent over her fingers. "But my friends call me Meri," she added with the barest whisper, "or Mac."

Wyatt watched her for a long breath before straightening. The hand she had assumed to be in his back pocket emerged from hiding holding a small bouquet of deep purple violets. He bowed low again as he offered them to her. "With my compliments, Miss McIsaac."

His fingers brushed hers when she accepted the pretty flowers. She was beginning to look forward to the thrill that raced through her whenever he touched her. Burying her nose in the delicate blooms, she hid her face a moment and inhaled their faint sweet scent as he resumed speaking in his newly acquired supercilious manner.

"I was hired to be the marshal of Little Creek, and soon found the town was plagued with a rash of burglaries." He paused dramatically and rocked back on his heels, tucking his thumbs into his belt loops and gazing at the top of the arbor. "However, I was brilliantly able to resolve all but one of the thefts."

Meri grinned at his impudence. "You surprise me, sir."

"The horse theft was solved immediately by my quick action. I had the thief rounded up before she knew what hit her."

She rolled her eyes as he glanced down to check her reaction to this statement but refused to rise to the bait. "Next…?"

"It took a wee bit longer, due to a slight cleverness on the part of the next thief, but I soon solved the mystery of the bank robbery with my usual dazzling detective skills."

This time she laughed outright at his unmitigated arrogance.

A satisfied grin marred the haughty upturned face, until a look of abject despondence replaced the smirk, and his head fell forward abashedly. "But alas, I have been unable to resolve the most grievous theft."

Meri had never seen puppy-dog-sad eyes retain such a deep, mischievous gleam. "So even your brilliance has its limits?"

"Repeat offenders are sly, hardened characters and more difficult to apprehend. Especially when they don't even realize they've committed a theft." His head shook remorsefully.

"How can a thief not realize they've stolen something?"

"This particular thief happens to be rather forgetful."

"So an absentminded thief has outwitted our brilliant marshal? How can that be?"

"Shocking, I know. It has been a rather severe blow." Again, his glossy head bowed in contrite shame. "This thief cannot seem to remember my name even though she has stolen my most valuable possession."

Too late, she realized the clever trap she'd blindly walked into. She crossed her arms as best as possible, considering one arm was in a sling, and narrowed her eyes at the merry hazel ones that peeked at her through thick lashes. "And what, pray tell, am I supposed to have stolen this time?"

All traces of humor fled, and his eyes glowed with a fierce look that took Meri by surprise. Her own eyes widened, and her heart stuttered.

He scrutinized her with a long, measuring look before responding in a low voice. "My heart, fair lady. You've stolen my heart. And I don't know how to function without it."

Meri searched him for any trace of teasing or humor but found only resolute earnestness. "I've never heard of anyone living without a heart," she said tentatively. She had to clear her throat of a sudden lump. "Would it help if I gave it back?"

"No. It wouldn't fit anymore. Someone has taken up residence in it."

Silence fell again. Meri forgot to breathe. She had two choices, fearful retreat or bold advance. After a short but hard-fought internal struggle, she chose boldness. "Would it help if I offered a replacement?" She'd forgotten to notify her mouth that she was being bold. It barely broke a whisper, and Wyatt had to step closer in order to hear. His closeness very nearly destroyed her hard-won bravery.

"What do you mean by a replacement?" he asked cautiously.

"Would you take mine in exchange for yours?" Fear swamped her heart, and she ducked her head as she made the request, unable to look at him. Silence fell and was almost unbearable, but she dreaded looking up to find rejection on his face.

Gentle, calloused fingers touched the tender skin under her chin, and lightning raced through her at the unexpected contact. Like velvet steel, they softly, inexorably forced her face up out of hiding. The second she saw his expression, she understood he'd been waiting for her to look at him before replying.

Expectation filled his eyes as he searched her face. She timidly allowed him to look his fill. "Do you mean what I hope you mean?"

She'd never heard that tone of anxious longing from him before, and a surge of confidence replaced shyness. She'd discovered the key to a new language. What had been undecipherable before was beginning to make sense. "You called me a forgetful thief, but the charge can just as easily be leveled at you. You said I didn't know I'd stolen your heart, yet *you* didn't realize you had stolen *my* heart. So you see, Marshal Wyatt Cameron, I'm in good company. It takes a thief to catch a thief."

Hope birthed a huge smile, and Wyatt moved to the bench. "Do you mind if I sit down? I find my knees are suddenly in need of support." Meri started to move her legs off the seat, but Wyatt stopped her with a hand gently laid atop her slippered feet. "Let me."

Ever so carefully he tucked her skirt modestly around

her legs, lifting them and sliding under to sit on the bench and lowering them again to rest across his lap. He kept one hand on her ankles and rested the other arm along the back of the bench as he admired the pretty, rich color that sprang to her cheeks.

She was absolutely beautiful, and he longed to kiss her, but he didn't want to scare her away. Besides, he'd seen the curtain move in the kitchen window and figured they had an audience. "Since we seemed to have exchanged hearts unknowingly, might I have the honor of calling on you, Miss Meri? I miss my heart, you know."

Her eyes twinkled before her lashes veiled his view. "I'd like that, but I do have one request, Marshal."

He narrowed his eyes in mock sternness. "And what might that be, Mac?"

Her lashes swept up. "Yes. That's it."

Wyatt cocked his head in confusion and felt his brows knit. "Huh?" Not exactly the most eloquent speech he'd ever uttered.

Laughter spilled unhindered from her lips and danced along the fragrant air.

"It's not healthy to mock the marshal, young lady. Please explain yourself!" He jostled her ankles lightly in emphasis and felt heat race up his arm.

"I was going to request that you call me Mac occasionally, but you beat me to it." She grinned, blushing slightly.

He grinned right back and shook his head. "Women! My father said I'd never understand them."

Two pairs of laughing eyes met and held and awareness sizzled the air between them. Wyatt found himself leaning toward her.

"How 'bout something to eat?" Mr. McIsaac stood by the arbor holding a tray.

Wyatt straightened and glanced at Meri. Another blush

deepened the pink of her cheeks, and she tried to twist her legs off his lap. He quietly stilled her movements, holding her in place. "I don't know about Meri, but I'm hungry. I think we misplaced lunchtime somewhere along the way."

"Meri still has a little trouble handling food one-handed. Could I impose on ye to help her since ye're already so nicely situated?"

"You make me sound helpless," Meri protested.

They ignored her as Wyatt took possession of the tray while McIsaac pulled the little table within Wyatt's reach.

"I'll take yer hat into the house out of the way. Holler if ye need anything." He gave Wyatt an approving nod and wink, and Wyatt released the breath he'd unconsciously held.

"Would you care for a sandwich, Mac?" He offered her one of the small plates from the tray.

She blinked in charming confusion, looking from the closing screen door back to him. "Why do I get the impression someone is being hustled?"

She must have seen her father's wink. "Maybe you just have a suspicious nature, dear. Sandwich?"

Her frown held no heat, and Wyatt could see her searching for a comeback. He distracted her by asking a blessing on the food and filling her plate. There was little conversation as they ate, Wyatt keeping her supplied with food, drink and napkins as needed, but there were plenty of tentative smiles on her part and not so tentative on his.

When they'd finished, and Wyatt had replaced the dishes on the tray, Meri suddenly blurted, "I won't be here."

"Hmm?" He glanced at her, idly fingering the bow decorating the soft kid slippers on her slender feet.

"We're going home tomorrow. I won't be here." Panic colored her words.

Wyatt stretched his arm along the back of the bench again and allowed his fingers to rest against her shoulder. "I think I remember the way to your ranch. And if not I'll refresh my memory when I escort you home tomorrow."

"But what about your job?"

"What's the use of having a deputy if the marshal can't take an evening now and then to court his girl?"

The shock in her eyes would have been funny if it wasn't so sadly genuine. "You're courting me?" she squeaked just like a mouse.

"Does it mean something else out here when a fella asks to call?" Wyatt watched confusion cross her face again and waited patiently for her response. When it came, it was halting and muffled.

"I…I'm not sure. I've never had anyone ask me before."

The men who had overlooked her were idiots. And he was extremely grateful. "Leave it to a Virginia boy to be the only one to recognize a true gem in this land of fool's gold." He assumed a haughty tone again, and she grinned nervously in answer.

"What happened with Mr. Samuels?" She changed the subject so abruptly, it took him a full second to catch up.

"We delivered the prisoners to the county jail without any problems, and after the hearing, the judge ordered them held for trial, which has been scheduled for next month. Your father will probably get a notice to go testify along with Jonah and myself. I figure Samuels and Mullins will go away for a long time afterward."

She asked a couple more questions, and they chatted for several minutes before Wyatt regretfully announced he needed to return to his office. "May I walk you to the house, or do you want to stay out here?"

"I'm ready to go inside."

Wyatt lowered her feet to the ground, and offered her his arm. His heart swelled as her hand curled around it.

Arriving too soon at the kitchen door, he again brushed his lips across the back of her slim, firm hand. "Until tomorrow."

She nodded, the hand resting in the sling caressing the hand he'd touched with his lips.

Knowing he'd see her tomorrow didn't soothe the ache of having to leave, but he forced himself to turn and start back toward the office.

He heard the kitchen door open before Meri spoke. "Oh! Your hat!"

Walking back, he took it from her hand and swept her a gallant bow before settling the hat on his head. "Good afternoon, my fair lady."

A completely un-Meri-like dreamy sigh whispered past his ears as he left, and a jaunty whistle sprang to his lips. Turnabout was fair play. She'd sailed over the barriers around his heart altogether too easily, but it looked as if he'd knocked down a few of her own today.

Chapter Twenty

Meri's departure from the Kilburns' home was accomplished only after much to-do and many hugs the next day.

Franks delivered a freshly groomed, gleaming Sandy who nickered eagerly at sight of his mistress. Tying him to the back of the wagon, Franks hugged Meri, careful of her injured shoulder. "They be a lot a answered prayers 'roun' here lately, Miss Meri. I's shore grateful He healed you."

"He did, Franks—in more ways than one. Thank you for praying and for taking such good care of Sandy."

"Anytime, Miss Meri, anytime."

Naoma Van Deusen was next in line, and after an admonition to take it easy, she whispered loudly, "I hear a certain marshal can't stay away from the doctor's house lately. I knew you would catch his eye if you put your mind to it."

Her exuberant hug left Meri wincing, and as she disentangled herself from the self-satisfied matchmaker, she looked into the eyes of Wyatt. He'd ridden up on Charger, and from the grin on his face, it was clear he'd heard the not-so-quiet statement. He dropped one eye in a lazy wink. Meri's reproving look failed miserably due to a grin that impeded its progress.

The Kilburns took care to avoid her sore shoulder, and Meri was warmed by their gentle hugs. The time spent in their home had given her a new love and appreciation for this couple who'd dedicated their lives to caring for those around them, and she was profuse in her gratitude. Dr. Kilburn promised to ride out later in the week to check on her, cautioning her to allow herself time to heal before she went riding around the countryside like a wild Indian.

McIsaac grinned, vowing to keep his daughter quiet. "I believe it's me own turn to hover tiresomely." He and Doc assisted a grumbling Meri into the back of the wagon padded with thick quilts and pillows. "If I had to ride home in the back of the wagon, lass, so do ye."

"You're enjoying this entirely too much," she groused.

"Aye, that I am."

Meri propped a pillow against the side of the wagon and leaned in to it, primly folding her hands across her lap. She borrowed Wyatt's look of hauteur. "Home, driver."

Laughing goodbyes filled the air as McIsaac climbed onto the wagon seat and clucked to the horses. Wyatt turned Charger to ride alongside where Meri had a bird's-eye view of him.

As McIsaac threaded the wagon through town, several people waved and called out cheery greetings. Danny and Billy ran out of the mercantile and hopped onto the back of the wagon as it passed to hand Meri a slightly sticky peppermint stick to "help make the trip more comfortable." Meri thanked them, smiling at Mr. Van Deusen who waved from the doorway.

The boys amused her, jabbering of their new status as Little Creek's detectives and bragging how the town would be safer now that they were on the job. When they reached the bridge over Little Creek, they promptly forgot their detective status and ran down the creek bank to terrify the local crawfish population.

McIsaac commenced singing a fine old Scottish ballad in a not-too-rusty tenor, and Wyatt quickly added his baritone. One song became two, and when the second one ended, Wyatt suggested a third that drew a nod of approval from McIsaac.

O, my luve is like a red, red rose,
That's newly sprung in June.
O, my luve is like a melodie,
That's sweetly played in tune.
As fair art thou, my bonnie lass,
So deep in luve am I;
And I will luve thee still, my dear,
Till a' the seas gang dry.
And I will luve thee still, my dear,
Till a' the seas gang dry.
Till a' the seas gang dry, my dear,
And the rocks melt wi' the sun;
And I will luve thee still, my dear,
While the sands o' life shall run.
But fare-thee-weel, my only luve!
O, fare thee weel, awhile!
And I will come again, my luve,
Tho' 'twere ten thousand mile!
Tho' 'twere ten thousand mile, my luve,
Tho' 'twere ten thousand mile,
And I will come again, my luve,
Tho 'twere ten thousand mile!

Meri had sung along many times when her father had crooned the familiar ballad to her mother, but never before had the song stirred her so deeply. Never before had the words *my bonnie lass,* or *my only luve* been directed at her in a lovely baritone; emphasized by a pair of luminous hazel eyes.

She was trembling by the time the song ended and closed her eyes to hide the sheen of tears. She'd always chuckled when some old book hero serenaded the heroine beneath a balcony, but it wasn't a laughing matter. It was one of the most heart-touching moments of her life, and her emotions were about to leak all over the wagon bed.

Meri swallowed past the lump in her throat and joined the singing when they switched to the lively old "Will Ye Go Lassie?" tucking the experience deep in her heart. There would be plenty of time to examine the moment in detail in the quiet of her room.

"Ye huv a fine singing voice, laddie, and a knowledge of the auld songs, I would be able to tell ye were a Scotsman even if I didn't ken ye carried a guid Scottish name." Faither's brogue was in full force as he spoke over his shoulder.

Wyatt was riding abreast of Meri in the wagon, putting him slightly behind McIsaac. "Aye, me granfaither spoke the Gaelic and taught all the wee bairns the auld songs." Wyatt mimicked McIsaac's brogue perfectly, and Meri laughed as he grinned at her, obviously proud of himself.

The remainder of the ride flew by and, all too soon, they slowed to a stop at the front porch of the ranch house. Their arrival acted as a signal. Ms. Maggie, Barnaby and the rest of the ranch hands swarmed the wagon.

"Is anybody left to watch after the cattle?" McIsaac's voice was gruff, but his eyes twinkled brightly.

"Boss man, when they heard she was coming home today, I had a near mutiny on my hands. All of a sudden nobody wanted to be a cowboy anymore; they were too busy taking baths and stinking up the bunkhouse with their hair tonics and smelly potions. This bunch of dandies would start a stampede if the cattle caught sight or smell of them. I figured it was safer to keep 'em home today. Maybe you can do something with them."

It was the longest speech Meri had ever heard from Barnaby, and she swallowed a giggle at the sight of the cleanest, reddest-faced ranch hands she'd ever seen. Wyatt, still mounted on Charger, reached to give her a hand up as she rose to her feet to address them. "Thank you for the warm welcome. I've missed each of you, and I'm very glad to be home."

Rough voices called out greetings as they jostled each other for the best position at the back of the wagon to help her down. Meri hesitated, wondering how to handle the situation. Whom did she allow to help her descend? Wars had started with less provocation.

Her quandary resolved itself when a strong forearm circled her waist and lifted her easily out of the wagon to sit across muscular thighs.

Wyatt reined Charger around the wagon, circling until they stood at the porch's edge, and Meri heard a muttered, "So that's how the land lies…" as Wyatt lowered her gently to her feet on the porch.

Wyatt tipped the brim of his hat slightly. "Thank you for allowing me to escort you home, Miss McIsaac."

"Are you leaving so soon?" She couldn't keep the disappointment from her voice.

"I need to get back, but with your permission, I'd like to call on you Saturday afternoon." He spoke firmly and clearly as if some of the assembled men might have trouble hearing, but their eyes and ears were firmly glued to the little tableau playing out before them. They weren't missing a single word.

"I would be honored, Marshal Cameron." Meri tilted her head like a queen bestowing a favor.

A roguish grin twinkled through hazel eyes and promised retribution, but the onlookers saw only the matching nod. "Until Saturday then."

All eyes followed Wyatt as he departed and disappeared over the rise. When they turned back to the porch, they found Meri regally ensconced in one of the rockers. She rested her aching shoulder and reigned as queen while her humble subjects paid tribute with little carvings, pretty rocks, new leather reins and additional small trinkets.

After a Ms. Maggie—enforced rest in her room, a welcome-home feast finished the day in grand style. When she tumbled into bed that evening, tired and sore but not quite sleepy, she replayed the events of the day, smiling as the strains of a Scottish ballad filtered through her thoughts. Excitement and apprehension concerning Saturday threatened to keep her awake, but a weary body prevailed and worry surrendered to dreams of a handsome, singing lawman.

Wyatt had to force himself to wait until Saturday to return to the McIsaac ranch. After all, he did have a job to do, but the three days felt like a month. At times a vague fear that Meri's soft smiles were simply gratitude for catching the men responsible for her and McIsaac's injuries would trouble him. At other times, a memory, like the heart-in-her-eyes look she'd worn when he'd sung the Scottish ballad to her, would leave him grinning like a simpleton.

Friday afternoon he was passing the front window of the Van Deusen mercantile, and the new window display caught his eye. A delicate parasol sat unfurled next to a handsome picnic basket. The image of Meri twirling the parasol over her shoulder as they sat together on a picnic blanket halted his steps and turned his feet toward the mercantile door. Before he could change his mind, he entered the store, plucked the parasol and picnic basket from the window and carried them to the counter where Mr. Van Deusen carefully wrapped the parasol in brown paper.

Wyatt was counting his blessings for the quiet, reserved Thomas and the absence of the voluble Naoma as he picked up his parcels and thanked the storekeeper.

Thomas nodded, waiting until Wyatt was at the door before speaking. "Happy courtin', Marshal."

The bell over the door jingled a jolly laugh as Wyatt exited, feeling an unaccustomed heat in his cheeks. Hurrying to his room at the back of the marshal's office, he tucked the items out of sight underneath his bed. He was guardedly eager to court Miss McIsaac; he wasn't quite so enthusiastic to be teased for his previously unknown romantic streak. He'd never seen Meri carry a parasol, but he had a hunch she might like it. After all, she had worn that fancy purple dress to church with her hair swept up so pretty. The parasol would just complete the picture.

Saturday morning he painstakingly tied the slender brown package to his saddle and rode toward the ranch. Keeping Charger to a fairly sedate canter, he tried to bring his attack of nerves under control. For the first time in years, he'd cut himself shaving this morning because of unsteady hands. When Jonah arrived after breakfast to watch the office, he had simply shaken his head and laughed at Wyatt's bloody face.

He topped the rise above the ranch and gingerly felt his cheek. Good. The bleeding had stopped.

A slender figure stood from the porch rocker and walked to the edge of the porch.

Wyatt took off his hat and gave a short wave. Meri lifted a hand in acknowledgment, and his nervousness vanished.

For the first time since he'd met her, she wasn't turning and running when she saw him. The times he'd seen her after she'd been shot didn't count; she'd been too injured to run away if she'd wanted to. This time she was not only waiting on his arrival, she actually came forward to greet him.

Wyatt gave a whoop and jammed his hat farther onto his head. Charger lived up to his name, flying down the lane to the house. They came to a sliding halt at the porch, and Wyatt leaped off the horse and onto the porch in an effortless dismount.

Meri hadn't batted an eye as the horse had raced toward her and slid to a snorting halt nearly at her feet. Nor had she flinched when Wyatt had landed in front of her on the porch. That was his girl. Fearless almost to a fault.

Wyatt reached for her hand and kissed it. "You are looking remarkably pretty today, Mac." She was, too. Her eyes sparkled, and her pink blouse brought out the glow in her cheeks.

A smile accompanied her thank-you as the porch door opened, and Ian McIsaac stepped out. He greeted Wyatt and waved them toward the rocking chairs before picking up Charger's reins and leading him toward the barn.

Wyatt started to sit, but upon remembering the package he'd brought, sprang to his feet and off the porch. Running toward his horse, he brought a startled Ian to a stop and untied the paper-wrapped parasol. "Sorry. I forgot something."

Meri was chuckling and shaking her head when he

landed back on the porch. "Should you see a doctor for those fits?"

"Keep it up, Mac, and I won't give you your surprise."

Eager curiosity filled her face as she looked at the slender object in his hand, but the question she asked wasn't what he was expecting. "Would you like a glass of lemonade after your long ride?"

He nodded. She filled a glass from the pitcher on the table and handed it to him before filling the second glass and sitting carefully.

He sat down in the other rocker before draining his glass. "How are you feeling? I notice you're not wearing your sling."

"I'm fine, and I don't need the sling as long as I keep my arm quiet." She eyed the package across his lap.

He grinned. "Getting curious?"

Her eyes flew back to his innocently. "No."

He laid the parcel across her lap. "Go ahead. See what's inside."

Her hand shook a little as she untied the string and slowly unwrapped his gift. A smile bloomed across her face, and she fingered the parasol's lace. "It's so pretty."

"I'm glad you like it. I thought we'd go for a stroll. I'd like to see your home, and this will keep the sun off your pretty face." His mother's romantic streak was apparently alive and well in her son.

A soft blush suffused her face. "I'd like that."

She stood, and he offered her his arm, taking the parasol from her as they stepped off the porch. Opening it, he held the sunshade over her head.

"I'm perfectly capable of carrying a parasol," she protested without force.

"I would hate it if you strained your poor shoulder carrying my gift." Wyatt grinned and tugged her a bit closer as they walked away from the house, pleased when she didn't argue further.

Ms. Maggie was ringing the bell for the noon meal the minute Meri finished giving him the grand tour of the ranch grounds. When the meal was over, Ian McIsaac excused himself to talk with Barnaby, and Ms. Maggie shooed Wyatt and Meri to the front porch.

The ranch lay silent and drowsy under the afternoon sun as they settled into the rocking chairs. Wyatt toed the porch and set the rocker in motion, listening to its faint creak for a moment. "Would you tell me about your mother?"

She was quiet for so long, he was afraid he'd upset her. "I, uh…" She blinked rapidly and a tear slid down her cheek. "Fiddlesticks! I don't cry the whole year after her death, and now I cry at the slightest thing."

"I didn't mean to upset you. You don't have to tell me anything, if you don't want to." Wyatt regretted his stupidity, cringing as another tear followed the first.

She shook her head. "No. I want to tell you about her. Just ignore my leaky face, please." She leaned her head against the back of the rocker. "Growing up, it was Faither, Mither and me against the world. There weren't a lot of children around when I was small, and my whole world was my folks and then our ranch. We had so much fun together, even in those early hardscrabble days." She smiled a little. "Faither is the dreamer and planner. Mither was our rock." She laughed deprecatingly. "She was very even-tempered, not like me at all. When Faither or I got too excited, she'd calm us down. On the other hand, she had the driest sense of humor and could raise our spirits whenever either of us got down. And then, out of the blue, she became sick."

She broke off on a sobbed breath and another tear wet

her cheek. Wyatt dug out his handkerchief. He leaned over and ever so gently blotted her cheeks.

Watery brown eyes met and clung to his. "Thank you." The words were so quiet he saw rather than heard them. He nodded and pressed the handkerchief into her hand.

She sniffed. "When we realized just how ill she was, I starting praying like I'd never prayed before, but one night, she slipped away. Faither was beside himself. I stayed strong for him even though the only world I'd ever known was shattered. When he started healing, he wanted to talk about her, but the only way I could cope was not to think about her. The better Faither got, the angrier I became. The morning before he was shot, he simply mentioned her on the way into town, and I nearly snapped his head off." She ducked her head. "I was feeling guilty about that and running away from another of Mrs. Van Deusen's matchmaking attempts when I ran into you. I'm sorry I took it out on you."

Wyatt covered the hand that was gripping the arm of the rocker with his own. Her eyes flew up and met his. "I'm tough. You didn't hurt me. You just very effectively grabbed my attention."

"I didn't mean to." Her cheeks went pink, and her eyes widened. "I mean…"

He smiled and squeezed her hand. "I know what you mean. You caught me by surprise, too. I had a plan, I had a dream and I wasn't going to pursue a woman until I had those accomplished."

He heard her quick intake of breath before she spoke. "Are…are you pursuing me?"

Chapter Twenty-One

Wyatt grinned. "Yes, ma'am, but if you have to ask, I must be going about it all wrong."

Her hand had been curled over the arm of the rocker when his own had covered it. Now, however, she turned her hand until it was actually holding his, and he felt the pulse in her wrist racing madly. She cleared her throat. "No. You're not."

Wyatt's heart swelled at her shy glance, and for a moment, there was no need for any words to fill the silence.

"What is your dream?" She shifted slightly in the chair to face him better and grimaced a little.

"Are you hurting?" He was a cad for keeping her out here so long. She was injured.

"Sit down. I'm fine. I just rubbed against the back of the chair a little too hard."

He hadn't realized he'd stood, but he hovered over her for a long minute to make sure she was really okay before he sat back down. "Wouldn't you be more comfortable inside?"

"No. Now quit dodging the question. What is your dream?" A smile softened the order.

He grinned right back. Did she have any idea how

much she'd changed his dream? "I've long wanted a place of my own to raise good-quality horses—mix Charger's speed and bloodlines with some of these tough Western horses like your Sandy to produce a line that has both speed and endurance." It seemed so small compared to what he wanted now. He scooted his rocking chair closer to hers and reached for her hand again. "And maybe raise a family of my own."

She looked out across the front yard, her fingers tightening around his. "That's a nice dream. Do you have a particular place picked out yet?" A slight tinge to her cheeks belied the casual-sounding question.

Wyatt rubbed his thumb over the back of her hand. "No. I'm still looking." His eyes traced her profile. He could easily look at her all day.

She took a deep breath. "There's good horse land around here." She glanced toward him and just as quickly glanced away again. "And Franks could get you started with a couple of good mares." She paused slightly. "If you're interested." Her shy uncertainty was endearing and encouraging.

"I'm very interested." In everything about her.

Meri twisted to face him, her eyes bright with cautious hope. "You are?"

Wyatt smiled and nodded. "Any place you'd recommend?"

Her face lit up, and she immediately began to list the good and bad points of various pieces of land, growing more animated the longer she talked. She attempted once to pull her hand away to emphasize a point, but he kept his grasp until it nestled back down.

His heart busy with plans, Wyatt relaxed into his chair, content for the moment to enjoy the expressive face of his new dream.

* * *

Meri twirled in front of the mirror for a final inspection, the skirt of the new dress flaring softly around her slim high-button shoes. Mother-of-pearl combs held her hair off her face, the length falling in soft waves down the back of a green calico dress sprinkled with tiny yellow flowers. She'd picked the fabric because the colors reminded her of the green-and-gold flecks in Wyatt's eyes while making her own hair gleam with golden highlights, and the cut flattered her figure with its slim bodice and full skirt.

"Hurry up, lass. We'll be late if ye don't quit fussin'."

Meri quickly pinned on a little straw confection of a hat, barely acknowledging the small twinge when her shoulder protested the movement. Picking up her Bible, reticule and lace parasol, she hurried from the room and down the stairs to her father and the awaiting buggy.

It had been a month since Meri had returned home, and Wyatt had ridden out to the ranch every subsequent Saturday afternoon. They would play checkers, stroll around the ranch, or as Meri healed, venture farther afield on horseback. On Sundays Wyatt would meet them at the church door, and he'd become an expected fixture in the McIsaac pew.

Meri smiled, admiring the lace-patterned shade the parasol cast over her skirt as the buggy rolled toward town and Sunday services. It was all frills and femininity, and she loved it. Because every time she went for a stroll with Wyatt, he insisted on carrying it. Which meant she had to walk very close to him.

The days stretched long during the week after seeing Wyatt on Saturday and Sunday, and she quickly found that absence truly did make her heart grow fonder. Occasionally Wyatt would make it out for supper during the week, but as she had resumed riding Sandy, her path somehow always wound up heading into Little Creek and the marshal's office.

Meri fingered the fabric of her dress. The mercantile and dressmaker had certainly benefited from her frequent trips to town, and she had the new dresses to show for it. Her feminine vanity had come to life with a belated vengeance.

Wyatt was waiting to assist her from the buggy, and he escorted her inside the church building. The service flew by with Meri endeavoring to pay attention to the music and sermon instead of Wyatt's nearness. Closing her eyes, she focused her wandering attention on the verses the pastor had read instead of the arm laid casually along the back of the pew, just brushing her shoulders.

Thank You, Lord, that You defend us and that Your joy is our strength. Thank You for defending me against the evil intentions of Mr. Samuels, for showing me that I am not strong when I try to stand on my own, but I am strong when You are my strength. Help me to remember joy isn't found in my circumstances, it's found only in You. Wyatt shifted, turning her attention back to him. *Father, I'm in love with this man, and I think he loves me. Would You give us wisdom, and if he does love me, would You remind him that he hasn't told me?*

"Amen."

Meri's eyes flew open in surprise as Wyatt's voice uttered the single word. Had she spoken aloud? No. The congregation was standing, gathering their belongings and chatting with one another. Service was over.

Wyatt grabbed her hand and hustled her toward the back door. After greeting the pastor, he hurried her outside to the buggy. Hands spanning her waist, he lifted her onto the seat.

"Where's the fire?" Meri asked, amused as he loosed the horses from the hitching rail before climbing into the buggy. "Wait, this isn't Faither's buggy."

"Nope." Reaching behind him, he pulled out Meri's parasol, opened it and handed it to her.

She took it and glanced curiously at the uncommunicative man beside her, but he ignored her silent question. She'd left the parasol under the seat of her father's buggy before services started and hadn't seen him or Faither move it.

Wyatt guided the horses around the other conveyances parked about the churchyard, clucking to them as they turned onto the road. Meri looked back at the church building as the horses broke into a quick-stepping trot. They'd departed the building so quickly no one else had exited the doors yet; everyone was still inside visiting.

"This could be considered kidnapping, you know," she said seriously, hoping to get an explanation out of him.

"It would be, if your father didn't know my plans."

"Aha. So you had a conspirator in your nefarious schemes." She twisted on the seat to see him better, her back brushing the armrest.

"Yup."

The man made Mr. Van Deusen look like a blabbermouth. "May I know what your plans are?"

"Nope."

"I must warn you, I get very hungry when I'm kidnapped. I hope you brought food." She twirled her parasol and watched it spin over her head.

"Been kidnapped often?"

"Dozens of times, but they always brought me back and told Faither I ate too much."

Wyatt had kept both hands on the reins, looking steadily down the road and keeping a straight face at her foolishness, but now he shifted the reins to one hand. His free hand snaked around her waist and pulled her up against him on the bouncing buggy seat.

"That's better. Can't have you so far away you think you can escape."

Meri loved riding Sandy alongside Wyatt and Charger, racing each other or merely exploring together the past few weeks, but a buggy ride had its own distinct charm. Especially when a handsome lawman had his arm wrapped around you.

Silence surrounded them as the scenery rolled by, but she was more absorbed in the delightful sensations caused by her traveling companion than the passing landscape. They headed in the direction of the ranch, but before they reached the rise that allowed them to see the ranch buildings, Wyatt turned the horses off onto a trail that climbed gradually to a high meadow. The sun was shining brightly and butterflies were busily flitting around the wildflowers dotting the large expanse of open ground.

Wyatt pulled the team to a stop under the trees that fringed the edge alongside a cool, clear stream. Hopping down, he turned and reached for Meri, swinging her to the ground easily. "Would you care to have a picnic with me?" He reached into the back of the buggy and held up a large picnic basket.

Meri looked around slowly and grinned. "Well…since I'm hungry and since you seem to be the only other person around…I suppose I'll have a picnic with you."

Wyatt's eyes danced. "I appreciate your kindness. If you'll give me a couple of minutes to tend to the horses, we'll eat."

He set the basket down and moved to the horses. Unhitching them, he led them to the water for a long drink, hobbled them and turned them out on the grass to graze.

Retrieving the basket, along with a thick quilt, he offered his arm to Meri and led her farther up the sloped meadow to a large, shady tree that stood magnificently alone in the center of the field.

Meri helped him spread the quilt and sat down, legs curled to the side. "I've always loved this spot."

"That's what your father said."

"He knows we're here?"

"I didn't tell him specifically, but he probably guessed."

He busied himself filling two plates with delicious-looking pieces of fried chicken, sliced cheese, fresh tomatoes, pickles, biscuits and cold baked beans. She accepted the food and cup of lemonade he handed her, closing her eyes when he offered a quick blessing. They hungrily dug into their food; comfortable silence highlighted by the sounds of trickling water in the distance and birds flitting back and forth over their heads.

Meri thought back to her prayer in church; at the rate they were going, there would be no confession of feelings today. In all the times they'd been together recently, she'd never seen him this quiet and enigmatic. She finished her food and set the plate aside.

"Dessert?"

"Not right now, thank you." She watched, fascinated, as Wyatt refilled his plate and continued eating. Where did he find room for it all? There wasn't an ounce of spare flesh anywhere on the man.

When he finished, he set his plate aside and flopped back, head cradled on his crossed arms. He closed his eyes and let out a satisfied groan. "That tasted good."

"It did. You're a man of many skills, Marshal," Meri teased, standing to her feet to put some distance between herself and the man who overloaded her senses just by his very presence.

One eye slid open lazily. "I thought we settled this."

"Settled what?" Meri feigned innocence and didn't wait for an answer but turned to stroll across the meadow.

A growl sounded. She looked over her shoulder to see him surge to his feet quicker than she thought should have been possible. She was running before she realized what she was doing, pulse racing harder than her feet when she heard him drawing closer. Changing directions unexpectedly, she managed to evade him, lifting the hem of her skirt to keep it from tangling around her ankles and wishing she were wearing her much more practical split skirt.

Feeling him behind her, she darted to the side again, but he was anticipating it, and muscular arms closed like steel bands around her. She emitted a surprised squeak and stumbled to a rather ungraceful halt. She tried to step away but the arms refused to yield their captive. He turned her to face him.

Heart racing and breath coming in quick little gasps, she looked up into his face.

"I can't have you running away with my heart if you can't remember my name. You just might forget you even have it, and then where would I be?" He held her loosely, but there was no escaping the arms that enfolded her, or the eyes that devoured hers.

"Do I still have it?" she whispered. Her eyes fastened on an eye-level shirt button.

The sinewy bands around her tightened, drawing her inexorably closer, and she braced her hands against an expanse of rock-hard chest.

"Ah, Meri," he crooned. "Don't you *know* I love you? You irretrievably have my heart whether you want it or not. I'm just hoping you do." One hand came up to lift her head, knuckles lightly grazing her chin as his thumb caressed her jawline.

"You love me?" She thought she uttered the words, but his hand on her face was causing her heart to do all sorts of acrobatics, and she wasn't at all sure her tongue was still in proper working order.

"Didn't you realize I love you? I said you had my heart." One hand caressed the wavy hair hanging down her back.

"I wasn't sure…I mean…I hoped so, but you didn't say it…specifically… I don't know. I guess I'm pretty naive when it comes to things like this." Meri ducked her burning face and leaned her head into his chest to hide from his keen eyes.

Both arms enveloped her and held her close, the silence allowing her to hear the steady thump of his heart. "Well?"

Meri felt the vibration of the low question rumble through his chest. Captivated, she waited for it to happen again.

He shook her a little. "I'm waiting."

"Hmm?" She wanted to place her ear to his chest and hear that interesting rumble again.

His hands shifted to her arms, and he nudged her back a step, leaning down slightly to peer into her eyes. "Do *you?*"

She smiled into his eyes. "Yes. I love you." It felt as wonderful to say the words as to hear them.

They were barely out of her mouth when he hauled her back to his chest. She fully anticipated a kiss, but he only tucked her head under his chin and held her tight as a gusty sigh of relief escaped him. "Thank You, Lord!"

Meri's heart mirrored his prayer of thanksgiving. *He loved her.* Her arms tightened around his waist as she smiled and inhaled the scent that was Wyatt Cameron.

She was abruptly pushed back, and hazel eyes peered intently into hers. "I have a solution."

"For what?"

"For remembering my name. Permanently."

Her breath froze. He sank to one knee and gathered her hands in his. "Miss America Catriona McIsaac, would you change your name to mine?"

Tears sprang to her eyes, and she hastily blinked them away so she could see his face clearly. She wanted to remember this moment. "Yes." The answer barely whispered past her lips.

He looked at her with hopeful uncertainty. "You'll marry me?"

"Yes." She nodded. "I'll marry you." That came out a little stronger.

A huge smile lit his face, and he stood, gathering her tenderly in his arms. Her hands slipped up to his shoulders. "Wait." He leaned back slightly. "Yes, I'll marry you, what?"

She smiled a bit mistily. "Yes, I'll marry you. Thank you for asking."

"That's not quite what I had in mind." He leaned in and placed a tiny kiss on her nose.

Breathing was highly overrated. "Did you not want me to say yes?"

"You little minx. Of course I wanted you to say yes. But who are you saying yes to?"

She circled his neck with her hands, sliding her fingers into his closely cropped hair. "Yes, I'll marry you, Wyatt Cameron."

A huge smile bloomed across his face and took what little breath Meri had left. "That's what I wanted to hear."

His eyes caressed her face, and she rose up on tiptoes to meet him halfway. He leaned down and settled his lips against hers in a first kiss. The world rocked and then stood still and silent except for the sound of each other's heartbeats. Wyatt tightened his grip and straightened, lifting Meri off her feet as he continued kissing her.

The kiss lasted a lifetime and was entirely too short. He twirled her around, throwing his head back and laughing joyously. She was dizzy when he set her down, leaning in for a second kiss that trailed over her eyes, cheeks and nose before landing hungrily on her lips.

She could get used to this.

When they finally pulled apart, breathless, he tucked her head under his chin and snuggled her close. They stood that way for several minutes, simply enjoying the moment. Finally he snuggled her under his arm, and they walked back to the forgotten picnic blanket.

"Do you want dessert now?"

"Yes. I'm suddenly hungry again," Meri admitted, surprised.

"Good." He helped her sit down and knelt by the basket. "Close your eyes."

She did and listened to the sounds of his rummaging around.

"Okay. You can open them." A plate holding a large piece of a dark-colored cake topped with cream balanced on his outstretched hand.

Meri shot him a puzzled grin. "Gingerbread?"

"Yep. It will forever remind me of you, our first picnic together and the spice you bring to my life. I had Ms. Maggie bake it for me when I asked your father's permission to marry you yesterday. I thought it'd be the perfect way to finish our picnic today."

Meri blinked, stunned. Her father had known and hadn't said anything? A smile blossomed slowly; God had answered her prayer this morning before she'd ever even prayed it. "You were certain I'd say yes?"

"No. But I had a backup plan in case you said no."

"What?"

"I didn't intend to let you go until you said yes." He winked and laughed when her attempted scowl shattered into a pleased grin.

Taking the plate, fork and quick kiss he offered her, she dug into the gingerbread. Never before had it tasted quite so delicious.

Epilogue

Summer flew by in a flurry of preparations for a late-September wedding.

Wyatt purchased the meadow and surrounding acreage from Meri's father, and the town threw a house- and barn-raising social. The house was small but cozy with plenty of space to build on as needed, and the barn had ample capacity for Charger and Sandy and the other horses they intended to raise.

Meri would be near her father, Wyatt was close enough to town to continue in his capacity of marshal, and Jonah had decided to remain permanently as deputy. Moreover the town council voted that in view of the recent bank robbery and expanding population they would hire a second deputy as soon as Wyatt found a suitable candidate.

The trial of Mr. Samuels and Mr. Mullins had ended; their fates decided by a judge and jury. Mr. Samuels would spend the rest of his life in prison, but Mullins was sentenced to death for his role in multiple shootings and robberies.

The townsfolk continued to shake their heads over the fact that one of their own deceived everyone so completely. There were a few, however, that argued they'd been suspicious of him from the start.

The bank reopened its doors for business, but the new manager was finding it slow going to rebuild the trust that had been broken concerning the credibility of the bank. Meanwhile Mr. Van Deusen had picked up business since he had a good-size safe in his store, and for now, many people preferred to trust him with any savings they had.

Meri and Wyatt continued to fall deeper in love as the days passed. There were serious discussions and occasional arguments, lighthearted moments and of course, the inevitable teasing. One such moment transpired a couple of weeks after their engagement while they were planning the layout of their new home.

Meri was admiring her handsome husband-to-be as he stepped off the layout of house and barn when a thought occurred to her. "You know my middle name, but I don't know your full name." He continued pacing off measurements as if he hadn't heard her, so she trotted over to him. "Are you named after your father?" Again he didn't answer. "Are you ignoring me?"

"No, just the question." He continued his careful measuring steps.

"Why?" She matched his stride.

"Because it isn't important."

Meri stepped into his path and slammed her fists onto her hips, eyes narrowed. "You pestered me for weeks to use your name and now you won't tell me what it is?"

"You're a pest, and you know my name." He reached to move her out of his path, but she dodged his hand.

"Not all of it."

He sidestepped, but she stuck like a bur in front of him, ignoring his attempt to bait her and intrigued by the faint pink tinge just above his shirt collar.

"Are you blushing?"

He closed his eyes and sighed heavily. "Why are you making a big deal over this?"

"You *are* blushing," she crowed. "And it wasn't a big deal until you started evading the question. Now I'm curious, and I'm not letting you go until you tell me." She wrapped her arms around his waist and grinned up at him.

His own arms draped loosely around her shoulders, and he leaned in to brush his lips lightly over hers. Meri stretched up to deepen the kiss and forgot everything but the feel of his mouth on hers for the next few blissful moments. When he pulled back, she sighed happily and leaned her head on his chest. They remained in that position for a full minute before she recalled her mission.

"I haven't forgotten that you haven't answered my question, and I'll keep after you until you tell me."

"Of that I have no doubt, so…I'll tell you after we're married."

"But that's not 'til September."

"Uh-huh, it'll give you something to fuss over 'til then." He laughed when she growled at him and kissed her forehead, but he refused to give in.

She eventually changed the subject, a little miffed that he was having fun at her expense. After a couple more tries over the next few weeks, she put the question aside and focused on other things. The man was quite possibly more obstinate then she was, and she was head over heels in love with him. Best of all, she was fully loved in return. In spite of his refusal to share his full name.

At long last the day of the wedding rolled around. McIsaac walked his daughter down the aisle to the accompaniment of the newly arrived piano purchased with dessert auction proceeds, presenting Meri's hand to the marshal who'd captured her heart. The service was sweetly solemn, and when they exchanged their vows, Mrs. Van Deusen employed her handkerchief to dab teary eyes.

When Pastor Willis directed, "You may now kiss your bride," Wyatt eagerly obeyed. Meri emerged from the assault on her lips, breathless, blushing and beaming. The congregation broke into cheers and applause, and Pastor Willis presented them as Mr. and Mrs. Wyatt Cameron.

Following the ceremony everyone moved to the shade of the trees and feasted on a bountiful wedding luncheon. There was plenty of food and gifts for the bride and groom, as well as congratulations, well wishes and lots of good-natured advice. When the cake had been cut and served, Wyatt and Meri made their way to a shiny new buggy decorated with white ribbons and left the festivities to wind down without them.

Once out of sight and sound of the gathered wedding guests, Meri wrapped her arms around Wyatt and snuggled into his side. She peeked up at him through her lashes. "We're married, Mr. Cameron."

"I do believe that's what the preacher said, Mrs. Cameron." He squeezed her close and kissed her slowly, quite forgetting the animals attached to the other end of the reins.

In time the absence of motion alerted them to the fact the horses had taken advantage of their freedom to graze along the roadside, and Wyatt tightened up the sagging reins. Meri looped her arms around Wyatt's arm as he gently reminded the horses of their responsibility to carry them home, and a comfortable silence fell as they reveled in each other's presence and quick stolen kisses.

They were within sight of their home when Meri spoke. "Now that we're married, I believe you have something to tell me."

"I do?" He dropped a kiss on her upturned lips.

"You do. Now quit distracting me and 'fess up. Why wouldn't you tell me your name?"

He laughed. "Because wives can't testify against their husbands, and you weren't my wife yet."

Meri gently slapped his arm. "Be serious. What's so bad about your name?"

"It's a sad story." He sighed so tragically that Meri giggled at the affectation. "A month or two before I was born, mother was reading Shakespeare's *Twelfth Night*. She fell in love with one of the names in the book, and when I was born, she decided to burden me with it. Mother was the only one who ever used it, but I finally convinced her to stop about the time I was ten. I was tired of having to fight the boys who laughed at me when they heard her use my full name. And I think Mother was tired of patching me up."

Meri had read *Twelfth Night* years ago, but couldn't recall any names that would explain Wyatt's reluctance to share his full name.

He took a deep breath; released it. "My full name is Wyatt Valentine Cameron."

Meri kept a straight face with much difficulty, but her eyes were sparkling with glee. "I don't remember a Valentine in the book." She loved his name, and he looked absolutely disgusted.

"He was a minor character—Duke Orsino's attendant. Do you see why I dislike it?"

"No, I'm like your mother, I love the name Valentine."

"Thank you," he said dryly, "but you didn't have to grow up with it. Please don't use it in public, or I will have to resort to drastic measures."

Meri shrieked as his fingers tickled her ribs, and the horses flinched at the sudden outburst. Her giggles filled the air as the horses pulled the buggy up to the barn and stopped, looking back as if exasperated at the foolishness behind them.

Wyatt swung down from the buggy and reached for his new wife. He cuddled her close, ignoring her wiggling, and walked to the shady side of the barn to set her on her feet. "Stay there." His twinkling eyes softened the command.

He unhitched the horses and turned them into the grassy paddock, making quick work of hanging up the harness. Then he returned, swept her into his arms again and walked toward the sparkling new little house. Stepping onto the porch, he opened the door and carried his bride over the threshold, kicking the door closed behind them.

"Have I told you today that I love you, Mrs. Cameron?"

Meri sighed happily. "If you did, I've forgotten. Say it again, please."

Her arms wound snugly around his neck, her fingers luxuriating in the feel of his hair. She was content to stay in the safe haven of his strong arms forever.

"I love you, Mrs. Cameron." His nose touched hers.

"*I* love *you,* Wyatt Valentine." There was a twinkle in her eyes as she spoke.

He groaned, resting his forehead against hers. "Why do I get the feeling I'm going to regret wanting you to use my name, Mac?"

"That's Mrs. Cameron to you, and you asked me to call you by your name. I'm going to be a good, dutiful wife and obey you." It was hard to be prim and innocent when you were giggling.

He pulled his head back and gave her an incredulous look. "I'll believe *that* when I see it."

"Oh!" Meri's eyes widened as a thought suddenly occurred to her.

"What?" His eyes narrowed suspiciously.

"We should have waited to be married until February 14!"

"And that's exactly why I didn't tell you my full name, Mrs. Cameron." He plopped down onto the lovely new divan and started pulling pins from her elegant chignon.

"But it would have been perfect! On Valentine's Day, I would marry my very own Valentine!"

Wyatt snarled menacingly and tickled her ribs until helpless giggles pealed forth, filling the room with the happy sound.

"Stop, Wyatt Valentine Cameron!" she gasped breathlessly, futilely trying to escape.

"Hmm…if that doesn't work, maybe this will shut you up." He nestled her close, imprisoning her lips with his own in a bone-melting kiss.

Meri began to giggle again, and Wyatt pulled back, puzzled. "What's so funny?"

"If this is the consequence of using your full name, I'll never call you anything else, Wyatt Valentine!"

Wyatt Valentine Cameron was more than happy to mete out her punishment swiftly and thoroughly.

* * * * *

Dear Reader,

It is a beautiful spring morning as I write this. My windows are open, the birds are singing, the trees are sporting bright new frocks and the breeze carries hints of fragrant blossoms. My little corner of the world is coming to life after a dreary winter, much like the fictional town of Little Creek, Colorado. Although it is springtime in the Rockies, it is still very much winter in Meri McIsaac's grieving heart. But a spring thaw is on its way. In the shape of a bossy marshal.

I hope you enjoy Meri and Wyatt's story, and I thank you for picking up my first book.

I would love to hear from my readers; you can visit me at www.facebook.com/ClariDees or drop me a line at cdeesbooks@gmail.com.

Until we meet again,
Clari Dees

Questions for Discussion

1. As the story opens, the storekeeper's wife is giving unwanted advice to Meri McIsaac. Does Meri handle the situation appropriately? Why or why not? How do you handle unwanted advice?

2. Meri's best friend is Franks, a former slave. Do you think this would have been an unusual friendship in 1883?

3. Meri is still struggling with the loss of her mother almost a year after her death. Do you think this is realistic? Why or why not?

4. What do you think of Meri's attitude when she meets Marshal Cameron for the first time? Should she have handled his teasing differently? How do you handle someone teasing you?

5. Meri is a rough-and-tumble ranch girl, but she isn't comfortable in a town setting. She prefers her horse to lots of people. What about you? Do you prefer to be with lots of different people, or do you prefer your own company and a few close friends?

6. When wounded Mr. McIsaac takes a turn for the worse, Meri asks the elders of her church to come pray for him. Is this something you would do? What did you think of the outcome?

7. Wyatt Cameron is attracted to Meri, but he has reasons for not wanting a serious relationship. What were those reasons? Do you think they were valid?

8. Mr. Samuels was not a well-liked man. Did he bring it on himself? Do you think this contributed to his problems? If someone had tried harder to befriend him, would it have changed his self-destructive course?

9. When Meri finally confesses her anger, she is able to move past her mother's death. Have you ever been angry? How did you deal with it?

10. Did you enjoy Meri and Wyatt's story? Did you like the setting? Was the ending satisfactory?

COMING NEXT MONTH
from Love Inspired® Historical
AVAILABLE FEBRUARY 5, 2013

BLESSING
Deborah Bedford

Disguised as a boy, Uley Kirkland must testify as a witness to attempted murder, but when she falls for Aaron Brown, the defendant, she realizes she'll do whatever it takes to save Aaron's life—even risk her own.

COURTING MISS CALLIE
Pinewood Weddings
Dorothy Clark

Ezra Ryder, disillusioned by women seeking him for his wealth, disguises himself as a stable hand. But when he falls for the beautiful Callie Conner, his deception may ruin their hopes of happiness.

THE RELUCTANT EARL
C. J. Chase

Leah Vance risks social ruin by selling political information to pay for her sister's care. When Julian DeChambrelle, the dashing former sea captain, catches her in the act, they're both pulled into a world of danger.

GROOM BY ARRANGEMENT
Rhonda Gibson

Eliza Kelly is mortified when she mistakes blacksmith Jackson Hart for the mail-order groom her friend arranged for her. Both are afraid to fall in love, but could a marriage of convenience make them reconsider?

REQUEST YOUR FREE BOOKS!

2 FREE INSPIRATIONAL NOVELS
PLUS 2
FREE
MYSTERY GIFTS

Love Inspired.
HISTORICAL
INSPIRATIONAL HISTORICAL ROMANCE

YES! Please send me 2 FREE Love Inspired® Historical novels and my 2 FREE mystery gifts (gifts are worth about $10). After receiving them, if I don't wish to receive any more books, I can return the shipping statement marked "cancel." If I don't cancel, I will receive 4 brand-new novels every month and be billed just $4.49 per book in the U.S. or $4.99 per book in Canada. That's a saving of at least 22% off the cover price. It's quite a bargain! Shipping and handling is just 50¢ per book in the U.S. and 75¢ per book in Canada.* I understand that accepting the 2 free books and gifts places me under no obligation to buy anything. I can always return a shipment and cancel at any time. Even if I never buy another book, the two free books and gifts are mine to keep forever.

102/302 IDN FVXK

Name	(PLEASE PRINT)	
Address		Apt. #
City	State/Prov.	Zip/Postal Code

Signature (if under 18, a parent or guardian must sign)

Mail to the Harlequin® Reader Service:
IN U.S.A.: P.O. Box 1867, Buffalo, NY 14240-1867
IN CANADA: P.O. Box 609, Fort Erie, Ontario L2A 5X3

Want to try two free books from another series?
Call 1-800-873-8635 or visit www.ReaderService.com.

* Terms and prices subject to change without notice. Prices do not include applicable taxes. Sales tax applicable in N.Y. Canadian residents will be charged applicable taxes. Offer not valid in Quebec. This offer is limited to one order per household. Not valid for current subscribers to Love Inspired Historical books. All orders subject to credit approval. Credit or debit balances in a customer's account(s) may be offset by any other outstanding balance owed by or to the customer. Please allow 4 to 6 weeks for delivery. Offer available while quantities last.

Your Privacy—The Harlequin® Reader Service is committed to protecting your privacy. Our Privacy Policy is available online at www.ReaderService.com or upon request from the Harlequin Reader Service.

We make a portion of our mailing list available to reputable third parties that offer products we believe may interest you. If you prefer that we not exchange your name with third parties, or if you wish to clarify or modify your communication preferences, please visit us at www.ReaderService.com/consumerschoice or write to us at Harlequin Reader Service Preference Service, P.O. Box 9062, Buffalo, NY 14269. Include your complete name and address.

Love Inspired HISTORICAL

The wrong groom could be the
perfect match in

GROOM BY ARRANGEMENT

by **Rhonda Gibson**

Eliza Kelly thought her humiliation was complete when she
identified the wrong train passenger as her mail-order groom.
She was only trying to tell Jackson Hart that the madcap scheme
was *not* her idea. When the blacksmith decides to stay, he offers
the lovely widow a marriage of convenience. Between caring for
an orphaned youngster and protecting Eliza, Jackson feels whole
again. If only he can persuade Eliza to marry him, and fulfill
their long-buried dreams of forging a real family.

Available in February wherever books are sold.

www.LoveInspiredBooks.com
LIH82954

All Laura White wants is a second chance.
Will she find it in Cooper Creek?

Read on for a preview of
THE COWBOY'S HEALING WAYS.

The door opened, bringing in cool air and a few stray drops of rain. The man in the doorway slipped off boots and hung a cowboy hat on a hook by the door. She watched as he shrugged out of his jacket and hung it next to his hat.

When he turned, she stared up at a man with dark hair that brushed his collar and lean, handsome features. He looked as at home in this big house as he did in his worn jeans and flannel shirt. His dark eyes studied her with curious suspicion. She'd gotten used to that look. She'd gotten used to people whispering behind their hands as she walked past.

But second chances and starting over meant wanting something new. She wanted to be the person people welcomed into their lives. She wanted to be the woman a man took a second look at, maybe a third.

Jesse Cooper took a second look, but it was a look of suspicion.

"Jesse, I'm so glad you're here." Granny Myrna had returned with a cold washcloth, which she placed on Laura's forehead. "It seems I had an accident."

"Really?" Jesse smiled a little, warming the coolness in dark eyes that focused on Laura.

"I pulled right out in front of her. She drove her car off the side of the road to keep from hitting me."

Laura closed her eyes. A cool hand touched the gash at her hairline.

"Let me see this."

She opened her eyes and he was squatting in front of her, studying the cut. He looked from the gash to her face. Then he moved and stood back up, unfolding his long legs with graceful ease. Laura clasped her hands to keep them from shaking.

A while back there had been an earthquake in Oklahoma. Laura remembered when it happened, and how they'd all wondered if they'd really felt the earth move or if it had been their imaginations. She was pretty sure it had just happened again. The earth had moved, shifting precariously as a hand touched her face and dark eyes studied her intently, with a strange mixture of curiosity, surprise and something else.

Will Jesse ever allow the mysterious Laura into his life—and his heart?

Pick up THE COWBOY'S HEALING WAYS
by Brenda Minton,
available in February 2013 from Love Inspired.

LIEXP0113